Bit by the Bug

Kat's head fell back on her shoulders and she opened her mouth wide, gasping for breath. Her heart beat hard in her chest and she tried to focus on the sound of his voice, trying to place it. 'Dr Vincent?'

'Shit!' Kat screamed, sitting up in bed, breathing hard. Her arms flailed as she felt all around her. The bed was empty. Tossing the blankets off, she practically jumped off the mattress as if burnt by it. It was just a dream – a potent, erotic, sinfully wrong dream. Her heart was still beating hard and her body was tense, no longer feeling the relief of her dream state orgasm. Instead, unfulfilled arousal caused her nipples to ache.

Why in the world was she dreaming of the awkward Dr Vincent?

Other Cheek titles by the author:

FIERCE COMPETITION

OPPOSITES ATTRACT

For more information about Michelle M Pillow's books
please visit www.michellepillow.com

Bit by the Bug

Michelle M Pillow

In real life always practise safe sex.

First published in 2006 by
Cheek
Thames Wharf Studios
Rainville Road
London W6 9HA

Typeset by SetSystems Ltd, Saffron Walden, Essex

Printed and bound by Mackays of Chatham PLC

ISBN 0 352 34084 3
ISBN 978 0 352 34084 9

Dedication:

To Dena, Loren and a Notebook

To Malinda and the Family Curse

Note from Author

Though the American Museum of Natural History in New York is an actual museum, the DJP Scientific Department of Entomological Research mentioned in this book as part of it is a fictional facility and department. This novel is a complete work of fiction. All characters and events are of the author's imagination and not to be confused with fact. Any resemblance to living persons or events is merely coincidence.

For factual information about the American Museum of Natural History you can visit their website at http://www.amnh.org/.

Chapter One

'So you're saying you want me to deflower your son?'

Kat Matthews stared at Mrs Mimi Richmond in disbelief, knowing her tone was dry with sarcasm and unable to help it. How else could she say it, though? The woman wanted to hire her to 'be' with her son. It was preposterous. It was the new millennium and yet, here she was, sitting in a posh hotel suite looking at a woman who couldn't be more serious.

Kat had known Mimi for a total of four days – four very long days she had spent vacationing with her own neurotic mother at the trendy Colorado ski resort. For some reason Beatrice Matthews thought she needed to spend alone time with each one of her daughters on a yearly basis so they could bond. As she had five daughters, she took five vacations each year. If not for Kat's great desire to photograph the Rocky Mountains for her portfolio, it was a mother-daughter trip she would never have taken.

'Oh, no, no. Nothing so risqué as all that, I assure you, Katarina.' Mimi looked at her husband, Vincent, and laughed. It was the sort of laugh that managed to mock those around her even as it amused herself. It was a rich laugh, not boisterous rich, but the kind of rich that came backed by Mr Richmond's multi-million dollar bank account. 'Dear, didn't I tell you she was utterly charming?'

Mr Richmond didn't answer his wife. He merely nodded from where he paced the hotel suite talking on his cellular phone. Mimi didn't seem discouraged by her husband's lack of response. She laughed lightly and waved at him in dismissal before turning back to Kat.

Nothing about this situation made sense. Kat tried to smile, but just one look at her would tell anyone she really didn't belong with these people. Her long dark blonde hair was piled beneath a black Betty Page style wig. The dark colour was a stark contrast to her paler complexion. Though she knew she was very fashionable and chic in appearance, she couldn't afford a designer wardrobe except for a few second-hand pieces and those she borrowed from her sister, Zoe. Her faded blue jeans with the hole in the right knee and the oversized black turtleneck sweater with sleeves extended over the backs of her hands just didn't match the flashier Mimi.

Everything about Mimi Richmond was designer, from her white leather Sergio Rossi heels to her Elie Tahari white stretch twill pants and matching blazer. The older woman positively glittered: her diamond earrings, her diamond tennis bracelet, her diamond brooch and neck-laces, and – Kat tried not to laugh at this part – her diamond navel ring. Yes, the fifty-plus year old had her belly button pierced. Though, to be fair, the woman was in wonderful shape.

Mimi's short red hair complemented her ageless face. It was a face bought and paid for from the best Califor-nian plastic surgeons. She exercised fanatically and looked barely out of her thirties. However, Mimi was self-proclaimed proud of her age and told everyone who would listen how she achieved her timeless good looks. In fact, as far as Kat could tell, the woman didn't have a filter between her brain and her mouth. She'd talk about almost anything – things others would've been ashamed to admit to.

Kat didn't move. It was clear that though money could

buy many things, sanity wasn't one of them. Whatever had compelled her to come and meet with these people?

Oh yeah, she thought, slightly dejected. Even the voice in her head was sarcastic today. I came because they're rich. Mom said they wanted to talk about a job and I need the cash. Silly me for not automatically assuming that meant prostitution.

Kat turned to Mr Richmond as he sat down next to his wife, suddenly thankful they weren't swingers trying to hire her for themselves. Though, it was surprising to see he was off the phone long enough to look at her, let alone join the bizarre conversation. Just as she thought it, he opened his mouth and his cell phone rang. Mimi rolled her eyes making a sound of exasperation as her husband answered the call. As the man talked, Kat absently sang cartoon theme songs in her head to pass the time and to keep herself from jumping off the couch and running away. Tapping her toes, she knew she'd give almost anything for her New York apartment and a pair of pyjama pants right now. Mr Richmond spoke for a few minutes about business before hanging up and turning back to the still silent women.

The Richmonds looked her over in thoughtful contemplation. Kat tried to smile, feeling really awkward by this point, but her cheeks were too stiff to move. The white love seat she sat on was comfortable – so thick she was actually sunk down into its cushy depths. She glanced at the door and determined it would take too long to get out of her seat to make a proper run for it. The cushions held her trapped in their cloudlike padding.

For lack of anything better to do during their indiscreet scrutiny of her person and the awkward silence that accompanied it, Kat glanced around the room. The executive suite was huge. It had to be over a thousand square feet. The white walls and carpet added an elegant, almost untouchably sterile appeal to the place. The dark-brown boardroom table on the far side of the long living area was covered with stacks of papers. A vase of calla lilies had been pushed aside to make room for the mess. The Richmonds were supposedly on vacation, but it looked as if Mr Richmond was spending most of his time conquering the mountains of paperwork on the table, as opposed to the beautiful mountainous ski slopes outdoors.

Swallowing nervously, Kat turned her attention back to the couple. They eyed her expectantly from a matching white couch, as if they expected her to speak. She really had nothing to say to them.

'We would like for you to date our son,' said Mr Richmond finally. He was just as eccentric as his wife in his bright silk Italian suits and gold jewellery. His hair was slicked back from his face and he had a little moustache that didn't touch the top of his lip. He looked more like a stereotypical mafia kingpin than a businessman. All that was missing was the strong Jersey accent.

Ba-da-bing. Forget about it.

Kat tried not to laugh as she found herself staring at his moustache, fairly sure it was slicked with oil just like his black hair. Her fingers itched for the camera she'd left back at her hotel suite. She'd give almost anything to get a close-up of the ridiculous thing with her macro lens. Already she could imagine blowing the photo of it six feet wide and hanging it on the wall.

Realising she was still staring at his facial hair, she again glanced around the hotel suite and tried not to laugh. These people could not be serious. The poor kid must be awkward indeed if his parents had to get him dates. Either that or he was a completely spoiled brat no one wanted. She hadn't seen him around the hotel, but got the image of a larger than life jerk with his mother's obnoxious laugh and his father's phone addiction.

'Oooh, cocktails!' Mrs Richmond announced, the sound abnormally loud. The woman waved her hands in excitement and again laughed in her high-pitched tone. A servant dressed in a black and white maid's uniform leaned over, reaching out with a pewter tray filled with drinks. Kat glanced at her watch. It was ten in the morning.

'I'll have one of those,' Mr Richmond said, his voice booming as loud as his wife's had, as he reached for the tray. He raised his brow at Kat and she politely shook her head in denial. 'Suit yourself. More for us.'

The couple laughed. Kat tried to smile, she really did, but it was hard with all the deprecating thoughts running through her head. These people were certifiable. On the plus side, they were so absorbed in themselves they didn't seem to notice her sarcastic ways.

'You see, we wouldn't expect you to . . . how was it you so charmingly put it?' Mr Richmond looked at his wife for help.

'Hmm, yes, deflower,' Mimi said between sips of liquor, only to mutter, 'Charming.'

'Yes, deflower, thank you, my darling. We wouldn't expect you to do anything like that,' Mr Richmond assured her. 'That would be crazy.'

'Ah,' Kat nodded. Don't laugh, she told herself. Do not laugh. You're smirking. Quit smirking. It's rude to smirk.

'Dear, I believe our son has probably already been deflowered, don't you think?' Mimi tilted her head to the side, actually pondering the question.

'Oh, I should hope so,' Mr Richmond agreed. Then, still looking at his wife, he said, 'Well, if she wanted to sleep with him, I suppose it would be fine. A man is a man after all.'

'Yes, we'll leave it up to them,' said Mimi.

Kat could only watch them in bewilderment. I'm dreaming, she thought. That has to be it. I'm in bed and I'm dreaming and in some morbid way, I don't want to wake up. I actually want to see where this train wreck is going. No. No wrecks. End it now. Be polite, yet firm. Say no and then run away.

'Mrs Richmond, Mr Richmond,' Kat began as diplomatically as possible.

'Mimi, dear, call me Mimi,' Mimi said, smiling.

'Vincent,' Mr Richmond said.

'Ah, well, OK. Mimi. Vincent.' Kat tried to look pleasant even as she felt her face strain. 'I appreciate the fact you want your son to have dates and all, but hiring me to be his friend maybe isn't the best way to go about it. Have you ever thought of just having a dinner party and inviting eligible women to attend? Or perhaps a blind date? Work associate's daughter?'

A stripper from Las Vegas? she added silently.

'We tried those already,' Mr Richmond said. 'It didn't work out and quite frankly we've run out of friends with eligible daughters. The boy is constantly forgetting to come to dinner and when he does he hardly says a word to any of them.'

'That is not true. He does talk to them sometimes. He just doesn't talk about anything interesting.' Mimi shook her head. 'Bugs. Who talks to a woman about bugs? I can barely get Cathy Herrington to come back for a visit. She is still convinced our house has spiders. We told her he was just talking nonsense and I assured her I had the house sprayed. I even showed her the bill as proof.'

Bugs? Kat took a deep breath, cringing on the inside. 'He's not in high school is he? I mean, this isn't for a prom or anything, is it?'

'Oh, no, of course not,' Mimi assured her. She took a sip of her drink mumbling, 'He's, um, thimeehraree.'

'Excuse me?' Kat leaned forwards. Why was she even listening to this?

'He's thirty-three,' Mr Richmond said, toying with his cufflink.

'You want to buy your thirty-three-year-old son a girlfriend?' Kat asked, unable to stop the blunt words of surprise. Biting her tongue had never been a strong suit, though she somehow managed before the sarcastic 'Does he live in your basement and collect comic books?' came out.

'Not buy,' Mimi said. 'More like hire.'

'I'm sorry, I think you have the wrong girl for the job –' Kat started to stand. Mimi's look stopped her.

'But you're an actress,' Mimi insisted. 'Your mother told us you're an out of work actress. We want you to think of it like a job.'

'I haven't acted since high school. It was one play in my freshman year,' Kat answered. What had her mother been going on about now? Actress? The thought was laughable. The production had been a flop and the drama teacher had cast her as an old Chinese man. There was nothing wrong with the casting *per se*, except she was a young girl from a French-Swedish background who couldn't do accents to save her life.

'Oh, well I'd say that was being out of work,' Mimi snorted, laughing so hard she jiggled her glass. Liquor sloshed over on her hand. 'Oh, dear, well.' She shrugged licking the drops from her skin before taking another drink. Mr Richmond's chuckle joined hers.

'I'm not an actress,' Kat insisted.

'Oh, touchy,' Mr Richmond whispered under his breath to his wife. The woman nodded.

'I'm a photographer,' Kat said.

'She told us that as well,' Mr Richmond nodded, though he hardly looked impressed. She didn't think he would be. This was a man who only understood business and making money. He'd have no concept of true art.

'You just keep plucking away.' Mimi leaned forward and pinched Kat's cheek, smacking it soundly. 'You'll get there someday. In the meantime, I think this is just the perfect way to hone your acting skills.'

'So, let's get down to business.' Mr Richmond fingered his cell phone, flipping it open and shut as he talked. 'You pretend to be interested in our son. Get him to take you out a few times, maybe bring you over to our house for dinner so we can see him with a woman who isn't going to slap him and run away.'

'Sundays are good,' Mimi interjected. 'Maybe for brunch. Oh, no, make that dinner. There is always something so elegant about dinners.'

'Let us see that he's actually starting to date,' Mr Richmond continued to explain. 'Maybe give us a chance to study him in action, see what he's doing wrong so we can help.'

'You know,' Mimi gestured her hand in wide circles, 'get his feet wet so he's not so shy around women. You'll be his practice date.'

'We're not going to be young forever,' Mr Richmond said. 'And he'll have to marry someday. The Richmond name must live on. God knows my good-for-nothing nephews will never see to it.'

'I don't want grandchildren.' Mimi turned to him.

'But, you'd make a perfect grandmother,' Mr Richmond assured her.

'Oh, honey, you think so?' Mimi leaned into him, puckering her lips and making little kissy noises. 'Well, a granddaughter would be nice, after you get your heir of course. It would be great to have a girl to take shopping with me. Oh, we could wear matching little pink Chanel suits with the black patent leather trim.'

'I just don't think that I –' Kat tried to interrupt their side conversation, but was again cut off.

'Anyway, our son works all the time, just like his father.' Mimi frowned at her husband, pouting out her bottom lip. 'You know you do, dearest.'

'He's alone,' Mr Richmond added, looking at Kat. 'Can you blame us for wanting to see him happy?'

'No, I can't, but –' Kat pulled her Fendi knockoff purse close to her hip, readying to make an exit just as soon as she could gracefully stand from the thick couch.

'Oh, art show, you forgot to tell her about the art show,' Mimi said.

'Art show?' Kat perked up. Her grip loosened on her purse.

'At a little gallery, Faux Pas of New York,' Mimi said, her eyes narrowing. 'Maybe you've heard of it? Howard Faustino is a close personal friend. He was just over at our country house for dinner the other evening talking about how he wished he could find some new young hot talent to shoot into stardom. Know anyone who'd be interested in something like that?'

This wasn't fair. Kat's palms started to sweat and her heart raced. Faux Pas was only the 'IT' gallery in all of the United States. It was huge. It was big time. International exposure. Accolades. Artistic validation. Money.

Artists would do anything to get just a shot at being in the same room as Howard Faustino, let alone getting him to look at their work – even if it was only to tear it apart with disdain. If Faux Pas hung her photographs, she'd get any job she wanted. She'd make so much money off of one show she'd move out of her almost crappy studio apartment with the constantly running toilet and noisy plumbing. Her career, her standing as an artist, her work would have validation.

'Just a few dates,' Kat clarified softly, trying to control her shaking. 'That's all you want?'

'Just a few dates,' Mr Richmond repeated. 'Three months tops.'

'Maybe four,' Mimi said.

'Yes, three or four.' Mr Richmond nodded. 'At least for the summer.'

'Maybe some of the fall.' Mimi paused and said to her husband as an aside, 'It would be great if he had a date for the annual Halloween Ball which Candace always throws. Maybe Kat can talk him into actually wearing a costume.'

'Hmm, great idea, I didn't think of that.' Mr Richmond nodded thoughtfully. 'Yes, until the ball. Perfect.'

To Kat, Mimi continued, 'Get his feet wet. All we want is for him to start seriously dating.'

Kat didn't move. It was April twenty-fifth. Halloween was the end of October. Suddenly just a few dates had turned into a little over six months. Was Faux Pas really worth it?

Hell, yes!

'Show him what it's like to go out and get him to talk about something other than work.' Mimi pressed her lips tightly together and Kat wondered at the subtle gesture. The hairs on the back of her neck stood up and she got the feeling something was wrong with the whole picture. Either that or they were purposefully not telling her something. Mimi cleared her throat and continued, 'Consider it his secret date training. Let him make his mistakes on you, help him and when he's date ready, you're done. You know, don't run away when he's rude or tries to brush you off or is awkward.'

'He's just shy around women,' Mr Richmond said.

'What if he's not interested?' Kat asked. 'It's possible I'm not even his type.'

'Oh, don't you worry about that,' Mimi said. 'I'm sure Vincent is just going to love you. Besides, you're an actress. You'll be able to give him whatever type he likes.'

'Vincent?' Kat asked, glancing at the man across from her with a sick feeling in her stomach.

'Yes, our only son, my namesake and heir,' Mr Richmond said. 'Dr Vincent Richmond the third.'

Kat pulled the black wig off her head and dropped it on her suitcase. Scratching her scalp, she fluffed her long dark-blonde hair before giving it a quick comb through with her fingers. The locks were currently streaked with navy blue chunks and oddly crimped from the intentionally trendy mess of spikes and braids she'd worn that morning. Kat chuckled. She'd put the wig on to freak out her mother when she met her for a late lunch in the hotel restaurant.

Falling onto her back on her hotel room bed, Kat was glad to finally have some alone time. Her room was small compared to the Richmonds' executive suite, but at least there was some colour to the walls and bedspread – not like their untouchable, sterile white. Pastel swirls decorated the comforter and the colour was mimicked by the unobtrusive, bland landscape paintings on the wall. The mauve carpet was new, as was the cheap dresser that doubled as a TV stand.

A large mirror reflected her image back to her. She looked misplaced in the middle-class suburban family style hotel room. With her smudged black eyeliner and dark-blue glitter lipstick, she'd be better fitted to a youth hostel. Kat grinned, the overdone look was mostly to annoy her mother. At twenty-seven, she still loved getting the best of the woman. However, to be fair, after twenty-seven years of having an artist for a daughter, Beatrice didn't seem too bothered by Kat's eccentricities anymore. She always encouraged her daughters to be themselves.

After her meeting with the Richmonds, she'd spent all day shopping with her mother. Mostly, Beatrice window-shopped and Kat did her best to concentrate on finding the perfect photograph. If her mother knew what the Richmonds wanted with her, she didn't let on. In fact, she seemed to be under the impression Kat was going to take some family portraits of them. Kat let her mother think what she wanted.

It was late, but she didn't care as she reached for the phone. She needed to talk to someone – someone normal, someone her kind of normal, someone with a great voice, a way with words and a helluva sexy body.

Dialling, she didn't have to wait long for Jack to answer. An actor by trade, Jack Knight was exactly the type of guy she needed in her life. He was vain enough to take care of himself, narcissistic enough to have his own life and confident enough to answer the phone for a little late night fun.

'Ugh, yeah,' Jack's deep voice answered, groggy with sleep and yet still adorably masculine. She could just picture his messy, shoulder length brown hair tousled about his head, his full mouth partly open in heavy breath, his lids lowered over his eyes like she'd seen them so many times. When he woke up, it always took him a few moments to come to his senses. He'd blink several times, moan softly before his green eyes would clear and a cute little perfect dimple indented his left cheek. 'What? Who's there?'

Kat had been silent as she waited for him to wake up. Her body stirred at the thought of him, at the memory of his bold touch. There was no love, not beyond that of a friend, but that is what made Jack so perfect for her. They didn't have the mess of emotions between them. It was uncomplicated. It was as close to perfection as she imagined ever finding. They understood each other on an artistic level and could appreciate the fact that nothing would ever amount to the burning needs inside of them. Not just the flesh. Sex was merely an expression of their physical human natures. The burn inside them was the desire to be more than they were, the drive to make something perfect – a photograph, a scene, the one moment that would scorch the pages of history for all time. Art was their life but, more importantly, their life was their art.

'Hey, baby,' Kat purred into the phone, only to giggle. 'I promised you a booty call this week.'

'Hmm, hi booty, I was about to give up on you.' Jack chuckled.

'You alone, Mr Knight?'

'You know I don't see anyone but you.' Jack groaned and she could hear the sound of the phone being jostled on his end.

Kat rolled over on her back, turning towards the large mirror. Stretching out her body, she looked at the long line she made on the bed, seeing it as if the mirror was a frame and she a picture frozen forever. She often saw things as if they were photographs. Lifting her knee slightly, she dropped an arm over her head and posed in a more appealing way.

'Love me too much?' she asked. 'No one else compares?'

'No one else understands me like you do, princess. All the other women I meet want something I can't give them.' Jack laughed.

'Your heart?'

'My soul.'

'You are a soulless bastard, aren't you?' she teased. Jack's loyalty was perfect. Before they'd even started fucking, they'd gone to the clinic together to get tested. They were both clean and since they always used protection there was never a risk of children. Jack didn't fuck around on her and he had no reason to lie to her if he did. He didn't want to contract anything and Kat couldn't say she blamed him. It didn't make them exclusive, but it did make them picky. Their arrangement had been that way for nearly four years now.

'Did you call to bust my balls, Kat? 'Cause my new director is doing the busting just fine without you helping him out.'

'No, baby, I called to listen to you play with them.' Kat giggled.

'Mmm.' The sound was incredibly sexy. 'Things not going well?'

'Well enough. I might have a line on a job when I get back.'

'Go all the way to Connecticut to get a job here? That's pretty funny.'

Kat didn't even bother to correct his mistake. She had sisters if she needed someone to listen to her innermost thoughts and friends if she wanted to debate the current state of America's affairs – not that she ever did. Jack she kept around for another reason altogether.

'I don't want to talk about work,' Kat said. 'I need you, baby. I wish you were here with me. Right now.'

'Oh yeah, and what would you do to me if I were there right now, princess?' Jack's breathing audibly deepened.

Kat knew the man liked to sleep naked so there was no point in asking him what he was wearing. Rolling up on the bed, she unbuttoned her denim jeans and pushed them off her hips. 'First, I'd make you peel every inch of shiny tight black leather off my body.' She fell back on the bed, kicking off her boots and socks before pushing completely out of her blue jeans. Lying on the bed in her panties, she pulled at her knit sweater. 'You know the leather I'm talking about, don't you?'

'Oh, yeah. The outfit I got you from the studio prop room last Halloween.' Jack groaned. He'd stolen the costume for her as a joke. The studio he'd been working for was on location from Los Angeles and they hadn't even missed it.

'That's the one. I'd make you peel it off my body, slowly revealing my legs, my ass, my wet hot pussy.' Kat pulled the corded phone back from her ear and lifted the sweater off, tossing it aside. More comfortable, she rested on her back, lightly running her hand over her flat stomach. Her black lace panties and sturdy white bra didn't match, but it didn't matter. This was fantasy. 'My corset beneath the leather is tight, cupping under my breasts, exposing them and pushing them up so they're high and perky. Mmm, and I'm wearing crotchless panties.'

Jack made an animalistic noise. 'You have a beautiful voice. I love it when you talk like this.'

'And I love it when you talk like Lord Angus,' Kat said with a giggle. Angus had been one of Jack's favourite roles. He talked like a Scottish laird for months while the play had been in rehearsal. Unfortunately, the show was shut down after only one night and no reviews of his performance had been written. Jack was lucky to have gotten half his paycheck from the ordeal. It was a joke between them that at least he'd gotten something from his time as Angus – a sexy accent.

'Do ye now, lass,' he murmured, affecting the soft burr. 'And where are we?'

Kat involuntarily trembled. There was just something about American girls and accents. She didn't care if it was stereotypical, it was very true. Just hearing Jack affect one always turned her on. It was exotic. Closing her eyes, Kat wiggled on the bed. 'Forget the leather. I'm on a bed of furs in a tunic gown and we can hear the sound of a celebration beyond your tent as your men celebrate their victory.'

'Aye.'

'You've just won a giant, vicious battle and your muscles are hard and sweaty from the fight. I was captured amongst your enemy and brought to your tent by your men as part of the spoils of war.' Kat quickly sat up in the bed, leaning over the side to grab a large lifelike pink vibrator and a tube of lubricant from her bag. She tossed it next to her and again lay on her back.

'Ye have nothing to fear,' Jack said in the thick accent.

'Oh, but I do, because you peel back your kilt, reveal-ing your hard thick weapon. It's just as hard as the rest of you as you wrap your fist around it.' Kat ran her hand lightly over her stomach, liking their fantasy game. 'Frightened, I try to escape by crawling off the bed, but you stop me. I try to fight you off, but you're too strong. You rip my gown from me in your haste to see me naked.' Kat tugged at her bra and panties, quickly getting them off her body so she was naked on the bed.

'Where ye goin' wench? There's nowhere to run. No one here will help ye.'

'Your eyes light up with devious intent as you look at

my huge breasts and you automatically want to thrust your cock between them and come on my neck.'

'Aye, I do.'

'You pin my arms over my head.' Kat lifted her hands, bringing them together at the wrists. 'I know you're going to fuck me good. I can feel your hard, giant cock along my thigh.' She arched on the bed, make-believing she was held down by the conquering Scottish laird.

Jack's heavy breathing continued as he whispered into the phone. She couldn't understand what he was saying, and the odds were he was just making up Gaelic words for the sake of the part, but she let the game take over completely. She could practically feel him, the pressure of his body to hers, the idea of the Scottish laird so vivid in her mind.

'And then you surprise me by kissing me. You steal my breath and weaken my will to fight you. Your strong chest is against mine and our hearts are beating so fast.' Kat reached for her vibrator, holding the phone with her shoulder as she lubricated it.

'I trap your small body beneath mine,' Jack continued the story without missing a beat. 'I feel you getting wet as I suck a breast hard into my mouth. As your resistance fades, I let you go and you touch me, running your hands along my chest. You've never seen a warrior so handsome and strong, so in control. You beg me to conquer you as I did your people.'

Kat gave a small passion-infused smile towards the phone. Jack's arrogance was in his voice, but she didn't mind. He played the dominant role well. 'Oh, yes, conquer me, m'lord.'

'I bid you to kiss every inch of me, worshipping my flesh with your tongue. You can't resist. My body is like a drug and you beg to be fucked. I throw you down on the furs and your legs fall open in invitation, ready for my cock to ram into you. You gasp as my cock edges closer to your sweet pussy. You know I'm huge and I'm going to tear you apart with my colossal size. You beg me to take it easy on you, telling me how you've never had one so big, so huge, so handsome, so . . .' Jack paused when Kat giggled.

'Jack, stop trying to make me laugh. You're ruining the moment.'

'Sorry,' he chuckled, 'couldn't resist. It was starting to sound like those novels Zoe reads and I just got into the part of the beefcake.'

Kat turned on her vibrator, letting the wet tip run along the crease where her thigh met her pussy. She waited until Jack gave the word signifying he was ready as well. There was movement on his end of the phone and she imagined he was looking for some lubricant of his own. Hearing a snap of a plastic lid, she smiled, easing the vibrator towards her clit.

'Ah, that's it, lass. Dinna worry, I'm goin' to fuck ye good.' Jack continued to talk dirty to her, using the accented words of the Scottish conqueror. Kat parted her thighs, running the vibrating rubber cockhead along her folds. She pressed along her clit, circling it, mixing the cream of her body and the lubrication to ease the vibrator's way.

'Tell me what you're doing with your hands,' Kat said.

'I've got one on my balls, squeezing them, and the other is filled with heated lotion on the tip of my shaft, ready to thrust. It's hot and wet just like your pussy and my cock is so hard and ready for you.'

'Fuck me, m'lord,' Kat moaned, loving how Jack could easily keep up with the fantasy, not like some lovers she'd had in the past. Sure the plot was something out of a romance novel like Jack said, but that's what made it so much fun. When Jack put on a role, it was as if he was fucking both her mind and her body. He was no longer Jack, he was the fantasy. 'Give it to me.'

'Aye,' he growled, letting his voice drop into a heated murmur.

Jack grunted and moaned. Kat, following his lead, thrust the vibrator deep into her pussy, filling it with the thick length. It buzzed, hitting perfectly inside her as she rocked it along her G-spot. A thin attachment at the base vibrated her clit helping to build the pleasure inside her body. The conversation became a series of shared grunts and half-spoken sentences. She longed to have Jack on top of her, right there in the room with her. She wanted to feel his weight against her body, knowing for that moment she wasn't alone. Holding the phone to her ear with her shoulder, she flipped over using the bed to help hold the vibrator in place as she lifted and fell in a steady rhythm on top of it.

'Jack,' she whispered into the phone, gasping as the orgasm built to a trembling peak. She held the phone tight, her heart beating hard in her chest, her flesh just starting to bead with sweat.

'Argh,' Jack grunted, the one sound he made when he found release. It took her a few seconds longer but soon she was coming with him.

Kat fell forward on the bed, smiling and relaxed. She shut off her vibrator and tossed it aside on the bed. Who knew, she might want it again before the night was over.

'Hey, Kat, thanks for calling, but I have to go. I have an early day tomorrow. I want to get down some lines before the director gets to rehearsal and some of us guys are going to meet up early to practise.'

'Uh, sure, I'll get in touch when I get back in town. Bye.'

'Night, princess.'

Kat crawled over and hung up the phone. Resting naked on the bed, she again turned to the mirror and held completely still except for the rise and fall of her chest. Seeing her dishevelled image looking back at her, she admired the realistic way her make-up was now smudged along her cheek in a dark glittering streak.

Staring at herself for a long time, she didn't move. Her

head raced with thoughts of her work, this chance at Faux Pas, of what pieces she'd need for her own art show in such a place. And, as she drifted off to sleep, she thought once of Dr Vincent, a sad, awkward man who needed his parents to buy dates for him.

Chapter Two

Upper West Side, Manhattan, New York City. One week later...

'A doctor?' Zoe whispered, leaning forward and bracing her arms on the table. The white linen tablecloth wrinkled slightly and she instantly pulled back, smoothing it.

Kat nodded at Zoe. She was one of her younger sisters. Zoe's short, shaggy haircut fitted her slender face and long neck perfectly, giving her a very pixyish look. Right now she wore it streaked with subtle hints of brownish red. Both of them had matching dark-blue eyes. Out of all her sisters, Kat was closest to Zoe. They just seemed to get each other.

It was late afternoon and the small, trendy Italian restaurant, Sedurre, wasn't very busy. In fact, the last customers had just left and the only waitress was in the back doing side work in preparation of the evening rush.

The long, skinny building could only fit two rows of tables down each wall, leaving a single walkway for the waitresses to go down the middle. Brown vinyl booths were along the sides in the far back, surrounded by more crowded tables. The walls were white, matching the table cloths and linen napkins, and the décor was minimal. There were a few Italian influenced paintings of Venice and Rome, but aside from the vases of fake flowers, that was it.

Even though extremely cramped during the rush, the restaurant was popular. Kat liked to think it was because her sister was one of the cooks. Already, Zoe had proven herself every bit as talented as the sous chef. Kat was positive her sister would some day make head chef, even possibly open her own restaurant.

'Can you believe it? They've actually hired me to date the man,' Kat said. She had told Zoe everything. How could she not? It was just too weird. This was definitely a time in a girl's life when she needed a sister's opinion.

'And did you really use the word deflower?' Zoe laughed.

'Yeah, I'd been on an old novel kick and panicked. Besides, what did you expect me to say? "Hey, so you want me to rock your son's world?" That's real classy.'

'This whole thing sounds strange if you ask me.'

'After what I've told you, can you imagine what kind of offspring Mimi and Vincent would've produced?' Kat shivered just thinking about it. 'I mean, ew.'

'To be fair, our parents had all of us and we're –' Zoe paused, shrugging, '– not them.'

In total there were five Matthews sisters – Megan, the oldest at twenty-nine, then Kat, Zoe, Sasha and the baby, Ella, who would be graduating from high school that month. All of them had the same fair complexions. Zoe, Kat and Ella all had their mother's blonde hair. Megan and Sasha took after their father's dark brown. After so many girls, their parents had given up on ever having sons – though they remained hopeful for sons-in-law. So far, not one of the Matthews sisters showed any signs of settling down.

'I can't believe our mother actually set it up,' said Kat. 'Do you think she knew what Mimi wanted to ask me to do?'

'Mom's just weird. Who knows what she was think-ing? She probably thought it was the only way to get you out on a date. Either that or she divined your future in the tea leaves again.' Zoe laughed. 'Remember when she was convinced Sasha was going to get hit by a car if she went outside and made her spend the entire day in bed until the signs passed?'

'Oh, gawd. I don't know how dad does it,' Kat said. 'That woman drives me crazy.'

'She means well,' Zoe lightly defended their mother.

'It still doesn't mean she's not crazy. Anyway, what do you think about this whole dating the doctor thing? I need a quick analysis of the situation.'

'Hmm, okay, first thought. Why would a doctor who comes from a rich family need help getting dates? This is New York. Why isn't he on the most eligible bachelors list?' Zoe frowned. 'I don't like it. He must be a real cretin or mean to old people or something.'

'But, Faux Pas,' Kat insisted, nearly wiggling in her seat just saying the words.

'Well, I didn't say you wouldn't do it,' Zoe answered. 'Of course you'll do it. I mean, Faux Pas. You land a prestigious show like that and all the fashion magazines will have to pay attention to your work. Everybody pays attention to Howard Faustino's artists. There'll be no more scrounging for jobs. In fact, you'd probably have more than fashion mags at your door with offers. The field will be wide open.'

'I know.' Kat bit her lip and squirmed around excitedly in her chair. Her heart beat so fast at the very idea of her career taking off in such a way. It was all her dreams, right in front of her, about to come true. She'd sacrificed everything for her work, for her dreams of making it big – not that there had been much to sacrifice. She'd never had any serious boyfriends, or at least none she seriously felt anything for beyond great sex.

'You can date an ugly, awkward man for six months. Besides, all dating consists of is getting together every once in a while. Let's see, once a weekend for six months, that's like twenty-four dates, minus a few because you can skip them for work – once you get a job.'

Kat lifted her glass of water and nodded in agreement. Yeah, she really needed to find a job.

'Mark some off as group dates, which will be important if the guy is such a creep that you positively cannot be seen alone publicly with him.'

'Group dates,' Kat agreed. 'Perfect idea.'

'That's only like twenty dates, less if it takes him a while to ask you. Then you're just creating opportunities, like showing up where he is, running into him "coincidentally". That sort of thing. Twenty dates is very doable and it will be less than that if he has to work weekends. Most doctors do because of staff rotations.' Zoe took a deep breath, nodding. 'What hospital does he work for?'

'He's not that kind of doctor. He's, ah, I forget how to pronounce it. I have it written down somewhere.' Kat glanced at the black camera bag she carried instead of a purse, but didn't touch it. The paper it was written on was at home by Sasha's computer on which she had looked up the word. Sasha was a college student at NYU and Kat let her use her apartment to study when she couldn't get work done at the dorms. Her sister had left her laptop behind last time she dropped by. Since it had a wireless network card, they could steal bandwidth from one of Kat's neighbours and connect to the internet. 'He's one of those non-medical doctors. An ety-*something*-ologist. I looked it up, but basically they study the origins of words and stuff.'

'Ah, one of those English professor guys. I see now why he's not on the bachelor's list.' Zoe nodded knowingly. 'You should take him to visit dad. I'm sure they'd have plenty to talk about. Maybe they buy their tweed suits at the same place.'

'Oh, hell no,' Kat said, shivering at the very idea. Their father, Douglas Matthews was a retired English professor. He'd worked at several private schools, most prestigiously Harvard. Usually he wasn't one to pressure his daughters, but if he found a guy like Mr English, he'd probably start harassing her as much as her mother did to settle down.

Zoe laughed, hitting her flat palm on the table in exaggerated mirth. 'You could double date with mom and dad!'

Kat shivered in abhorrence of the suggestion. There was no way she'd double date with her parents!

'Ha, ha, ha, very funny,' she said dryly. 'My luck, dad would want me to settle down and marry the guy.'

'What's wrong with that?' Zoe asked. 'It just might turn out to be true love.'

'Have you been reading those romance novels again?' Kat asked, shaking her head. 'I swear, romance is an addiction and I for one have better things to do. Besides, I like being addicted to coffee better than being addicted to love. Coffee serves a purpose. It keeps me awake. With love, you have only two emotions – gushy or heart-broken. Both are completely unappealing and have no place in a modern woman's life. I won't say it doesn't exist, just that it's foolish to wish for it. There are so many more fulfilling things than being someone's Mrs.'

'You're hopeless.' Zoe sighed. 'Not that I think you would fall in love with an intellectual.'

Kat knew what her sister meant and didn't even pretend to be offended. It was true, she usually only dated artistic people – painters, musicians, actors, poets, men who thought like she did. Life was an adventure, to be taken at leisure. She looked at love the same way. Why stress over the love of one person, when you could have the love of family and friends? Such a type of love that came with no strings and was uncomplicated – or at least ideally it should be.

'Huh, I'll have to contemplate that one later,' Kat said, more to herself.

'What?' Zoe asked, confused.

'Oh, nothing, the supposedly uncomplicated love of family.' Kat waved a dismissing hand.

'You lost me that time.' Zoe frowned.

'Never mind, it's not important.' Kat laughed. 'Yeah, this poor man probably really does wears tweed suits and has a comb over. Maybe I can do him some good. I'll take him shopping and spruce him up a bit. He'll be my makeover project. With any luck, he'll find a real girl-friend and I'll be off the hook in less than a month.'

'You know, that's not such a bad idea. Hook Mr English up with someone else more his speed and then it's not your fault he stops dating you. You did say that his parents just want him to get out there.' Zoe shrugged. 'Could work.'

'It's definitely a plan.'

'So, how are you going to do it?'

Kat reached down to the side pocket of her camera bag and pulled out a book. She handed it to her sister.

'Five hundred big words everyone should know and love. A guide to intellectual conversation,' Zoe read. As she handed it back, she said sarcastically, 'Sounds dreamy.'

'I thought it might help if he got all smart on me.' Kat grinned. 'Want to quiz me? I've got two pages almost memorised.'

'Ah, tempting, but no,' Zoe laughed.

'Who knows, maybe if I whisper big words in his ear, he'll get all excited,' Kat dropped her tone to a sultry pout, 'pneumonoultramicroscopicsilicovolcanokoniosis.'

'What in the world is that?' Zoe laughed, shaking her head.

'It's a disease in the lungs caused by breathing parti-cles of some kind of volcanic dust.'

'And that will turn him on?' Zoe made a playful move to grab the book from Kat. 'You've lost it, sweetie.'

Kat jerked her arm back, still holding the book. 'It happens to be the longest word in the English language. I looked it up.' Kat laughed. 'I guess some guy made it up in the nineteen-thirties, but it still counts.'

'Huh, I thought it was that children's song mom used to sing to us all the time when we were growing up, "Supercalifragilisticexpialidocious".'

'Nope –' Kat took a sip of water, '– common misconception.'

'That is it. Miss Katarina, you have got to go.' Zoe stood up. 'We've officially run out of things to talk about when we start discussing big words. Besides, I've got some chicken back there that needs prepping.'

'I'm going, I'm going. You don't have to throw me out.' Kat slipped the book back into her bag. 'Besides, you know I'd never stand between a cook and her chicken.'

'You want me to make you a sandwich before the boss gets back?'

Kat's smile fell. 'No, I'm fine.'

'Have you eaten today?' Zoe persisted. 'You're looking thin.'

Kat forced the smile back over her face. She was hungry, but she had to stop taking her sister's charity. The last thing she needed was Zoe losing her cool new job because of her. 'You're one to talk. Whoever heard of a skinny chef? You should gain at least –'

'Kat,' Zoe drawled, 'quit avoiding.'

'Fine, yeah, a quick sandwich,' Kat agreed. She stood, slipping the camera strap over her head so it went across her chest and back with the bag resting on her hip. She'd designed it out of a side pack she found on clearance. It was much easier than hauling around the usual awkward rectangular shaped camera bags. 'I am a little lightheaded.'

'Hmm,' Zoe walked back towards the kitchen. Reaching around the corner, she pulled out a sack. Kat laughed. Zoe already had a lunch made for her. 'Too bad this date job doesn't actually pay in cash.'

'I know,' Kat said, before thanking Zoe for the food. 'But, if it does pay off the way I want it to, then I won't have to worry about cash and I'll buy you your own restaurant with my millions.'

'I'll hold you to that,' Zoe said, pointing a finger at her.

'I'll talk to you later. I'm going to go and do some recon, see if I can't figure out who the guy is and why he's so awkward. According to his parents, he works downtown, not too far from here. Maybe I'll catch a glimpse of him and see what I have to work with. Who knows, maybe the whole makeover thing could be fun.'

'Did you ever think maybe he's gay?' Zoe asked, tilting her head thoughtfully to the side. 'It'd make sense as to why he doesn't date.'

'Ugh, don't curse it.' Kat leaned against the outside door, and pushed it open without using her hands. 'I can pretend to be many things, a boy isn't one of them.'

'Good luck,' Zoe called. Laughing, she pointed at Kat's head. 'Oh, and I love the pink. *Très chic.*'

Kat reached up and touched a long strip of her bangs. The hot pink chunks framed her face while the bulk of the heavy brown locks were piled high on top of her head. Grinning, she said, 'Thanks. I did it last night when I couldn't sleep. Though, I'll probably have to take it out for Mr English.'

'Who knows.' Zoe winked. The waitress came out of the back with a tray and began clearing a table. The sisters ignored her. 'Mr English might like a little freaky freaky in the bedroom.'

Kat rolled her eyes, letting the door close behind her as she stayed inside the restaurant. She might pity date the poor man for purely selfish reasons, but she wasn't going to give him pity sex. 'No way am I sleeping with him. The last thing I want is some nerdy English guy falling in love with me. Besides, freaky freaky is why I keep Jack around.'

'Kat!' Zoe scolded. 'You are not still seeing Jack, are you?'

'What do you mean still? I've been with him for four years.'

'I know.' Zoe shrugged. 'I just keep hoping you'll give him up. He's not right for you.'

'What? It's not like I'm going to marry the guy or any guy for that matter. A single girl's got to get her kicks somehow and Jack's good at accents.' Kat grinned, again pushing the front door open to let in the unseasonably hot air. 'I like to think of Jack as a giant sex toy that never runs out of batteries. Besides, just like a vibrator, he never complains when I get rid of him afterward. I just tell him I'm inspired to work and he leaves.'

'Kat!' Zoe shook her head. Kat could tell her sister was trying really hard not to laugh. The waitress just grinned at them, chuckling to herself.

'Ah, you know you love me.' Kat winked.

'Yep, you are the bane of my existence.' Zoe waved a hand and turned to go towards the kitchen.

Kat smiled, stepping out into the bright sunlight. Opening the paper bag, her grin only widened as the smell of food wafted over her. Now this is why she loved Zoe. She took out half the cut sandwich and sniffed the delicious grilled chicken smothered with homemade mozzarella, fresh basil, sliced tomatoes and a creamy ranchlike sauce Zoe had invented. On the bottom of the bag was an extra sandwich for later.

Who needs true love when I have sisters, she thought, as she took a very unladylike bite.

The address she was looking for was several blocks away and it was fairly hot out, but Kat decided to walk it. With traffic, she'd probably get there faster on foot and she couldn't really afford to waste money on a cab ride anyway. Eating as she strolled, she navigated her way along the busy sidewalk.

Horns honked, drowned out by the sound of busy street workers drilling away. Kat ignored the sounds, having tuned them out long ago. For the most part, she minded her own business, but her eyes were always searching the crowds, looking for that one must-have photograph. It didn't look as if she'd find it today, but she never knew.

She finished the first sandwich, wrapped up the second one and put it in the side pocket of her camera bag for later. Stopping in front of a window she quickly adjusted her hair, using the reflection as a mirror. Kat really didn't have a plan, but knew it was best to be prepared in case she found an opportunity to meet Dr Vincent. With that in mind, she dug a couple of breath mints out of her bag.

'Vincent,' she said, thoughtfully studying her reflection in the glass. She wore faded denim jeans and a black jersey tunic that was split down the front, starting at the ruched material between her breasts and falling softly below her hips. The slit showed a splash of hot pink. It matched her hair and had actually been the inspiration for her to colour the pieces framing her face. Scrunching up her face, she lowered her voice into a breathy, seductive murmur, 'Hello, Dr Richmond, know any big words?'

The shoulder straps on the T-shirt were wide, but still left her arms bare like a tank top. She glanced around to make sure no one was staring at her before reaching down the front to grab her breasts and lift them up to show more cleavage. Next, she pulled her hands out and quickly adjusted the underwired bra. A quick squirt of the perfume conveniently kept in the side pocket of her camera bag and she was ready to go meet the man who'd make all her dreams come true.

Kat laughed. Most women seemed to think men themselves were the ultimate goal – marriage, family, pretty little homes in the suburbs to raise the kids in. Not Kat. If marriage happened, it happened. If not, then not. Her whole life was not built around the desire to make someone else happy. Just because she wasn't in love didn't mean she wasn't complete. Her first love was her photography, the burning desire to make something real, tangible, moving, potent, the need to capture the small moments that made life what it was. And, if some of those moments happened to be taking photographs of designer clothing for top selling magazines, then so be it. Kat was happy doing what she loved. Fashion, after all, was an important, if not immortal part of society.

The front entrance to the building Vincent worked in was narrow and poorly marked. Kat actually walked past it and had to turn back around. She stopped, glancing up the side of the tall brick structure. It wasn't much to look at, nestled between larger retail stores and set back from the street by a small row of steps. A little weathered plaque next to the door read, 'DJP Scientific Department of Entomological Research'.

'This is it,' she whispered to herself, taking a deep breath. Kat wasn't nervous about meeting a man, so much as what that man represented. She made herself a promise. No matter how bad or obnoxious he was, she'd get him to ask her out on a date. Vincent Richmond was her chance of living her dream – a chance at Faux Pas.

Kat reached for the wooden door and pushed it open. It was painted a dark green with white accents around the edges. The interior was dim compared to the bright sunlight outside and it took a moment for her eyes to adjust. White, naked walls surrounded her. The small, square foyer was empty except for a wooden desk with an ugly yellow corded telephone and a wooden chair. The furniture was scuffed at the corners, attesting to its age. The floors were wood, the boards a little uneven, and they squeaked terribly when she stepped on them. Wrinkling her nose, she tried not to sneeze. The room was covered in dust and had the musty scent of old books.

'I can't stand it!' The enraged feminine voice came from the long hall behind the desk.

Kat took a slow step into the reception area at the

angry sound, curious to see what was going on. She heard loud, stomping footsteps before a short woman turned the corner and stalked towards the front.

'The advisors said he was difficult. Difficult, my ass! That arrogant son of a bitch man is impossible. Five times those damned things got out. I am not looking for his stupid pets again. I did not sign up for this! I don't care if they do fail me. I'm so out of here.' The woman was talking to herself, angrily jerking her arms. Her neat bun was pulled to the nape of her neck, a severe look that made her appear older than she probably was. The khaki pants with the high waistline and the tucked in white button-down shirt didn't help matters. Narrow black glasses slid down her nose and she pushed them up with an irritated thrust of her middle finger. Seeing Kat, she paused in her tirade.

'Hi,' said Kat, smiling at the woman.

The woman actually harrumphed at her, before answering, 'Good luck with him. He's all yours. I'm out of here.'

'But –?'

'I don't care how good this job looks on the resume or how much it pays,' the angry woman continued, going to the desk and pulling out a pink backpack. She threaded it over her shoulders. 'It's so not worth it. There's a reason why that man goes through assistants like he does. It's a wonder any of us last more than an hour. Oh, but we do, don't we? No wonder they offer us scholarships to get us in here. But, I tell you, I'd rather pay off a student loan than put up with this shit.'

'Ah,' Kat's mouth opened to say more, but the woman only brushed rudely past her, continuing to mumble.

'I told him I quit, but he probably didn't hear me – like usual.' The woman pulled open the door. Glancing down the hall from which she came, she growled, 'Impossible!'

'Okay,' Kat said under her breath when the woman was gone. 'That was interesting.'

'Margaret!' a man yelled. 'Margaret, I need your help.'

Kat stepped closer to the desk, her curious nature again getting the better of her as she waited to see who had made the woman so mad. Watching the hallway as a man turned the corner, she stiffened.

She instantly looked him over, studying him with a photographer's eye, taking in every last detail and memorising it. The man was adorable in an absent-minded professor kind of way. She found herself completely enamoured with the image he presented her. He wasn't drop dead gorgeous by any means with his tired, messy appearance, or at least from what she could tell he wasn't. An overgrowth of dark facial hair hid most of his features from view, including his lips, and the hair on his head bushed out, falling over his forehead. Safety glasses covered his eyes, the clear plastic obscuring the true colour of his irises underneath, though they looked to be a deep, solid brown.

Still, there was something very appealing about him. Though messy, his hair fell in thick waves of dark brown, curling loosely around his head. It was mussed up in such a manner that made Kat think he'd been pulling at it in frustration. He wore a white lab coat, dark charcoal grey pants and casual black leather slip-on shoes. The shoes looked designer from a distance, but it was hard to tell.

'Margaret!' Seeing her, he stopped and adjusted his safety glasses. 'Oh, there you are Margaret. Very good. He's disappeared again. I need your help.'

When she didn't move right away, he lifted the safety glasses and put them on his head, as his eyes narrowed in on her. They were bloodshot and had dark circles underneath them attesting to the fact that this man hadn't slept for some time. Kat was even more enthralled. The curious artist inside her screamed for answers.

Who was he? What kept him awake? Why was he

screaming for Margaret? Why did he think she was Margaret?

'Well, come on then,' he said.

'I'm Kat,' Kat said. 'Not Margaret.'

'What? Oh, right, Kat,' the man answered, straightening slightly. 'I'm always forgetting that, aren't I? So sorry. Kat.' He nodded his head and repeated her name softly as if doing so would help him remember it, 'Kat. Kat. Kat.'

She just watched, her hand absently straying to the latch on her camera bag. The man was absolutely distracted. He was looking right at her, but she had a feeling he wasn't seeing her at all. She could envision his mind racing with thoughts.

'You think I'd remember your name as you've been working so long for me.'

Kat didn't move. He still thought she was his employee? Having seen the fashion nightmare that just walked out of the office, she wasn't sure whether to laugh or cry.

'I will try to remember, Kat,' he promised. She decided he had a nice voice, deep and low. The kind of soothing tone a girl could fall asleep listening to. 'Sorry, I guess my other assistant must have been Margaret.'

'That's perfectly all right,' said Kat, not moving.

'Come on, you're not paid to stand there.' He motioned, as if to insinuate she was to follow him down the hall.

'But, I'm not paid,' Kat said, slowly moving to go after him. How could she not? The man was so strange, she found herself utterly fascinated. True, mildly attractive nerds weren't usually her type, but there was something all too appealing to his lost looks and his wild hair. Besides, there was a kindness in his voice, in the tone of it that she detected right away. Maybe it wasn't a tone so much as it was a feeling she got when she heard it.

The man stopped again. He shook his head before fumbling to pull up his lab coat. She leaned to the side, getting a better view of his trim waist. The man was in shape, either he worked out or he was so busy he forgot to eat. Hmm, maybe science guy had a little more to offer than she first gave him credit for. Perhaps with a clean shave and a lab coat-free wardrobe, he'd be passable.

OK, why was she suddenly having very sexual thoughts about Mr Distracted? Maybe it was the lab coat and glasses, but her mind turned on a very wicked fantasy involving the man before her, a science lab and being fucked from behind.

Get a hold of yourself, Kat, she told herself.

Even so, her body stirred, becoming moist between her thighs. Maybe playing patient and mad scientist would be a better scenario. He could do naughty little science experiments on her with his tongue.

Whoa, Kat, reign it in.

'Sorry, I must have forgotten again.'

His words jerked her out of her fantasy and she blinked several times, trying to follow what he was saying.

'Don't hesitate to remind me in the future.' Shoving his hand into his pocket, he pulled out a wallet. He began walking, digging through the wallet for cash. 'How much do I owe you?'

'Ah, nothing,' Kat said.

'That's ridiculous. You can't work for free. I know the college calls this an internship, but still, I prefer it if you made something as my assistant. I remember what it is like to carry a full class load and an internship.'

He stopped at a door. The glass window in the door was frosted over and a gold plate read, 'Laboratory 1A Dr Vincent Richmond, PhD Entomology'.

This poor adorably lost man was Dr Richmond? Her Dr Richmond? This was the guy she was supposed to date? Kat took a deep breath. This was going to be harder than she'd first thought.

Step one. Get him to actually look at her.

Vincent grabbed the doorknob, opened the door and turned seemingly all at the same time. In his hand was a hundred dollar bill.

'Take this,' he said, thrusting it back at her. 'I'll figure out the difference later. Right now we have work to do.'

Kat looked at the money, very tempted to put it in her pocket. He shook it expectantly. She wasn't a saint, but she also wasn't so mean as to rob this preoccupied man.

'But, I'm not –' she tried to say, but he sighed heavily, stopping her.

Vincent grabbed her hand and put the money in her palm. His fingers were warm, but he didn't let his touch linger. She frowned as he turned away, ending any discussion over the money. She watched him closely, but he didn't even look at her. His hands were on his hips as he looked up and down the laboratory studying the floor and ceiling in turn as he walked beside the long line of tables.

Row upon row of narrow drawers filled one of the walls. They were each marked with a white sticker written on in small precise script. The stickers were labelled with a letter and several numbers. Opened books were piled high on one of the tables. Some had highlighted passages in them, others were marked with paperclips. A notepad, filled with the same script that was on the drawers, was by the books. They were compiled of long lists of Latin words and strange notations.

The door had said this was a laboratory, but Kat found the room odd for a lab, though the old brown tables and the library atmosphere were probably suited to a guy who studied word history. Cluttered along the edge of the long counter, there were beakers, microscopes, an array of instruments from tweezers to little slides and some sort of machine that looked like it belonged in a science laboratory, but Kat had no idea what it did. She'd failed science in high school and never went to college.

There'd been no point. Ever since she was little, she'd wanted to be a photographer. She deduced easily that the drawers had to be filled with old texts and maybe the equipment was used for carbon dating or whatever it was these types of men did.

'I don't work for you.' Kat set her camera bag on the table. Thinking she'd seen movement on the floor, she glanced down. It was nothing.

'Sorry, what was that?'

'I don't work for you,' Kat repeated.

Vincent stopped, standing very still as if it took him a moment to process what she said. Slowly, he turned. 'You can't quit on me. I've had too many quit on me this year.'

'But –'

He held up his hands and came back to where she waited by the door. As if seeing her for the first time, he blinked, his eyes roaming over her face and clothes. 'Ah, wow, you're . . .'

Kat waited. Beautiful? Pretty? Sexy? Dateable? This was more like the reaction she was used to from men.

'. . . ah, different,' Vincent said, not exactly in pleasure. He frowned at her pink hair. 'Did that happen here? Did you have a chemical spill? I hope you filled out the proper paperwork. I'm not sure what I have around here that would cause such a reaction in human hair, but is that why you're quitting?'

Kat tensed. Different? She was different? This nut job was one to talk. He didn't even know his own assistant's name or what she looked like.

'Here,' he reached for his wallet, 'I'll pay to get your hair fixed, only don't quit. Please. I'm so close to a breakthrough, I can feel it. I've got too much going on right now and the college won't send me another assist- ant until the autumn semester.'

'I coloured my hair like this on purpose,' she said, dryly.

'Oh.' He looked surprised. 'Ah, well, it's lovely.'

His tone was hardly convincing. So, the man didn't like her hair. So much for Zoe's theory that he'd like a little freaky freaky in the bedroom. Not that she was going anywhere near this man's bedroom. Different? Did he really call her different?

Kat reminded herself why she was there in the first place. Faux Pas. She had to get him to date her. Since by the looks of him she could assume he never left work, maybe the best way to get him to date her was to work with him. Besides, she really needed a job.

'You're in luck,' Kat said, smiling brightly at him as if she hadn't a care in the world. What was it his mother had insisted? Part of the job was looking past his rudeness and not running away too quickly when he was ineloquent. 'I happen to be looking for a job. Your assistant, who I can assume was possibly named Margaret, quit on you. She walked out when I was walking in. She mentioned that you might not have listened to her when she told you.'

Vincent frowned and scratched his beard. He glanced around the room, leaning over as if looking for something under the counters. His pet, perhaps? Kat glanced around, not seeing any dogs or cats lounging about. Could it be a rodent of some sort? A little mouse maybe? A shiver worked over her spine. She wasn't a big fan of mice, but she could handle it.

As if to himself, he said, 'Someone was talking. I wasn't really listening.'

'Hmm, that would've probably been her,' said Kat, nodding. 'People tend to appreciate being listened to.'

'What?'

'I said, how much does this gig pay?'

'Do you have any experience in a laboratory?'

'Do you have any other job applicants vying for the position?'

'Uh, good point,' Vincent said. 'Say, five hundred a

week in cash, eight hour days, Monday through Saturday. Sundays off.'

'Five-fifty,' Kat counter offered.

'Deal,' he said. 'Now, help me look.'

'I would've taken five.' She watched him lean over again to look under the table.

'I would've paid six. I'm desperate.'

Kat hid a smile. Maybe on a good day he wouldn't be so bad. It was possible he was under a lot of scientific stress. Maybe his boss was breathing down his neck for him to get something done. There might be some sort of enormous book find he had to get dated for archaeological research purposes. Thinking of it like that, the job as his assistant might actually prove to be interesting. She could document the find or something.

Glancing around, she determined her first order of business would be to replace the burned out light bulbs and maybe dust the rows of drawers. Though dust added to the dingy atmosphere, and she'd be sure to get a picture of the room as was, it took away some of the scientific feel to the place. Scientists were supposed to be clean and tidy and she didn't want to work around dust all day. She made a move to walk behind him, only to stop as a big brown spider ran across the floor. Kat gasped, instantly crushing the insect under her boot. She shivered in disgust. There was nothing nastier than spiders.

Make that first order of business to get some bug spray, she thought, as she scraped the bottom of her boot on the edge of the table to get the spider's remains off.

'So what kind of pet are we looking for?'

'Pet?' Vincent asked. 'No, no. I'm looking for the *loxosceles reclusa*. I was milking it when I was distracted and it got loose.'

'I'm sorry, what am I looking for?' Kat craned her neck, looking around the laboratory.

'Oh, ah, the *loxosceles reclusa*, the brown recluse,' he answered, sounding distracted. 'It's a spider about a half an inch long with eight legs, six eyes in a semicircle on its head and a fiddle-shaped mark on its cephalothorax.'

Kat tensed, glancing back to where she'd scraped off the squished spider. 'Say what?'

'Cephalothorax. It means upper body, like where you'd expect to see a neck.'

'No, I'm sorry, I'm still trying to get the fact – did you say you were milking a spider?' Kat would've laughed if he didn't look so serious.

'For the venom, yes. It's a hobby. It helps me relax so I can concentrate better, only I sometimes think too hard and lose hold of them and they get loose. The current antivenom isn't available on the market because of the possible side effects.' Vincent sighed heavily. 'This is taking too long. I have work to get done. I don't have time, I don't have time.'

Kat shivered. He said the whole milking thing like it was normal. 'Why would you even have a spider? Don't you . . .? I mean, your door says you work with old words and stuff, right?'

'My door?'

'Yes, your door.' Kat crossed over and pointed to the glass where it said 'Entomology' backwards.

'You're thinking of an etymologist. I'm an entomologist. Etymologists are linguists who research the origin of words. I study insects.' Vincent's beard shifted and he sounded amused, if not a little condescending. Was he laughing at her?

Wait, more importantly, did he actually think she'd keep a job working for a bug guy? Ugh! Let alone date Mr Bug Guy? Suddenly, it all made sense. His parents hadn't wanted to get into details about his job. In fact, it was quite possible they told her the wrong word on purpose, knowing she'd look it up before meeting him.

Didn't Mimi even mention he talked to his dates about bugs?

This was too much.

'If you see it, just trap it under a beaker and I'll do the rest. Don't let it bite you,' Vincent said, glancing around. 'Try looking in the corners. They like dry, dark locations, some place that can't be easily disturbed.'

'Like under my boot?' Kat asked, arching a brow. His face fell and his mouth dropped open as if she'd slapped him. Almost regretfully, she said, 'I think I squished your little friend.'

Vincent didn't move as he stared at her boots in disbelief. 'But, why would you do that? The bite is rarely fatal, especially in healthy adults.'

'It's a spider. I'm a girl,' Kat answered. She wondered if he even noticed the last fact. Maybe she needed a tighter shirt and a better padded bra. She thrust her shoulders back slightly to make her breasts stick out more. It was actually a little irritating that he didn't seem to check her out the way a normal man checks out a pretty woman. She didn't claim to be the be-all and end-all of gorgeous women, but she knew she was easy on the eye.

Already she could check gay off her list. She was pretty intuitive about those things and this man didn't give her that vibe. From what his parents had said, he hadn't been romantically involved with anyone for a while. Surely flying solo had to be losing its appeal. According to Jack, men could only masturbate for so long before going a little crazy.

So then, why wasn't he checking her out and trying to think of clever ways to get into her pants?

It didn't matter. This was all a mistake. Girls and spiders didn't mix – especially poisonous spiders that escaped their cages on a regular basis. No wonder his assistants quit on him. Just thinking about bugs made her skin crawl. She hugged her arms to her waist and slowly backed up. Glancing at the ceiling, she made sure nothing was going to land on her head.

'Listen, I don't think I'm the right person for this job. I mean, it's my first day and I already killed your, ah, test milker bug.' Reaching into her pocket, she pulled out the money he'd given her and put it on the table. 'Here's your cash back. Sorry about the spider. Have a nice life.'

Kat turned to go, reaching for her camera bag as she moved past it.

'Wait,' Vincent said. She heard him moving behind her but didn't stop as she opened the door. Every urge she had screamed to get out of the spider infested room. 'You can't leave. I need you.'

Kat stopped walking and slowly turned to him. If any other man had said those words in such a desperate, pleading voice, she would've thought it romantic. This man needed her to play spider hunter with him.

Ick. No thank you.

'I can't work with spiders,' Kat said emphatically. 'Sorry.'

'But, why?'

'Because I'm a girl.' Kat shook her head. She never in her life thought she'd be saying those words aloud. 'Girls don't like bugs. We scream like maniacs and stomp on them.'

'What's that?' he asked, glancing down to her camera bag.

Kat followed his eyes. Was this man always this distracted? She suppressed a long sigh. 'My camera. I'm a photographer.'

'Perfect. I can use a photographer. You can't leave. I can't put in for another assistant and I can't handle the workload on my own. You did say you needed a job.'

'First you need an assistant and now you need a photographer?' Kat arched a brow. If he asked her, she'd tell him he needed to get some sort of a life – perhaps one that included padded walls and a neurosurgeon. No wonder his parents resorted to playing matchmaker. He'd probably forget he was asking a woman out before the sentence was even finished.

'No, I need an assistant who can help me categorise specimens while I work. Photographs would be perfect and would make the museum directors very happy, which in turn would get them to leave me be.' Vincent watched her hopefully. 'I'll even move the live specimens to a completely different room. You'll work here in the collection room and I'll be in the other lab. Please, I really do need the help. I'm swamped as it is.'

'So, no live bugs?'

'Insects,' he said. 'I prefer the word insects.'

'So, no live insects?' She resisted the urge to roll her eyes at him. Insects. Bugs. Same thing. All gross. All creepy-crawly.

'No, I promise. At least give this a try. I'll even give you photo credit on all the pictures. The museum might even want to use them in brochures or in a book or something. That has to look good on a resume, right?'

'And I get permission to keep, sell or display copies of whatever I photograph?' Kat asked, already planning a new idea for an art show in her head. She wondered if she should point out to him that he hadn't even seen her work. He might not like it. Then again, to him one photograph was probably like any other. She decided to keep her mouth shut on that point.

'Yes, I'll get you a waiver from the museum or whatever it is you need to make it happen.'

'Which museum?'

'AMNH.'

Kat smiled. The American Museum of Natural History. 'Can you get me permission to photograph inside the museum so I can sell the prints?'

'Yes, I might be able to. Does this mean you'll stay?'

'And I get that six hundred a week you mentioned

earlier?' Kat tilted her head to the side. She flashed him her cutesiest little smile – a look most men couldn't resist. To her great surprise, the look actually worked. He smiled briefly as if at a loss for words and glanced away. Was that a blush on his cheeks? It was so hard to tell under all his facial hair.

'Fine. Six a week. In cash.'

'You got yourself an assistant, Dr Richmond,' Kat said. 'I'll see you tomorrow. Nine too late?'

'No, wait, tomorrow? But, you're already here. There is so much to be done.'

'And you have live bugs to move. If I see them out on the loose again I'll squish first, ask questions later.' Kat turned and made her way down the hall. Lifting her hand, she wiggled her fingers without turning around and said, 'I'll see you tomorrow, Dr Richmond.'

'Oh, fine, fine. Until tomorrow, then.'

'Tomorrow,' Kat repeated, not turning back around as she walked away.

Chapter Three

'Bugs? Oh, that is so cool, Kat!' Ella's voice came through the phone, full of the gritty tomboyish charm the youngest Matthews was known for. 'You say he actually milks live spiders. I saw this special on television about...'

Kat wrinkled her nose at the telephone, as she wound the cord around her fingers. Ella would think milking bugs was a cool job. She knew it was outdated to have a corded, rotary dial phone, but her last roommate, Kiki, had been terrified of getting brain cancer from the electrical waves emitted from a cordless – or some such nonsense. The poor woman wouldn't even use a microwave. After she moved out, Kat kept the phone because she was too lazy to go get a new one. She just called it vintage and left it at that.

Her sister kept talking, but she only half listened as Ella went off on a tirade. '...and with snakes, they grab their heads and stick the fangs through plastic and make them squirt the venom into a container...'

Kat lazily pushed back and forth in her office chair. As Ella continued to lay out the entire nature show she'd seen the week before, Kat idly adjusted cut pieces of photographs on her drafting table to create a collage. Deciding she liked the haphazard design, she held the phone with her shoulder and glued the pieces down on a small canvas.

'...anyway, it's so hot that you're working for a scientist. I wish I could come down and see the spiders. You are so lucky! I would give my left arm to have a job like that. I hate working at the restaurant. Waiting tables is so not cool.'

'You're the only girl I know who thinks bugs are cool. Let me work there for a couple of weeks and see what he's like. Maybe he'll let you come hang out.' Kat rolled her fingers rubbing off the excess glue from them. Strangely, her newest collage resembled a jagged heart with two cut up faces in it. It wasn't intentional, but neat just the same. 'Though, I'm warning you, he's odd.'

'Cool,' Ella said. 'Odd is definitely hot.'

Kat was inclined to agree, though with Dr Richmond she wasn't so sure. Maybe it was because he held her dreams in his hands and he didn't even know it. Or maybe it was because she'd had an instant, lustful reaction to him and he didn't seem to even care she was a woman. Any other normal guy would've been easy. Vincent was different. He was odd. There was no other way to put it.

'Kat, are you there?'

'What? Oh, yeah, I'm here,' she answered. 'I just drifted. Sorry.'

'Want to talk to mom?' Ella asked.

'No, I called for you. I'm going to go now. Hey, see if you can't come and stay with me next weekend.'

'Can't. There's this Academic Decathlon thing going on.'

'Weekend after that? Mr Bug Man wants me to work on Saturdays and I'll tell him you have to come with me. He's so hard up for help I doubt he'll care either way. That is if he even notices there's another person in the building with us. I tell you, the guy is very strange.'

'He sounds interesting to me.'

'He would.' Kat chuckled. 'Say you'll come, Ella. My apartment is too quiet. I pawned my television to buy some chemicals for my darkroom and there is no sound whatsoever. Well, unless you count the toilet.'

'You pawned your TV again?' Ella laughed. 'So, I take it you haven't found a new roommate yet? Need me to work on mom to get you some cash? I can tell her you haven't eaten in a week or something, but you're too proud to call home. I guarantee she'll be over there stocking your fridge and hiding twenties in your underwear drawer.'

'No, not again,' Kat said, chuckling. 'I was supposed to interview someone the other day, but they never showed.'

'That sucks.'

'It happens.'

'Let me check with mom, but I'm sure she'll let me come stay with you,' Ella said.

Kat grinned into the phone, excited to see her little sister. 'Call me tomorrow?'

'Yep.'

Kat hung up the phone, knowing Ella wouldn't expect a goodbye. She glanced around her lonely studio apartment. One wall was filled with pictures she'd taken of her and her sisters over the years. The smiling faces stared at her and Kat stared back. She didn't put them into frames, but instead glued them into a giant collage on the biggest piece of canvas she'd ever seen. The younger years started in the middle and spiralled out as they grew. It was a testament to their lives and she was still adding pictures around the edges.

The apartment was quiet. For what it was, the place was nice and only cost her 1600 a month. The building was a brownstone in a great location between Central Park West and Columbus, within short walking distance of the park.

Her kitchen and bathroom were small. She had a woodburning fireplace in the living room, high ceilings and wood floors. There was only one bedroom, but she hung a thick curtain down the middle and called it two. The pipes were noisy and she had to jiggle the toilet handle or else the water would run – like it was doing right now.

Kat didn't mind being alone, but she liked the feeling of someone in the other room better. Picking up the phone, she dialled her older sister and got voice mail, 'You have reached Detective Megan Matthews' personal line. If this is about a case, please contact the department and they will page me immediately. Otherwise, leave a message. Thank you.'

'Meg, honey, it's Kat again,' Kat said, twirling the cord, 'Do you ever not work? I haven't heard from you in weeks and I miss you. Anyway, I got a new job. You'd like it, Ella does. It's creepy and the guy I work for is weird. Well, he's cute in a weird way, but I'll never admit to saying it out loud so don't try to use it against me later. Or maybe it's just that I think he would be cute if I could actually see his face. His build is nice. Well, anyway, never mind because it doesn't matter. He is so not my type. Anyway, I miss you.' Kat paused. 'I said that already, huh. Well, I'm, ah, getting married. Call me.' Then, as an afterthought, she added, 'Don't tell mom. Or dad. Or the sisters. Call me. Love you. Miss you. Bye.'

Kat hung up the phone and smiled. That would make her older sister talk to her. Then, looking at the clock she frowned. Zoe would be in bed because she got up before dawn, but Kat wondered if it was too late to call Sasha. Desperate for something to pass the time, she tried to ring her college-based sister. It turned out Sasha wasn't in her dorm and after ten minutes' chatting with her sister's feminist roommate about being oppressed or some such thing, Kat told the woman goodbye and unwound herself and her chair from the cord.

Boredom set in and she regretted the late cappuccino she'd drunk at the apartment below hers. The woman who lived in it, Flora, was an elderly artist who loved company, but rarely had any. Kat had taken to stopping by to visit her, especially when she needed some caffeine.

She thought of her new boss, Vincent, and almost felt guilty about deceiving him. It wasn't like she was hurting anyone and the man was so awkward she'd really be doing him a favour. Frustrating thing was that he didn't even seem to notice her.

Nine o'clock was going to come too early, but it didn't matter. Picking up the phone, she dialled one last time. 'Jack, hey it's me. I'm back in town. Sorry I didn't call you earlier, but you know how it goes. So, anyway, why don't you come on over and see me?'

Vincent sat back in his chair, stretching his arms over his head before glancing at his wrist for the time. His watch was gone. Frowning, he glanced around. Did he put on his watch when he got up that morning? He honestly couldn't remember. Had he even been home that morning or did he spend the night in the office again?

Was it late? It had to be late. He couldn't tell because his laboratory didn't have a window and the clock on the wall had run out of batteries months ago. Either way, it felt late. Glancing around his sterile laboratory, the pristine metal countertops, the state-of-the-art scientific equipment, he sighed. It was very different from the dusty tomblike atmosphere of the collections laboratory.

Thinking of it only made him contemplate his side project of milking spiders for venom. He glanced over to the glass cages now sitting on the countertop. Seeing them only reminded him of the fact that one of his spiders was dead and his venom production would be down, which led to other thoughts altogether.

Kat. That was her name, wasn't it? Kat. Did he even get a last name? If he did, he couldn't remember it.

What in the world had compelled him to hire her, aside from the fact that he'd been up for days on nothing but caffeine and sheer will? The woman had no experience, but that could be a good thing. She wouldn't stand behind him, breathing down his neck as she asked question after annoying question about what he was doing, as if writing a college term paper from his answers. She didn't look the part of an assistant, not that he cared what she looked like so long as she came in and did her job. Though, she was strangely adorable with her choppy pink and dark-blonde hair and her round blue eyes.

Vincent frowned. Did he actually remember her eye colour? That wasn't like him. Sure, ask him how to spell 'papilionidae' and he could do so without flinching. But ask him to name three people he'd talked to that day and he was at a loss. It wasn't that he didn't care, it was just he had so much on his mind – important things, scientific things, lifesaving things.

No, it didn't matter that Kat was adorable or strange or that she had blue eyes. She seemed capable and self-assured and he needed someone who could catalogue the insect collection in an efficient way. Photos would be as good as anything else and the board would be impressed to have the specimens recorded somewhere other than in his laboratory drawers. There had been a photographic catalogue of them at one time, but the catalogue had been ruined and never replaced. And, if he didn't get them catalogued again soon, the museum would be upset and they'd be less inclined to let him keep working unsupervised. The last thing he wanted was someone breathing down his neck, whether it was a student or a museum supervisor.

However, he couldn't do the catalogue and continue to get his work done. If he didn't finish a significant amount of research into the genetic make-up of mosquitoes, he wouldn't be eligible for the grant money he needed to keep working. It wasn't his fault the college had been sending him their most dim-witted students – kids who resented interning in such a quiet, unexciting field. At least they thought it unexciting. Vincent loved his work. He liked the quiet. He liked making a difference and being on the forefront of saving lives. Not to mention he loved problem solving.

Rubbing the bridge of his nose, he decided to spend

the night in his office. His vision was starting to blur due to exhaustion and he didn't want to risk a miscalculation. One little mistake could set him back days. He'd learned that the hard way.

With a heavy sigh, he turned and left the laboratory. His feet shuffled as he made his way down the hall to his office. Closing his eyes before he even got there, his legs moved automatically over to the cot set up in the corner. He fell onto it, asleep seconds after his head hit the pillow.

Kat rested on her living room floor, staring at the ceiling, her arms spread out to the side, her legs parted and straight. The apartment was warm and she was overheated even though she only wore a pair of boy-cut pants and a white ribbed tank top with no bra. However, she didn't feel like moving to turn up the air conditioning.

'I miss my television,' she whined, though there was no one in the apartment to hear her complain. Groaning, she let loose a long sigh. She wasn't in the mood to read and didn't have any new books even if she was. There was always work, but she'd finished the last of the photographs she'd taken at the Rocky Mountains already. None of them were too impressive and she thought about selling them to a stock photography outlet for some extra cash. She'd sign away most of the rights, but she'd have spending money.

Hearing a key in a latch, she turned her head in the direction of her front door but didn't bother to get up. Jack had a key to the apartment. Actually, a lot of people seemed to have keys: Jack, her sisters, her downstairs caffeine buddy. The neighbour especially came in handy since Kat was constantly locking herself out.

'Kat?' Jack's soft voice reached her before he did. 'Kat, you still awake? I need to talk to you.'

'Mr Knight, what took you so long?' she asked, watching him enter the living room. He looked around, not seeing her on the floor. Kat studied him, waiting for his eyes to turn down. He had on the top she'd gotten him for Christmas, a blood-red cashmere sweater with aubergine raglan sleeves. It went well with the faded denim jeans and brown boots. Seeing his newly shorn locks, she frowned. 'You cut your hair.'

His green eyes found hers and he gave her a lopsided grin, as he ran his fingers through the shortened hairdo. 'Yeah, I had to. Military part.'

'That's not a crew cut,' she said. His hair was longer on top, flopping down along his eyes and the back was cropped shorter. 'Shouldn't it be buzzed? You know, high and tight?'

'European military, a couple of hundred years ago. I slick it back,' he explained. 'Want to hear my lines?'

Kat laughed. 'Not really. Can they wait until opening night?'

Jack shrugged, crossing over to her. Hands on hips, he looked down at where she lay on the floor. 'Just wham bam thank you ma'am, is it? Don't you ever get tired of treating me like a piece of meat?'

'Not really, sweet cheeks.' Kat rolled onto her side, facing his feet. Running her fingers up his foot to the inside of his pant leg, she laughed. 'Since when do you mind the fact that I use you for your body?'

He didn't laugh as she expected him to.

'Jack?' Kat asked, letting go of him and rolling onto her back. 'What is it?'

'I was thinking . . .'

Kat waited, trying not to openly cringe. Jack got like this sometimes – contemplative of their relationship, of their decisions, of what society expected of them. And by society, she knew it was really his traditionalist parents who believed sex equalled love equalled marriage and babies. She just didn't see that future when she looked at him.

Dr Vincent Richmond popped into her head. Now that was a man who'd most likely expect the traditional family dream out of life. Somehow thinking of the good scientist made her desire Jack less. Vincent presented a challenge and women always wanted what they couldn't have. Still, she'd be lying if she didn't admit that thoughts of Vincent in his sexy lab coat didn't plague her all day. It was those churning desires that made her call Jack in the first place. If she couldn't have the one she was fantasising over, she'd take what she could get.

What she could get? That didn't seem too fair to Jack. Why was she feeling cruddy all of a sudden, like she was about to do something wrong? Sex was not wrong, no matter what the puritans tried to tell them. Then, why hesitate? Why now? And with Jack of all people?

'... that we –' Jack paused, looking uncomfortable as he shifted his weight back and forth. She blinked, drawn out of her thoughts back into his conversation.

Kat watched him, feeling a peculiar sense of emptiness inside her chest. Suddenly, Jack didn't feel as comfortable as he had before she left for Colorado. She took a deep breath, trying not to be foolish as she ignored the sensation. Clearing his throat, Jack kneeled onto the floor next to her. Kat turned to watch him, staying on her back. She threaded her hands behind her head. 'What's up?'

'Marry me.' The words were earnest.

Kat choked, coughing in surprise. That was a new one. As soon as the shock wore off, she started laughing. 'Oh my gawd, Jack, you jerk!' She rolled up, slugging him lightly in the arm. 'I thought you really had something important to say. Warn a girl before you do something like that.'

'Sorry, had to ask at least once I guess.' He gave her one of his famous lopsided grins.

At least once? There was a finality to the way he said it.

'How's it going, Princess Katarina?'

'Better now that you are here, my prince. I've been bored.' A strange feeling passed through her at Jack's look. She didn't wish to analyse it.

'Pawned the TV again, didn't you?' He laughed, sitting down on the floor. Neither of them cared there was a couch nearby, or several chairs in the apartment they could've used.

'Yeah, I needed chemicals.'

'Don't you always? You're a darkroom chemical junkie.'

Kat grinned. 'Stop bath and developers are better than drugs, and being in the darkroom is a natural high. I love watching an image appear. It's the closest thing to magic in the modern age.'

'Mmm, so that's why we were smoking "the pot" at my apartment two weeks ago.' Reaching for her, Jack trailed the tip of his finger down the slope of her nose, letting it skate off her flesh like a ski jump only to land on her chin. 'The pot' is what Kat's mother called marijuana. It was a joke between the two of them. Playfully, she snapped her teeth after the digit. 'You do know that your sister's laptop over there probably plays DVDs, don't you?'

'Huh?' Kat didn't bother looking where he motioned. 'Don't own DVDs and Sasha threatened to kill me if I downloaded joke clips on it again. Something about viruses being attached to the video files.'

'You are sadly behind the times, dear heart.' Jack leaned over her, his mouth just a hair's breadth away from hers. She smelled his fresh breath, knowing he'd squirted breath spray in his mouth before coming inside her apartment.

'Yep, I'm a regular damsel in modern distress.' She leaned up, closing some of the distance. 'Just looking for my knight in shining armour to come and save me.'

'Kat, God save the man who tries to rescue you.' His

eyes narrowed and Kat wondered at his serious look. There was something going on with Jack. He was different than the last time she saw him, almost serious, or sad even.

'Jack –?' she began to ask, wondering if something had happened, but his kiss cut off her question. He thrust his tongue deep into her mouth in an instantly passionate embrace. The sudden shock of mint invaded her senses, a little warm but very pleasant. She pushed at him, her hands meeting the hard planes of his muscular chest. 'Jack, wait. What's –?'

'Don't talk,' he said, his lips whispering along hers in a gentle caress. It was as if he was searching for something in the touch. The beat of his heart was steady against her palm. 'Just kiss.'

Jack's mouth closed over hers once more, cutting off any coherent words. His hands were on either side of her, holding up his weight. Closing her eyes, she ran her hands over his flexed biceps. He had always taken such good care of himself and she loved touching him. Kat often teased Zoe for reading romance novels, but the truth was Jack was as close to a living hero as there was likely ever to be – buff, sexy, confident, tanned. And he came with no strings.

Did she mention he was perfect?

Then why was she hesitating to continue? Kat felt the strongest urge to push him away. Again she ignored the sensation.

Kat tugged on his shirt, pulling it over his head, determined to prove to herself that she still wanted him. The room was already warm and his body only heated her more. There was something comforting in the familiarity of his touch. They knew each other and there was no awkwardness. Slowly, he trailed kisses along her throat, nipping at her flesh. Kat giggled, running her fingers up into his short hair. She explored the silky texture of his new haircut and decided she liked it.

Pushing his head down, she arched towards his mouth. His face nuzzled along the valley of her breasts as he tugged at her tank top. Jack rolled to the side, taking her with him as he fell on his back. The heated press of his cock strained against the stiff denim beneath her. Now, with both hands free, he reached to pull off her shirt.

Kat froze. Her mouth opened but no words came out. She wasn't sure what was going on. Sex with Jack was always great, but for some reason, she was feeling guilty. She thought of absentminded Dr Vincent, wondering why in the world the man would enter her head at such a heated, passionate moment. It's not like she had any promise to become intimate with him. Then why the guilt?

'Kat?' Jack whispered, confused.

'Jack, I . . .' There was a long pause. After four years, they knew each other well and some things didn't have to be said. But it didn't make what seemed to be happening any easier.

He sighed, nudging her with his body. She crawled off of him, sitting next to him on the floor. 'It's fine, Kat. I understand. Another time perhaps. Another life.'

Kat wondered at the soft, thoughtful sound. Trying to be nice, she said, 'I'm sorry, kissing you was perfect for inspiration.'

'Say no more.' Jack rolled up from the floor with a sigh. 'I read you loud and clear. You need to work.'

'But –'

'I have to get up early anyway. I'm meeting some friends for a workout at eight.'

Kat was slower to stand. She watched him tug on his sweater. His movements were jerky and he refused to look directly at her. 'Jack, is there something up with you? Do you need to tell me something? Do you need to talk?'

Turning to her, he cupped her cheek. Slowly, he glanced down over her body before meeting her eyes.

'Kat, there's nothing for you to be concerned over. I'm just preoccupied and busy, OK? I shouldn't have come tonight. I . . .'

Kat nodded in understanding, reading in his expression the words he was refusing to say – words she didn't want to say herself. 'Sure, but you know I'm here if you need me, all right?' She gave him a small grin and tapped the middle of his chest with her knuckle. 'And not just for sex either. We are friends. I can help you if you need me.'

'I know, doll,' he answered, adopting a 1920s gangster accent. With a light tap, he lightly clucked her across the chin. 'Take care-a you.'

'Take care-a you,' she answered, mimicking his tone.

Jack planted a quick kiss on her head and turned to leave. She couldn't let him go, not like this. What they had might not be true love, but the intimacy they'd shared for so long had brought them close. Kat did love him, in her way.

'Jack, wait. What's happening here? It feels like . . .' She bit her lip, trying not to cry.

'It feels like goodbye,' he answered, not turning to look at her. 'That's because we both know it is goodbye.'

'I don't . . .' Kat took a deep breath. Shouldn't there be more of an emotional outpouring? Uncontrollable sobs and begging? Sure, there was fear of being alone, sadness that a relationship was ending, but they were still friends and would see each other again. She had to trust in that much.

'Kat, don't. Tonight I'd decided something on the way over. We're not going anywhere. We haven't been going anywhere for four years. So, I decided that I would ask you to marry me. If it was meant to be, you'd say yes, fall into my arms and finally tell me you love me.'

'But, I tell you I love you all the time.' She took a deep breath, shaking slightly. 'And I mean it.'

'Yeah, you do, but this time it would've been different.

You would've said it like you needed me to survive. But you don't need me, Kat, not really. And though I love you, I don't need you either, not like a man should need a woman.' He glanced back. Words were coming out of his mouth saying one thing, but the pain was in his gaze. No matter what kind of brave face he put on it, this was affecting him too. 'There's no reason to make a scene, is there? This is what it is. We're too adult to lie to each other. I'll see you around. We still care about each other. We're still friends and we both agreed when this moment came, we wouldn't get all weird. So, like I said, I'll see you around.'

'I'll see you on opening night. I wouldn't miss your play for the world.' Kat watched as he walked out of the apartment. Part of her wanted to yell for him to come back, that even though this wasn't romantic true love, it was love and she didn't want to be alone. She liked how in sync they were, how he knew her. But to call him back wasn't fair to Jack. It wasn't fair to her. Taking a deep breath, she locked her front door, shut off her lights and went to her bedroom. She felt lonely, and she again resisted the urge to call Jack and ask him to come back. On a primal level she wanted sex, but in her heart she didn't want sex with him. Jack had been her crutch, a way to avoid all other relationships. Did he finally realise it, too? A tear slipped over her cheek. She cried for her, for Jack, for what they couldn't force to be between them.

Suddenly very tired, Kat pulled back her comforter. The bedding set was a matching camel-coloured floral pattern, complete with decorative pillows and a matching cashmere throw blanket. The ivory sheets and pillow-cases were four hundred and sixty thread count Egyptian cotton with a floral border embroidered along the top edge. Her mother had bought the bedding for her last birthday. Otherwise, she would've still been using the old cartoon character sheets she had when she first moved out of the house.

Kat bit her lip, trying to think of anything besides what had happened that night. If she didn't have Jack, she always had her career to focus on. But even her career didn't look too bright at the moment.

Kat saw a picture on her dresser of her sisters. It was sad that even Ella thought she needed her mother's help to make it in the big city. She'd done all right for herself, though even she had to admit getting the great apartment was mostly dumb luck. The old furniture in the room was painted white, only as a last ditch effort to save it. She'd gotten the lamp off the street corner out of a trash bin, painted it and rewired it until it looked halfway decent. But, somehow, looking around, she didn't feel it was good enough.

'You have to make this work for you, Kat. You have to make Vincent notice you,' she whispered, reaching for the lamp that suddenly looked so ugly with its black and gold crackle paint. 'It's time to make something happen for yourself.'

It was time to grow up. He might not have said it, but Jack was right in walking out on her. Or did she break up with him? It had happened so fast she couldn't be sure. It was all so confusing. Maybe they weren't broken up. No one had said the actual words. He'd only said goodbye.

Closing her eyes, Kat knew she should get to sleep. Her body was still aroused but she refused to pull out her vibrator to relieve the tension. She was too depressed, even for that. Tomorrow was the first day of her new job and she planned on making sure Vincent thought of her as invaluable.

Kat gasped, feeling hands along her sides. Did Jack change his mind and come back? It had to be him, as he was the only man with a key. Should she protest? Or maybe this was farewell sex?

Her mind was hazy and she didn't think to stop the

man from kissing her because it felt too good. The bedroom was dark, but she didn't think to be scared as a tongue brushed along her neck. His hands were everywhere, confident and sure. Then, suddenly she was astride a naked body, the feel of warm flesh potent and real.

Was this another of Jack's games? The sex with a stranger scenario? Should she stop him?

She leaned over, moaning as she kissed him, unable to find the will to stop what they were doing. Her hands instantly went to his waistband as she rubbed her pussy along his thigh, causing sweet friction between them. The stimulation to her clit sent little jolts of pleasure throughout her, causing moisture to gather along her folds. The man's hands were everywhere, running up and down over her body, cupping her breasts, pinching her nipples. Her body tingled in sexual excitement where a thigh pressed tight into her.

Kat dipped her fingers down between her thighs to find a large erection. He was stiff and ready as she touched him, stroking him as she worked her hand down into his crotch to cup his balls. Slowly, she pulled her hand away from his cock, needing to feel his body inside hers, wanting the sensation of being alive that only an intense orgasm could bring. With a firm pull, he tugged her forwards until she was straddling his hips.

She shivered in pleasure and anticipation. Her knees pressed into the softness of the mattress even as her finger grazed the harder surface of the man's chest. Kat rocked her hips against him, wetting him with her body's cream as she moved up and down along his shaft, not taking him inside. The firm texture of his cock pressed against her sex and felt so good she didn't want to stop. As if fascinated by her breasts, he cupped them, kneading them in his palms. He groaned, a truly masculine, tortured sound of pleasure.

Leaning over, she kissed him, tasting the minty freshness of his tongue against hers. He lifted her hips, angling his body to meet hers. A shock of pleasure hit her as the head of his penis touched her wet folds. He confidently thrust inside her, rocking his hips gently, working into her. Kat took him in, forgetting all about her momentary guilt from before as she felt the pressure of him deep inside her pussy.

'Ah, yes,' she said, breathlessly. He was unusually quiet, but she barely noticed. He might not be talking, but he was making all the right little noises in the back of his throat. His hand glided down her chest to her sex. The man knew how to work magic with his fingers as he stroked lightly along her folds to find the small pearl hidden there. Kat moved faster on top of him, her pleasure building.

He groaned, easily meeting the new speed. Her blood seemed to slow in her veins, as her hips jerked with the beginnings of release. She rolled her hips in a small circle, keeping his shaft deep inside. Kat grabbed her own breasts, tweaking the nipples. He didn't let up from her clit. She jerked again, gasping and stiffening as she came.

'Oh. Fuck.' The words were as stunted as his movements, as he shook violently, stiffening and trembling at the same time. The voice continued in a whisper, 'Fuck. Fuck. Yeah.'

Kat's head fell back on her shoulders and she opened her mouth wide, gasping for breath. Her heart beat hard in her chest and she tried to focus on the sound of his voice, trying to place it. 'Dr Vincent?'

'Shit!' Kat screamed, sitting up in bed, breathing hard. Her arms flailed as she felt all around her. The bed was empty. Tossing the blankets off, she practically jumped off the mattress as if burnt by it. It was just a dream – a potent, erotic, sinfully wrong dream. Her heart was still beating hard and her body was tense, no longer feeling the relief of her dream state orgasm. Instead, unfulfilled arousal caused her nipples to ache.

Why in the world was she dreaming of the awkward Dr Vincent?

'He has your career in your hands,' she assured herself, breathing hard. 'The dream was just a primal manifestation of your true desires.'

It was early yet, but she couldn't make herself crawl back between the sheets. She could still feel the touch of her dream lover's hands on her body. Weak and in a state of extreme arousal, she stumbled towards the bathroom.

'I must be more upset about Jack than I thought.'

But, as she turned on the shower, it wasn't Jack's hands she was thinking about or his voice echoing in the back of her head as she thrust her hand between her thighs. Stroking her clit, she rode her hand hard. Vincent's deep-brown eyes were burned into her mind as she brought her body to climax. Kat shook, as the water beat down on her sensitive flesh.

Breathless, she whispered, 'What in the world was that all about?'

Chapter Four

Vincent jolted awake, sitting up on his cot in sleepy surprise. Glancing around, he was disorientated by the sound of loud music being pumped into his room from outside the door. He blinked several times and it took him a moment to realise he was still at work and in his office. The music had a steady beat meant for club dancing – the kind of sound he'd never expect to be playing in his office building. It surely wasn't anything to which he'd have chosen to listen.

Blinking to adjust his vision to the dimness, he looked around the small room. The blinds were drawn, but light still streamed in from a small window, giving enough to see by. He had no idea what time it was, but judged by the fact there was light outside that he'd overslept. Normally, he liked to get an early start and, for that matter, a late finish.

His desk was full of folders, badly in need of filing. Somewhere under the pile were a laptop computer and a phone he rarely answered, though it did occasionally ring. The trash bin was overflowing with wadded up pieces of yellow notebook paper. Books lined the shelves along one wall. Many of the larger volumes were missing and he knew them to be scattered around the entire building.

It took him a moment to get his bearings, but slowly he noticed a large take-out coffee cup on the edge of his desk. It wasn't his. Was it for him?

Vincent pushed to his feet, stretching his arms wide. Amazingly, he felt rested, more so than he had in a long time. Picking up the coffee cup, he found it was full. On the side, someone had written on it in black permanent marker, 'Drink Me'. A bag next to the coffee read, 'Eat Me'. Curious, he opened the bag and found a pastry.

'Hmm.' He glanced around the room to see if there were any other changes as he quickly ate his breakfast. Taking a drink of the cooled liquid, he was glad to find it was just plain coffee – no frills or exotic blends, just good black coffee.

Drawn to the door, he took the cup with him. Where exactly was the music coming from? Who'd left the food? For a moment, he thought of his mother. No. That wasn't her style. She'd have come in with an army of maids and a chef, demanding he wake up to see what she was doing.

He was still dressed from the night before, down to his shoes. It wasn't the first time he'd fallen asleep like that. Vincent yawned, taking another sip as he walked down the hall, following the sound of someone yelling border-line obscenities into a microphone. Pushing open the door to the collection room, he paused, stunned by the sight of his workspace.

The room was brighter than he remembered and had a fresh smell to it, like lemon cleaner and disinfectant. On the long wooden table stood Kat, reaching above her head to change a light bulb. He'd momentarily forgotten he'd hired her the day before.

Her hair was pulled back into a messy bun, but the dark pink streaks were still there. She wore light pink cotton Capri pants and a white tank top that showed off a hint of her trim waist. Her back was to him, but he could easily see the dark pink bra beneath the T-shirt.

And was that a tattoo? Vincent tilted his head to the side, squinting to see what was on her lower back. A butterfly, maybe? By the bright colours, it wasn't based

on any real specimens, but a fanciful design with impossible swoops of the wings and unrealistic patterns. Before
he realised what he was doing, his eyes roamed down
over her butt. He might be overworked, but he was still
male. Licking his lips, he stared at her hips a little too
long. His body stirred with interest as the mass between
his thighs lifted and filled.

Suppressing a groan, he shook his head. He didn't have
time for this – for any of it. He was behind in his
mosquito research and his venom production was going
to be down due to the dead spider – not that anyone was
really waiting for those particular research notes but he
did keep himself on his own personal deadline. He didn't
have time to be staring at Kat's ass, no matter how sexy
and appealing it was to look at it.

'Ah! Damn it!' Kat jumped in surprise as she turned
around to find Vincent quietly standing in the doorway,
another distracted look on his face, though it was hard
to see more than his eyes through the waves of his sleep-
tousled hair and his overgrown beard. He still wore his
clothes from the day before, only they were wrinkled.
She'd seen that he slept in them when she went in to
give him his coffee and pastry. 'You scared the crap out
of me.'

Kat had come to work that morning only to find
Vincent asleep in his office. Secretly, she'd been glad of
it. After her erotic dream of him, she hadn't been in the
mood to hear his voice. It had been in her head since
she'd woken up.

The building had been left unlocked. This was Manhattan, and it wasn't safe to leave a place unlocked all night
– especially as hard as this man had been sleeping. He
could've been robbed blind and he wouldn't have moved.
When she got bored without company, she had turned
on the music. The man had slept through that as well.

'Huh? What? Oh, sorry, I...' He shook his head, his

dark eyes meeting hers as his words trailed off. Vincent looked confused as he scratched the back of his head, staring at her face.

'Well, good morning sleepyhead. I was about to go get some lunch.' Kat leaned over and turned the music to a low hum, refusing to entertain the notion of what Vincent would really be like as a lover. After hours of contemplation, she was certain her desire for him was just some messed up psychological concoction. She only wanted him because she shouldn't, because he held power over her even if he didn't know he did. 'Why don't you come with me?'

'Lunch?' Vincent blinked rapidly, passing the coffee between his hands to lift the sleeve to his lab coat. He glanced at his wrist but wasn't wearing a watch.

'It's about noon.' She looked down at him from the height of the table.

'Noon?' He questioned in disbelief. 'Noon? It can't be noon. Why didn't you wake me up? I've got –'

'A lot of work to do,' she filled in. 'I know. So you've said. Listen, from one workaholic insomniac to another, you were due for a crash. Now, I'd guess you are due for some food.' She looked him over. 'And maybe a shower.'

'Shower?' he repeated.

'Shave,' she added, really curious to see what he looked like under his facial hair. It would probably be a disappointment, but as a photographer, she found beauty in flaws. Besides, the curiosity was about to kill her. As she'd stared down at him sleeping, she'd been close to shaving him herself. She wondered if he would've even noticed the missing beard.

'Shave?' he reached for his beard and stroked it. The look in his eyes said he hadn't even thought about it.

'Yeah, where do you live? Is it close enough to walk or should I call you a cab? Please tell me it's not here in your office. Otherwise, I'll have to take you home with me like a stray.'

'Oh, no. I live on East Seventy-Eighth,' Vincent said absently.

'Pity, I could have used the roommate. Wait, you live on the Upper East and you're sleeping here?' Kat shook her head in disbelief. She suspected before that he might be crazy. This definitely confirmed it.

'It's just an apartment.' He looked like he believed every word.

'Hell's just a really hot place sinners go.' Kat grinned, looking around the room to avoid staring at him and that damned, oddly seductive, sleep-wrinkled lab coat. All the bulbs were replaced and the place was completely transformed from the dingy, dark place it had been that morning.

'What?' he asked, after some length.

'Never mind. It's something my mom says when we're not making sense.'

'Oh.'

Why was he staring at her all funny? She looked down, suddenly worried a spider might be crawling on her clothes. All day she'd been keeping an eye out for them and several times she was convinced she could feel something crawling on her skin, only to discover it was her imagination. It wasn't like she could depend on Mr Distracted to remember to move the poisonous little beasts.

'Wait.' Vincent blinked rapidly, as if just hearing what she'd said. 'Are you saying I'm not making sense?'

'Want me to call a cab?' She jumped off the table and avoided answering. 'Or do you have a car? It's a little too far to walk, though I think some fresh air as well as food would do you wonders. It might even make you more productive, what with all the work you have waiting for you.'

'No, there's a shower in the back and I have a change of clothes in the office – what have you been doing all morning?' He set his coffee down and gingerly placed his palms flat on the counter. 'Where are the notes I had stacked here?'

Kat watched as he looked over the table as if they would magically reappear. She'd picked up his notes, putting them into order the best she could. Camera equipment was partially set up around the room. Without him to tell her where to start photographing, she hadn't had much choice but to spruce the place up. She could only guess that the pinned insects she found in the drawers along the wall were what she'd be cataloguing for him.

'Over there.' She pointed behind her to the end of the wooden counter. 'Don't worry, I marked all your pages with little bits of paper.'

'But, I was organised!' He hurried past her to the stack she'd made of his mess. 'I liked it the way I had it. I could find what I needed.'

Kat rolled her eyes so he couldn't see. Impishly, she asked, 'Want me to clean your office for you?'

'Can you file?'

Frowning, she put her hands on her hips. 'Did you just ask me if I could organise things into the ABCs?'

'What, no, well yes, I suppose I did, but . . .' The poor man really did look perplexed.

'Well, I can't, OK. Are you happy? I never learned how to read. All I know how to do is take pictures. You don't understand how hard it is . . .' Kat dramatically sniffed and turned her back on him.

'Ah, are you . . .?'

It was really tough, but she managed not to laugh. Well, managed until he awkwardly patted her shoulder. She shook, trying to hold the sound back.

He must've thought she was crying, because he said, 'There, there. I'm sorry. I didn't know. Adult illiteracy –'

It was too much. Laughter poured out of her. 'Man, you are way too serious. Lighten up. Of course I can read. How else could I organise your notes for you?'

'That was a joke.' His tone was serious and bland.

'Thanks for the clarification, doc.' she chuckled.

'You are ...' His eyes roamed over her. She waited expectantly. Even though it was foolish, she still hoped he'd say something nice to her. 'Different.'

'Ask me to dinner,' she said, looking unflinchingly up into his dark eyes. When he'd come to comfort her, he'd stepped close and had yet to move back. The heat of his body radiated onto her, warming her in an instant reminder of the damned erotic dream. Though he looked a dishevelled mess, he smelled clean – like soap. It took all her control to keep the coy expression on her face. He blinked several times, as if he wasn't following her meaning. Well, so much for the direct approach. To save face, she added, 'You need to get out of this office and I have a feeling I'm the only person you haven't alienated who will put up with you for an evening on short notice.'

'I can't, no.' He stepped back. 'Thank you, but I have too much –'

'Work to do,' she interrupted. 'You've mentioned that.'

'Yes.'

'You know, all work and no play makes doc a dull boy.' She winked, pretending his rejection of her request for a dinner date didn't bother her.

'No, technically, being an entomologist makes me a dull boy,' he answered, heading for the door.

Kat stood in shock, watching him leave the room. Did he just make a joke? She was too stunned to even laugh.

By the end of her second week as Dr Vincent's assistant, Kat was pulling her hair out in frustration. The man was impossible, only popping his head into the collection room once a day to check the status of her progress. She'd tried everything to get his attention, from wearing tight midriff-showing shirts to purposefully standing too close to him, giving him indecent peeks at her cleavage, as she lightly touched his arm. All it seemed to do was run off him.

Today she wore her vintage blue strapless tunic, a silver scroll necklace, tight black slacks and very comfortable Mary Jane flats. She'd hoped the more conservative, yet still cute, outfit would turn his head. Kat sighed in frustration. If this didn't work, she'd have to try some politician wife's get-up and, if that didn't do the trick, she was joining a nunnery and giving up her dreams altogether.

No, stop thinking like that, Kat reprimanded herself. Dreams aren't meant to be easy. You just have to figure out how to crack this nut.

Dr Vincent hadn't paid her his daily visit yet. The man spent all his time in Lab Two working with his bugs. Lab Two was a place she didn't dare go. Turned out, Mr Bug Man also worked not only with poisonous spiders but mosquitoes. What was it with this man and bugs that bit people? Kat shivered each time she thought about it.

She was sure he'd forget to eat if she didn't get him food. At least it looked like he showered, though he had yet to shave and she had no idea if he even left the office. He did change his clothes on a daily basis and she could never actually complain about the way he smelled.

Once he did say something about the way *she* smelled. He'd stood there, leaning in, sniffing at her with the strange, normally distracted look on his face, before saying, 'You smell sweet. Better stop wearing the perfume. It will attract the mosquitoes if they happen to get out.'

It was the closest she'd ever gotten to a compliment from him. Though, needless to say, she did stop wearing the perfume.

'Kat, you're staring at the door again,' Ella said. Her sister sat on the long wooden table, kicking her feet as she traced her finger over the clear top of the collection case she held on her lap. It came from within the rows of drawers along the wall. Each case had a glass lid, which protected the specimens inside. Luckily, the insects were all dead and pinned down to the material covered bottom. Kat's job was to remove the lids and photograph each bug separately, getting not only the insect but the specimen number written alongside it. It was a tedious process for the most part, but she was building a cool portfolio. She'd be able to cut them out later and add them to her canvases. Plus, some of the close-ups she got with her macro lens were really exceptional pieces of art.

'I am?' Kat laughed. Ella had told her she was doing that a lot. 'Sorry.'

'So, tell me about this Dr Vin?' Ella set the drawer down gently. Her sister's blonde hair was pulled into two pigtails behind her ears. The long length was bound from root to end with cross straps of leather. Her army style combat boots, blue jeans and white tank undershirt purchased from the male clothing section of a discount store was an odd contrast to Kat's trendy chic. 'Does he have a nice ass?'

'I don't know,' Kat answered, giving a small laugh at Ella's blunt question. She suspected he did, but it was hard to tell underneath the tormentingly sexy lab coat.

'Is he old?'

'I already told you, his mother said he was thirty-three.'

'Yeah, but she misled you on the man's job. Does he look thirty-three? And if so, is it an old, hammered thirty-three, or a cute, still vibrant thirty-three.'

'I don't know how old he looks. Normal thirties maybe. It's hard to tell under all his beard hair.' Kat slid the lid over the tray she'd just finished and took the one Ella had been holding and started setting up for the next round of photographs.

'You haven't said too much about him at all. Either he's really bland, or you think he's hot and don't want to admit to it.'

Kat didn't answer. She hated when her sisters were too intuitive. It wasn't that she thought he was 'hot' *per se*, just that it was so hard to see his features under the mask of facial hair and glasses that she was burning with curiosity. Shifting uncomfortably, she refused to think of the almost nightly sexual dreams she'd been having of him. It seemed the more she tried not to fantasise about him, the more she did just that. Jack hadn't called and for some reason, she couldn't bring herself to be the first one to make contact – even if she needed sex with something other than her vibrator.

'Hmm, Chatty Katty with nothing to say?' Ella laughed. 'Now, I have to see what he looks like. Didn't you say he usually comes and checks on you by now? I want to meet him.'

'He's probably lost track of time, Ella the Fella.' Kat smirked as they used their childhood nicknames. All the girls had them – Beggin Megan, Glowy Zoe, Chatty Katty, Ella the Fella, and *Sha-zow!* for Sasha. Sha-zow was always said with the tone of a comic book action hero in the middle of a fight. What had started as them trying to annoy each other had become terms of affection as the sisters grew older.

Kat reached down and repositioned the tray of insects. She stood on the table, her camera pointed down. The photographs would come out better when she positioned her camera in such a way. Aside from photographing, she really didn't have too many more duties. Occasionally the phone rang and she would answer it when Vincent didn't.

Kat had convinced Vincent to give her a key so she could lock the front door when she left each night. It was better than trying to haul her equipment back and forth everyday for fear it would be stolen.

Checking the camera's focus, she added, 'I'll bet he's in Lab Two. He's always in Lab Two.'

'Hmm, I'll just go check.'

Kat blinked in surprise as Ella jumped off the table and made a move for the door. Curious as to what would happen if Ella disturbed Vincent's little sanctuary, she didn't try to stop her sister as she moved to watch the encounter. Kat had wanted to bother him at work often, but she didn't unless she had a great excuse.

Ella stopped and knocked on Lab Two's door. Glancing over her shoulder, she winked audaciously at Kat and called out in a no-nonsense voice, 'Dr Vin?'

It took a few tries, but the door finally opened. Vincent looked out in confusion. 'Are you looking for me, madam?'

Ella thrust her hand out and teased, 'Hi, I'm Margaret, don't you remember me? I'm your assistant.'

Vincent's expression turned from slightly confused annoyance to acceptance in an instant. 'You don't look a thing like Margaret.'

Kat frowned. Now how come he knew Ella wasn't Margaret?

'I'm teasing. I couldn't resist. I'm Ella, Kat's sister. I wanted to meet you. Hey, I hear you're milking spiders in here. That's just too cool. Please tell me I can watch. I promise not to get in the way unless you say I can help. In fact, I'll take a vow of silence for as long as I'm in there. Please let me help.'

Vincent glanced over Ella and smiled, though he did look at a loss for words. Ella had that affect on people when she went into super hyper mode. She pushed past him in enthusiasm, not giving him time to consider refusing, as she went where Kat wouldn't dare to go – in with the live bugs. The door to Lab Two shut as Vincent moved to follow Ella. Kat hurried forwards, pressing her ear to the door to listen.

'Oh, wow!' she heard Ella exclaim. 'Can I touch them? I mean, do they need to eat off human blood of something? Don't you ever get tired of letting them sting you?'

Kat frowned, standing up straight. Why was she suddenly jealous of her tomboyish younger sister? Then, she heard Vincent laugh. Kat gasped. He never laughed around her, not even when she made a joke. What was going on? Ella was in his presence for two seconds and suddenly he's laughing and being nice? She couldn't even get him into her presence long enough to strive for another date, let alone a whole conversation.

Slowly, she backed away, not wanting to hear anymore. Almost bitterly, Kat went to work. Thank goodness it was Saturday and she'd have tomorrow off. She definitely needed a break from Mr Scientist.

Chapter Five

Kat jumped in surprise as she heard the sound of a ringing bell. Looking around the collection's room, she frowned. No one was with her, but the sound had to come from somewhere. She listened closely, a frown on her face.

She was already in a bad mood because Ella hadn't come back out of the other laboratory. Kat had crept up to the door to eavesdrop more times than she would ever admit. Each instant, she'd only gotten madder as she heard the two of them laughing together.

'Why can't he be human around me?' she grumbled in jealousy. 'I get Mr Moody, and Ella gets Mr Cool.'

Kat hopped off the table where she was sitting. She'd refused to work, thinking that if Mr Science Freak was going to be rude enough to pay Ella more attention than his own employee, then she'd just sit around on the clock as revenge. He could pay her for doing nothing. However, sitting around made the hours go by slowly and she was bored out of her mind.

'Hello? I'm looking for Katarina Matthews?'

'Megan?' Kat said instantly, recognising her older sister's voice. She went to the door and opened it, excited.

Sure enough, there was Megan, looking like some movie star detective straight out of a suspense thriller. Her dark-brown hair was pulled back into a tidy bun at the nape of her neck. She wore a black stretch cotton shirt with raw-edged strip insets down the front and double button cuffs, and matching black wool stitched trousers cut to complement her long, lean figure. Sunglasses were pushed up on her head, the only accessory to her sister's ensemble other than the shiny badge at her slim waist.

'Oh, Megs, I missed you so much!' Kat rushed forwards and hugged her sister. 'It took you long enough to get in touch with me. I called you nearly two weeks ago.'

Megan laughed, briefly returning the embrace, though more standoffish than Kat's enthusiastic greeting. Kat took no offence, as Megan was always more stoic in nature. They all assumed it was a side effect of her gruesome job. Seeing the effects of homicide all day had to wear a person down.

'You know, it would serve you right if I called mom and dad and told them you really were getting married,' Megan said. 'You didn't actually think I would believe such a thing. Kat getting married, ha!'

'You're getting married?' Ella gasped, behind her. Kat turned to the youngest Matthews. 'Kat! How come you didn't...? Oh, no, it's not Jack is it? I thought you said you were no longer seeing him.'

'Whoa, easy.' Kat lifted up her hands. 'Slow down. I'm not getting married.'

'What, then who...?' Ella looked expectantly at Megan and then instantly gave a look of dismissal, as if the very idea of Megan being engaged was implausible.

'You broke up with Jack? Really?' Megan asked. 'When did this happen?'

'Few weeks ago,' Ella offered.

'Yes, no, yes,' Kat said. 'I don't know.'

'Kat didn't tell me you were coming today,' Ella said to Megan. 'I thought dad said you were working on that one case.'

'What one case?' Kat asked.

'Really, Kat, the huge one. Don't you ever read the papers? It's been on the front page.'

'No,' Kat answered.

The door to Lab Two opened and all three girls turned to see Vincent approaching.

'Hello,' Vincent said, brushing past Ella as he joined them in the hall. He held out his hand to Megan. 'You must be Detective Matthews. I'm Dr Richmond. We spoke on the phone this morning.'

'Oh, yes, hello, Dr Richmond,' Megan said in her 'all business' tone. 'Thank you for seeing me. I'll only take a moment of your time.'

'It's no problem, I assure you,' he answered. 'I'm happy to be of service.'

'What?' Kat asked, before she could stop herself. How did Megan know her Dr Science? 'You called him to check up on me, Megs?'

'Excuse me?' Vincent asked with his normally confused look.

'Oooo,' Ella said childishly, clicking her tongue as if a fight were about to start.

'No, I'm here to talk to Dr Richmond on police business,' Megan said. 'Dad mentioned you were working here and some of the guys down at the station said Dr Richmond was the person with whom to talk.'

'But, I thought you came to see me,' Kat pouted.

'I did. And to see Dr Richmond,' Megan said, unapologetically. 'He's helping me on a case.'

'You two know each other?' Vincent asked, glancing between the two women.

'She's my sister,' Kat said, solemnly. Then to Megan, she added, 'Why didn't you just call me? I could've arranged for you to come in.'

'Kat, please, I have a victim with no ID and a desk full of case files. Don't start with the whole jealousy thing. I'm here to see you, as well as to see Dr Richmond. Don't be mad because I'm being concise with my time.' Megan turned to Vincent. Kat said nothing. How could she protest when Megan put it like that? 'Can I buy you lunch? The photographs I was talking about are in my car.'

Kat bit her lip, knowing Vincent would refuse. He never left the office to eat.

'Sure, I'd be glad to. Just let me grab my wallet,' he said.

Kat gasped as he walked away, disappearing into the back office.

'Can we come?' Ella asked. 'Please. I'm starving and Kat doesn't have any food at her place.'

'I said we'd go see Zoe later,' Kat said, feeling guilty because Vincent hadn't paid her yet and she really didn't have food at her apartment.

'Sure,' Megan smiled, as if Kat hadn't spoken. 'Of course you can come with us. I assumed you would. Though, I think Zoe's off today so we'll have to go somewhere else.'

'How do you know all this?' Kat asked. 'You're always busy.'

'Dad faxes me family reports,' Megan said.

'Let's go,' Ella insisted. 'I wanna eat.'

'I'll get my purse,' Kat said in dejection.

'What's up with her?' Megan asked as Kat walked away.

'She's been trying to get ol' Dr Vin on a date. He won't even leave the office with her,' Ella said, with candour. 'She's probably just jealous he said yes to you.'

Kat flinched but kept walking. She knew Ella purposefully said it so she could hear but so Dr Vincent couldn't, just as she knew Megan would answer just as loudly.

'She has?' Megan's tone was full of amusement. 'But, he's not her type.'

'Oh, well, I'll have to fill you in on all of that stuff later,' Ella said in a hushed tone that was still audible. 'It's not something mom and dad know, so it wouldn't be on your report. But, we can't discuss it now.'

Kat went into the collection room, still frowning. Vincent had spent several hours with Ella and now was agreeing to have lunch with Megan. What was that? She was here every day and already her sisters had gotten further with him than she had in two weeks!

After she grabbed her purse, they all piled into Megan's nondescript black car the department had given her to use. The plain vehicle was as boring as Megan's wardrobe choices. Vincent sat in the front next to Megan and Kat was with Ella in the backseat. Pretending to stare out the window, she looked at Vincent's messy pouf of hair through the corner of her eye.

Ella poked her in the side for most of the trip, trying to pretend she wasn't doing it as she looked innocently out the driver-side window. Once, Kat managed to grab her finger mid-poke and Ella started laughing. The sound was odd in the quiet vehicle.

'I hope this is all right,' Megan said, turning the car into a parking lot.

'Yes, fine detective, thank you,' Vincent answered.

'Mmm, diner, rock on,' Ella said, getting out of the car.

Kat was slower to follow. Megan pulled a briefcase up that had been by Vincent's legs, and started to get out when he reached for it and said, 'Please, allow me.'

Kat suppressed a gasp of disbelief. He never offered to carry her camera bags for her. What in the world was going on here? Was he attracted to Megan?

The diner looked more like an overgrown mobile home without wheels. It had silver siding and bright neon flashing lights that read, 'Roxie's Place'. The front exterior wall was dented, as if a car had crashed into it at one point in its long history. By the design alone, it was apparent the place was old, probably built in the 1950s.

Kat took a deep breath, trying to relax.

OK, try and perk up, she told herself. There is no reason to be jealous of Megan and Ella. They're your sisters and it's not like you are in love with Dr Vincent. The dreams don't mean a thing.

Kat had never been to this particular diner before, but

it reminded her of the others she's been to in the city. Inside, dark-green booths ran down one wall by the windows and a long bar was near the other, set back to make room for the seating area. Rounded green barstools were bolted down to the floor, spaced beside the long countertop. The kitchen was in the back, visible through a high opening where plates of food sat under heat lamps.

The smell of hamburgers and grease from the deep fryer permeated the air. Megan led the way to a booth and Ella slid in beside her older sister. Vincent glanced at the empty seat, cleared his throat and motioned for her to scoot in first. Kat took a seat, moving over to make room for him. Ella winked at her, trying to look sneaky. Kat wanted to groan, hoping Vincent didn't see the secret 'you-go-girl' signal.

A waitress approached and Megan said, 'Three coffees', as she motioned towards her sisters.

'Same,' Vincent said. 'Coffee. Black.'

'Make mine water instead,' Ella corrected. Megan arched a brow. 'Gave up caffeine. It was a dare. Don't ask.'

'Cream for mine,' Kat said as the woman walked away. She wondered if the waitress even heard her.

'You mentioned something about needing help on a case?' Vincent said, getting right to the point. Kat studied him. He wasn't looking at her as he studied Megan, his expression all about the matter at hand. Did the man never loosen up? 'As I told you on the phone, forensic entomology is not my field of specialty.'

'According to the guys in our lab, you're the man to talk to when it comes to anything with more than four legs.' Megan dug through her briefcase before pulling out a file. The waitress came back, setting the drinks on the table. Before she could speak, Megan ordered, 'I'll have the chicken salad sandwich, light on the mayo, potato salad.' Pointing at Ella, she continued, 'Hamburger, no tomato, no onion, fries.' Then, motioning to Kat, she said, 'Grilled chicken, side of fries, side of ranch.'

'You always do that,' Kat said, making a face as she poured three little containers of liquid creamer into her coffee, turning it more white than black. 'What if I don't want grilled chicken?'

Megan lifted a brow. The waitress looked at Kat expectantly and stopped writing the order on her pad.

'Yeah, she's right,' Kat mumbled in dejection, picking up the sugar shaker. The waitress looked unimpressed. Megan suppressed a grin. 'Don't look so smug. You know, some day I'd like to order for myself like an adult.' Without stopping to stir her concoction, she took a sip of the coffee.

'Just saving time,' Megan said. 'I can't help that I'm always right.'

'Um, I'm not really hungry. Thank you.' Vincent lifted his coffee cup and blew lightly along the dark surface.

'You didn't eat today,' Kat said, toying with her mug. 'You should have something.'

Vincent glanced at her, blinking several times. 'Oh, all right. I'll have what's she's having.'

When Kat glanced at her sisters, they were both smirking at her in amusement. What? If the man died of starvation, she'd never get her art show.

The waitress left, still not having said a single word to the table. Megan pulled a folder from her briefcase and handed it across the table to Vincent.

'To tell you the truth, Dr Vincent, the guys in the lab are overworked at the moment. Any fresh insight you may have would be appreciated.' Megan looked at Kat. 'You don't want to look at that, sis, trust me.'

Kat had been staring at the folder, waiting for Vincent to open it. He glanced at her, leaned away, and cracked it open so the contents were hidden from her view.

'You say you found this on . . .' Vincent said.

'Yes, we did,' Megan answered.

'That doesn't make sense. This species of beetle isn't known for being particularly necrophagous. Ah, you see, when...' Vincent stopped talking and looked at Kat. 'Why don't we move to a different table so we can go over this privately?'

He stood. Megan grabbed her briefcase and nudged Ella so she'd let her out of the booth. Ella obliged, sliding back in as the two walked away.

'Well that was rude,' Kat said, staring after Vincent and her sister.

'Oh, I don't know. If they're discussing Megan's work, I'd say I'd rather have them at the other table when I'm eating.' Ella glanced over her shoulder to where their sister and Vincent sat a few booths away, heads leaned over as they flipped through Megan's files.

'It's just that I finally get him out of the office with me and he's over there, flirting with my sister.' Kat frowned, unconsciously dumping more sugar into her coffee in her irritation. Her hands shook as she set the sugar shaker down.

'Um, I hardly call what they're up to flirting.' Ella laughed.

'Yeah, you'd think that, wouldn't you?' Kat demanded, her eyes narrowed as she gave Ella a look of exasperation. 'But, that man only talks about work. What they're doing is probably his form of foreplay. You saw him –'

'And you didn't get him out of the office,' Ella interrupted. 'Megan did.'

Kat studied Ella, giving her a wry look. 'I'm curious, what were you two doing in the lab for so long?'

'Why, you gonna be jealous of me next?'

'Ella,' Kat warned.

'Nothing really. He doesn't say a whole lot, unless you ask him about his work.' Ella smiled as the waitress set their plates in front of them, thanking the woman before continuing, 'It really is fascinating stuff that he's up to.

That is one smart man. I mean like uber-genius, super smart.'

'What is he doing in there?' Kat asked, leaning forwards.

'You don't know?'

She shook her head. 'He never says. The closest he got was telling me not to wear perfume because his mosquitoes might bite me. Oh, and I swear he once muttered something about phallus worship. At least that was the makings of an interesting conversation. And,' Kat leaned halfway across the table, lifting up in her chair, 'for a moment I was relieved he actually had even an academic interest in sex.'

'Phallus worship?' Ella laughed in obvious disbelief.

Kat sat back down, grabbed a fry and dipped it in the small container of ranch dressing on her plate. Nodding meaningfully, she made a show of biting into the fry.

Ella again glanced back. 'That man actually said the word phallus?'

'Yeah, he said something about a vile in phallus, a vial of phallus.' Kat grabbed another fry. They were nice and crispy, just as she liked them.

Ella threw back her head and laughed. 'I think you mean viral encephalis.'

'Mmm, yeah, that's it.' She nodded. 'It's a type of phallus worship, right? Some kind of ancient form of it?'

Ella arched an eyebrow.

Lowering her voice, Kat again leaned forwards, 'I tell you. All that man does is play with bugs. How in the world am I supposed to fulfil my dream of an art show if he won't even spend more than a few minutes at a time with me? I've tried everything, even that Elie Tahari tan silk blend sleeveless shirt of mine. Not even a lingering glance. I've never had a man react like that to me. Just complete indifference. And you'd think a man that awkward would be desperate for female attention.'

'Kat, viral encephalis is a disease.' Ella gave her a strange look. It was almost as if she were disappointed. 'Mosquitoes have killed more people than any other insect in the world – viral encephalis, malaria, dengue fever, yellow fever. Vincent is working to stop that. He's literally trying to save hundreds of millions of lives by stopping the onslaught of malaria. If he can break the cycle of transmission on the mosquitoes' genetic level, he and others who are working on this project internationally can introduce a genetically modified insect into the populations and cure a disease or at least stop it from spreading.'

Kat stopped eating, a fry halfway to her mouth.

'Kat, I can't believe you don't know what's going on around you. Vincent is a real, true life hero. Not some flashy guy in a cool uniform, but a hero nonetheless.'

Kat automatically thought of Vincent's 'uniform', the lab coat. She really needed to get over that fetish.

'To him, every second he wastes is another life lost to malaria.' Ella shook her head, her dark-brown eyes wide in amazement. 'Have you even tried talking to him about any of this?'

Kat looked guiltily at her plate. Under her breath, she said, 'No, not really.'

'How is it you didn't even ask?'

'I've only been there for a few weeks,' Kat said, a little defensively. 'The man hardly talks to me. What was I supposed to say?'

Ella looked at her as if it were still no excuse. Kat knew Ella was going to be the sister who changed the world on a grand scale. They'd all known it since she was little. When she was five, the youngest Matthews had told her entire Kindergarten class she was excited about the Global Change Research Information Office being established. Ella used to sit on their father's knee, listening to him read the newspaper. Kat was twenty-seven and she still didn't know exactly what the GCRIO was or what it did and, as far as she was concerned, newspapers were building materials for art collages.

'Maybe if you stopped trying to impress him with Elie Tahari designer clothes and focused on showing him how smart and caring you really can be, you'd get closer to realising your dreams. Vincent's not like Jack. It's going to take more than midriff to get his attention.'

Kat had quickly lost her appetite in the course of the social lecture. Sitting back in the booth, she felt rotten as she picked up her coffee and swirled it in her cup. How was it her high school sister seemed to get it? How could Ella have all the answers? She was still a kid. 'What's that supposed to mean?'

'Ah, don't get mad. This is me you're talking to. It's just, Jack is self-absorbed.'

'No.' Kat shook her head. They might not be together, but he was still her friend. 'He's just extremely focused on his career.'

'Being focused solely on one's self is the definition of self-absorbed.'

'I'm not self-absorbed,' Kat said.

Ella raised a brow. 'I said Jack.'

'Oh,' Kat bit her lip, realising she was getting defensive. But, if Jack was selfish, that meant she was too. That's what had made them so good together, they understood each other and were alike in their desires to be more than they were. 'Well, I just think it's called being a hard worker. Just because Jack and I aren't a thing, it doesn't mean you can badmouth him.'

'Kat,' Ella began, only to be interrupted by laughter.

Kat gasped as she lifted up in her seat to spy on her sister and Vincent. That was Megan's voice. Did Vincent make a joke?

'Ha!' Ella said in an excited whisper. 'You are jealous. You like Dr Vin, don't you? Admit it, Kat. You want him.'

'I am not jealous.' Kat sat back down and glared at Ella.

'Oh my gawd, yes you are. You're jealous he's sitting over there by Megan.'

'I am not!' Kat hissed.

'Am not, what?' Megan asked, suddenly appearing by the booth.

'Nothing,' Kat said quickly, setting her cup down on the table. Her eyes sought Vincent, needing to know if he'd heard anything they'd said. By the look on his face, he hadn't. She breathed a sigh of relief.

'Oh, well, I just got a page and I've got to head into the station so you'll have to catch a cab. I'll see you two later,' Megan said before turning to Vincent. 'Doctor, thank you for your help. If you think of anything, please call.'

'It's no problem,' he assured her. 'Anytime. And I will, if I think of anything more.'

Megan pointed at Kat's plate, said 'Eat something, you're too thin', winked at Ella and left.

Vincent took his seat next to Kat. His thigh brushed up against her leg and a small shiver worked over her, making goose bumps rise on her flesh. The reaction took her by surprise and her breath caught. For a moment, she felt like when she was in high school and someone she liked sat too close to her. Her nerve endings actually jumped with life and she was all too aware of where he touched her. Kat's mind raced, but she couldn't remember him ever touching her. She was sure he must have in passing, but it never felt like this.

Nervously, she grabbed her coffee and tried to hide her reaction by taking a drink of the warm liquid. She didn't taste it, as her mind focused on Vincent's nearness.

Was Ella right? Was her sudden desire to reach over, grab his face and kiss him due to jealousy? She took another drink. That had to be what was happening. Vincent wasn't her normal type, even if he was a hero. His hair was messy and his beard too long. Though, he did have nice eyes – nice deep-brown eyes.

Kat realised she was gazing at him, her mouth slightly

agape as she took deep breaths. She squirmed in her seat, her panties moist as she became more and more aroused. His face was close, a little too close. Pulling back, she became conscious of the fact she'd been leaning into him, about to offer her mouth to his for a kiss. Looking at his lips, she wondered what it would be like to kiss him. From what she could tell, his mouth looked firm, even though it was hidden by the beard.

Studying him at such a close distance, she could see the definition of his cheekbones beneath his darker skin. There were definitely some of his father's features in him, but he didn't look completely like Mr Richmond. She found herself wanting to touch him, to run her fingers into his hair to feel and discover him.

'I was telling Kat about your work,' Ella said, interrupting the trance between them.

Instantly, Kat's attention was drawn to her sister. Ella was nodding slowly in encouragement.

'Oh, yeah, yeah, about the malaria,' Kat said, nodding as she looked back at Vincent. His eyes were no longer on her.

'Oh,' Vincent said. 'Can we get yours to go? I need to get back to the office. I'm expecting a call from South Africa later and need to compile some data.'

Vincent stood and walked away from the table towards the bathrooms.

Kat frowned, staring after him. 'See, El. I don't think the man likes me one bit. He doesn't even want to tell me about his job.'

Vincent took several deep breaths as he walked away from Kat and her sister. This was bad. He could not be attracted to his assistant. Though, his cock debated the fact quite effectively. It was so hard it became difficult for him to walk straight. Thankfully, he still wore his white lab coat, for it did a sufficient job of hiding his erection from view.

Well, it wasn't like she was really a scientist in training sent over from the college. Actually, she was just a girl he'd hired off the street. Vincent took a deep breath, walking into the bathroom to get away from her.

No, there was no justifying it. He could not be attracted to Kat. She wasn't his type. The woman had pink hair and a tattoo! She hated insects and she didn't know the first thing about his work. And not once did she care to ask him what he was doing – not that he really gave her the opportunity to inquire.

But, if Kat wasn't his type, then who was? Vincent wasn't sure he knew what his type was any more. It had been so long since he'd dated, let alone had sex. His parents had tried to set dates up for him on several occasions, but thankfully it appeared as if they'd finally given up on him. He wasn't interested in the socialites they always picked.

Maybe it was the fact he hadn't dated in a long time that made Kat so appealing. She was there during the day and she had a great smile. He liked her smile. Vincent wasn't one for noticing a woman's clothes, but the outfits she wore did demand attention. Yes, that's all it was. He'd been without feminine company for a long time and she was there.

Taking a deep breath, he looked down his body to where the tension between his thighs had yet to lessen. A men's bathroom in the middle of a New York diner was hardly the fitting place to take care of his needs, but did he really have a choice?

'Damn it!' he swore, pulling up his lab coat to adjust himself beneath his pants until he could get back to the laboratory.

'Whoa, buddy, sorry wrong room.' The thick Brooklyn accent was punctuated by the half laugh, half shock of the man's tone. Vincent looked up, horrified to see a big, burly middle-aged man in a red flannel shirt. 'They got motels for that kinda thing, ya know.'

'What? No,' Vincent began. It was too late, the man backed out of the door. Cursing, he lowered his lab coat and took a deep breath. He didn't mind helping the police detective, in fact he felt it was his duty as a scientist to help anyway he could, but the distraction could have come at a better time.

Not ready to face what was really on his mind – Kat – he went to the sink and washed his hands, splashing cold water on his face. When he looked up into the tarnished mirror, his attention was caught by the droplets shining in the yellowish florescent light. They adhered to his beard hair, whiskers that were wildly out of control. For the first time in a long time, he looked at himself, seeing what was actually there. His hair was overgrown and bushed into no particular style. He did brush it, but obviously it was past the point that dragging a comb through could do any good. And, if his beard grew any longer, he'd look like a member of an old rock band.

Running his fingers through the coarse dark facial hair to feel his face, he frowned. Even if he wanted the complications of a sexual relationship – which he didn't – what would make any woman want to be with him? At least any woman worth having. The look he'd just shared with Kat was surely one-sided. She was probably wondering why in the hell he was gaping speechlessly at her like a simpleton. There was no way a young beautiful woman like her would want a man like him. He looked ten years older than he really was and even Vincent had to admit, if he saw himself on the street, he'd automatically think he was a bum in need of a job and a hot meal.

'You don't have time for this,' Vincent whispered to himself.

Dr Speight was expecting a phone conference tonight and he still hadn't gathered all the information the man wanted. The only reason Vincent remembered he had the conference was because the man's project director had called early that morning to confirm it.

'I don't have time for this,' he said again, trying to will his body's arousal away. 'There is too much work to be done.'

With that in mind, he strode out of the restroom. Kat and her sister were already outside. Ella was hailing a cab and Kat held a takeout box in her hands. His beard was damp and the air sent a chill over him as the breeze hit his whiskers. As the cab pulled over to pick them up, Vincent reached to open the door. Ella beat him to it. He found himself disappointed as Kat slid in first, sitting by the door on the opposite side of her sister.

When the taxi stopped in front of his building, Vincent automatically paid the driver and stepped out. He was surprised when Ella stayed in the cab and gave the driver new instructions. As it drove off, he looked expectantly at Kat.

'She's going to visit Sasha in between classes,' she answered his unasked question. A strand of her pink hair blew across her face and he desperately wanted to touch it, to touch her. He held back. 'That's another sister.'

Vincent nodded, not knowing what to say to her. He'd always been aware of her as a woman, but his body had apparently caught up with his mind.

'OK, then,' she whispered to herself more than him as she brushed past him. 'Come on, doc, you have a lot of work to do. And just so you remember, tomorrow is my day off. I won't be coming in so don't freak out on me like last week.'

Vincent stared after her, watching the sunlight caress her bare shoulders for a brief moment before she disappeared inside. The image stayed with him as he moved to follow her. She must have hurried down the hall because by the time he made it through the door, she was gone.

Chapter Six

'A whole freaking month and a half,' Kat mumbled to herself, frowning at the collection room door. She'd come to work, do her job and leave. If possible, Vincent paid less attention to her as each week passed. Nothing worked – not the outfits, not the flirting, nor even questioning him about his hero work. In fact, when she asked about what was going on in Lab Two, he seemed more confused than usual. The saddest thing was that the closest she'd ever been to getting the man out of the office was when Megan came by and needed him for work – a whole month ago.

She turned back to her camera and adjusted the lens on the final tray of insects. Her job documenting the massive collection was coming to an end. Today she would finish the photographs. She'd been working slow, trying to make the job last so she'd have an excuse to be there. What would happen when she finished? Would Vincent have no more need of her? He never asked her to do anything beyond photographing the collection.

Her hair was pulled up at the sides and she pushed the heavy length over her shoulder, out of her way as she worked. She'd re-coloured the locks, taking out the pink. Not even the dye job back to natural dark blonde had gotten his attention. It didn't help she still had erotic dreams of him and didn't have Jack around anymore for sexual release. Vibrators really weren't any fun when a girl had to fly solo. There was no way around it. She wanted Vincent, at least once. It didn't matter what the reason was, if it was because he had power over her, or that she wanted him because he didn't want her. She did feel guilty about using him, but technically, she hadn't done that yet.

'Oh, good, you're still here,' Vincent said, coming into the collection room. Kat jolted in surprise, but didn't look up from her camera. Just thinking of the man had heated her blood and made the initial hints of arousal blossom within her pussy. Just hearing his voice compelled her body into full force desire. What was he doing here? He never walked across the hall to see her. In fact, she hadn't laid eyes on him for days, only heard his voice through the door as he told her what he wanted for lunch. She'd left it by the door like an offering.

Snapping the picture to cover the slight shake in her hands, she leaned back, took a deep breath and said, 'I'm done. That's the last one.'

'Oh. Already?'

Kat tried not to laugh. Already? She'd taken much longer than any creditable photographer would have, especially working eight hours, six days a week. Not hearing him move, she finally allowed herself to look in his direction. Gasping lightly, she stared at his face. 'You shaved.'

Vincent reached for his chin, only to bump it with a small present he held in his hand. It was wrapped in gold paper, with the kind of perfect ribbon decoration done in a department store. Clearing his throat, he looked around before placing the present on the counter. 'Yes, a couple days ago.'

Kat could only stare at his face. From the way the beard had bushed around his cheeks, she expected him to have rounded features. Instead, his cheekbones were well defined, set off by his straight proud nose. Full lips were parted, giving a hint of straight white teeth. Stubble shadowed his jaw, affecting his skin with a dark afternoon shadow. He rubbed his chin lightly.

Slowly, she drew her gaze higher. With less hair distracting from his features, his deep brown eyes were more pronounced. Kat knew she was staring and yet she couldn't look away. He was much more handsome than she'd imagined. Sure, he was no supermodel Jack, but he wasn't unattractive either. Far from it.

Not only had he shaved, but he'd also cut his hair. The dark locks were slicked back, reminding her of how his father looked. Thankfully, he didn't have the smarmy moustache and the same sense of gigolo style Mr Richmond favoured. No, Vincent always wore subdued colours and tasteful slacks beneath his lab coat.

'Is something –' Vincent paused, glancing over his shoulder, '– wrong?'

'You're . . .' Kat stopped as a shiver worked its way through her. She had been about to say cute, but couldn't force the word out. 'Ah, young. You're so young. With the beard, I hadn't realised.'

His mother had said he was thirty-three, but she wasn't supposed to know that.

'Hmm,' he murmured as he motioned down to the gift he'd brought into the room.

'Is that for –?'

'Ella,' he said.

'Ella?' Kat frowned. He bought a present for Ella? What in the world?

'Yes, she said she was graduating from high school. This is for her.'

Kat smiled, relieved by the way he said 'high school'. By his tone it was clear he thought of Ella as a kid, but the graduation had been three weeks ago. 'That's nice of you.'

Vincent looked around the room, as if he wanted to say more. Then, nodding once, he turned to go.

'Wait, what do you want me to do?' Kat asked.

'Do? Oh, well, give it to her if you don't mind. If it's a problem, I can ask Megan when I see her later.'

'Megan?' Kat gasped, taking an unintentional step closer to him. 'You're seeing my sister later?'

'She called earlier about her case,' Vincent said. 'We're going to meet up for dinner tonight.'

'You're going to dinner?' The words were out before she could stop them. 'With Megan?'

'Yes.' His tone was low and drawn as he considered her carefully.

Kat bit her lip. Now Megan definitely wasn't too young for him. 'Do you talk to her often?'

'Don't you?'

Kat shook her head, shrugging. 'Well, you know, she is rather busy with work. I don't want to disturb her.'

Damn her! Ella undoubtedly told Megan what Kat was doing with Vincent. How could her own sister betray her? Or was Megan trying to help her? Kat tried not to be jealous, but she couldn't stop the rush of feelings that overcame her. If Megan was trying to help her realise her goal, then why wouldn't she tell her? Or was it innocent? Was it really about work? There was only one way of finding out.

'Where are you going?' Kat asked, moving to take the present and set it by her equipment just so she'd have something to keep her shaking hands busy.

'I recommended Luna, though it's been a while since I've been there,' he admitted. 'They have a wonderful tortellini with gorgonzola.'

But you're supposed to take me out for tortellini with gorgonzola, not my sister! Kat took a deep breath, doing her best not to let her jealousy show.

'You're taking my sister to Luna?' Kat swallowed nervously. Her heart pounded wildly in her chest. Luna wasn't a 'talk about business' restaurant. It was romantic, with candlelight and private booths, and Megan making out with her shaved, sexy science man!

'Is that a problem?' he asked.

'Yes,' Kat blurted. 'What I mean is, Megan is allergic to pasta.'

OK, that was a bare faced lie.

'She didn't mention that to me,' he said.

'Yeah, she wouldn't. She's too nice, but it can't even touch her other foods. She wouldn't want to hurt your feelings if you suggested it. Her boyfriend is always getting on to her about being too nice.' OK, lie number two and three and possibly four. Kat couldn't keep track of them. Unable to look at him, she pretended to fuss with her camera, making unnecessary adjustments to the lens and manual settings.

'Oh, I see.' She saw him nod out of the corner of her eye.

'Yeah, they're pretty serious. Been together a long time,' Kat said. OK, soon she'd have spouted so many lies she wouldn't be able to keep them all straight. It was like verbal sewage, she couldn't make her mouth stop. But was it really her fault? Vincent was the one who'd cleaned himself up and gotten all sexy on her. 'I believe he's bought her a huge engagement ring and everything. And well, we all know how she feels about him. She'll say yes, no problem. But, he's a romantic. He'll probably wait to ask her on the Eiffel tower in Paris or something. Being a traditionalist, she won't mention it until it's a done deal.'

Oh, this was bad. He was so going to catch her at this. One word to Megan and her lies would all be undone.

Shut up, Kat. Don't say anything more! Change the subject.

'Do you have a better suggestion then?' he asked.

Yeah, don't take my sister out on a date, you idiot! Take me instead. I'm the one you're supposed to be dating!

'You know.' Kat turned to him and smiled, swaying her hips ever so slightly as she walked towards him. She pushed out her chest in a subtle move to get his attention. It was almost as if an alien life form took over her body, but obviously desperate times called for uber-slutty measures. 'Earlier, I asked what you wanted me to do. I didn't mean about Ella's graduation present, I meant about my job. I'm done photographing the collection. Everything is on digital file on my sister's computer. I can burn you a disc or make you a full set of prints, whichever you like.'

'Yes, um, please.' His tone was stunted and he blinked several times as she neared him. Kat didn't stop her leisurely advance as she kept her eyes directly on his. He continued to stutter over his words, 'Fine. Thank you. I mean, disc, digital.'

'So I'm done,' Kat lowered her tone into a husky murmur, letting a small pout come to her lips. If this was it, then what harm was there in trying? Stopping about a foot away from him, she waited for a sign that he wanted her to stay.

'You're . . .' Vincent's breathing deepened and he didn't finish speaking. His eyes drifted down to her breasts and she was glad she wore her lightweight cashmere sweater with the deep V neckline. The black material clung to her body, aided by the use of a padded push-up bra to make the ultimate cleavage.

Suddenly, her faded blue jeans felt a little too tight. Leaning against the counter, she traced her fingers along the edge, using it more for support than for anything else. Her stomach tightened as her sex heated and became moist. She was all too aware of him as a man. The fantasies had been implanted upon their first meeting and curiosity made them flourish.

'I'm what?' she whispered, letting her lashes sweep over her eyes. She desperately hoped he wouldn't call her different again. Kat wasn't sure which of them had moved but suddenly, they were so close she could smell cologne on his skin and feel the heat from his body.

'You're . . .' he looked down at her, the whisper of his breath tickling her cheek. He smelled really good. Every nerve in her body jumped to life, straining toward him, wanting to touch him. 'I should go.'

'Why?' Her voice had dropped to a husky murmur, but she didn't care. She was too aroused to think logically.

Both of them breathed audibly in heavy pants. Staying away from him was torture. Surely the arousal she felt wasn't one-sided – not right now, in this delicious moment of anticipation. Each second felt like a year, burning with unrealised passions.

Kat waited, knowing as his eyes bore into her that he wanted to kiss her. He stared at her mouth, licking his lips as if he could already taste her against him. But, to her surprise, he didn't make a move to close the distance.

I'm here to help him with this part. If I leave it up to him, we'll never get anywhere.

She slowly licked her mouth, dragging her tongue in a practised movement across her bottom lip. There was something alluring about his pristine white lab coat, which wasn't a surprise considering each dream and fantasy she had of him included him wearing it, about the scientific atmosphere of the building and about the man before her. Kat couldn't resist grabbing hold of the front of his coat. Warmth flowed through her fingers as she gripped the stiff material and pulled him forwards. He didn't stop her as she lifted her mouth to his.

She instantly thrust her hips forward into his as she deepened the kiss by small degrees, testing his response. To her surprise, and great delight, the stiff outline of his cock met her from beneath his clothing. What she felt for him was definitely not one-sided. How long had he been attracted to her? Why hadn't he said something, done something, earlier? Vincent made a weak noise and moved as if he would draw back from the intimate touch.

Tightening her grip on the lab coat, she refused to let him get away from her as she again rocked her hips forwards. His eyes closed and he stiffened as if he were waiting for her to act. Kat moaned, parting her mouth wider. She didn't trust her tongue inside him, but instead let him feel her breath entering his mouth. Her lower stomach rocked along his erection, caressing it naughtily as she slowly wiggled back and forth. With an audible sigh, Kat again kissed him, harder than before. The taste of mint welcomed her tongue as she explored the depths of his mouth.

Vincent made a strange noise in the back of his throat and suddenly grabbed her face in his hands. He took over the kiss, turning her so she leaned back against the counter. His stubble scraped her face, but she didn't care. There was a desperation to his passion, marked by the stumbling of his fingers as he moved a hand down over her neck to her chest. Eagerly, he grabbed her breast in his palm, squeezing it hard through the cashmere. Then, he jerked the V-neck to the side, pulling her bra to the side at the same time. Now, with one breast exposed, he took to fondling it once more.

The man had great hands, strong hands and he used them masterfully as he let the lengths of his fingers glide across the mound to tweak her nipple. Kat was so over-taken with surprise at his frantic passion that she forgot to move. She gripped his lab coat tight and heard one of the snaps pull apart, but the coat stayed on.

'Ah, damn,' he grunted, leaving her breast and her mouth at once so his hands could work on her jeans. With each tug, the denim crotch hit against her sex, stimulating her clit. Already she was wet for him, the cream of her body slickening her pussy as she wiggled to be free of her clothing.

Running her hands down his chest, she was pleased to discover the harder planes of his body. He was no body builder, but his muscles were firm to the touch and he threw off a great heat. Kat had fantasised too much about his lab coat so she pulled it up instead of jerking it off. He thrust a hand boldly down the front of her lace panties against her naked flesh, groaning as his finger slid easily into the folds of her sex.

With both hands, she managed to get his suit pants undone. The thin charcoal material slid to the floor and silk boxers were soon to follow. The lab coat hid his cock from view, but she easily took the thick length in her hand working her palm over the smooth, taut arousal.

Kat kicked off her shoes as he pushed her jeans further down her legs, exposing her lower body. The tighter denim trapped her calves when she spread them wide to allow him better access to her pussy.

Vincent lowered his head, pulling an erect nipple into his mouth. She moaned lightly as a jolt of pleasure coursed through her at the caress. Urgently, he pulled back and grabbed her by the hips. Instead of pulling her tight to him, he held her hips back. Roughly, he said, 'I don't have anything.'

'What?' She leaned up, confused.

'Condom.' He breathed heavily. 'I don't have a condom.'

'Oh,' Kat looked back and forth. Then, leaning down the counter, she grabbed the strap to her camera bag and pulled it towards her. Digging into the side panel, she took out her perfume, lipstick and a couple of wadded pieces of paper and dropped them on the countertop. The lipstick rolled onto the floor, clanking as it raced across the room. She wanted to cry out in frustration and almost did, but finally she found what she was looking for. Kat handed it to him. 'Here.'

Vincent blinked in surprise, but then nodded as he took the condom. Ripping the package with his teeth, he leaned over to put it on. Kat didn't help him as she instead ran her hands over his chest, kissing the flesh along his jaw to his ear. He grunted in pleasure as she bit the lobe only to suck it between her teeth. Her fingers glanced across his neck, feeling the hard beat of his racing pulse. Any more foreplay and she was likely to go mad from lust.

Vincent must have felt the same way, because he spun her around towards the counter. Stunned by the commanding manoeuvre, she braced herself on her palms and stared wide-eyed at the collection cases, as she bent over before him. Using his foot, he pushed her jeans down to her feet. Automatically, she kicked out of them, giving him better access to her body.

Kat tensed, waiting for the first intimate touch of his body to hers. Her fingers dug into the rough wood. Vincent didn't hesitate as he came up behind her. The stiff brush of material skimmed over her moments before the heated touch of his flesh grazed her ass. Vincent drew his cock along her cleft. The cold chill of the condom was soon warmed as he moved along her sex. With a hand on her back, he lifted her sweater and pushed her down to better angle her body. She felt his fingers run along the butterfly tattoo on her back, as if unconsciously tracing the design.

He thrust, stretching her body to his. Vincent groaned as he seated himself to the hilt. Kat gasped, instantly reaching down between her thighs to stimulate the sensitive bud hidden in her folds. As he pushed forwards, it jarred her sex against her hand. Vincent had complete control and he took it, holding her hip and her shoulder as he worked his body against her, riding her hard and sure.

'Oh, oh,' Vincent repeated over and over, the sound breathless. 'Oh, damn.'

The tension from the last month and a half built, making her come faster than usual. Kat slammed her palm against the counter, biting her lips as she tensed. There was something wicked and erotic about having sex in the entomology building. Knowing Vincent wore his scientist uniform only completed the fantasy. She'd wanted him, had thought about him taking her and now he was and it felt so good, so right. Even as she came, he didn't stop pumping his hips.

'Oh, oh,' he panted, as if nothing else would come out of his mouth.

Suddenly, he grunted, making an animalistic noise as he came. Jerking several times, his hand worked against her back and his nails dug into her skin. She gasped, straightening at the small pain.

'Ouch, watch it,' she said.

'I'm sorry,' he whispered, pulling out and away.

Kat wanted to laugh, but she was out of breath. He was sorry? She'd never had that reaction before. Slowly, she became aware her ass was exposed and she pushed up from the counter. When she turned, Vincent was buttoning his slacks. Spurred into action by his strange behaviour, she grabbed her jeans and panties, pulling them both on at the same time.

'I shouldn't have taken advantage of you,' he said, as he zipped his fly. 'I'm your employer.'

Kat did laugh that time. 'Doc, I highly doubt you could take advantage of anyone.'

'I can be, ah, forceful,' he said, as if offended.

She started laughing so hard, she snorted. 'Yeah, OK.'

'What?'

'I think the important question on the table is do I still have a job?'

'Kat, I don't want you to think this is … that I'm keeping you here for …'

'Sex,' she supplied, smiling brightly.

'Yes, that is not the reason. You're quiet, you leave me to my work and you've done a great service.'

'Hmm.' Kat crossed her arms over her chest. Teasing, she said, 'I never heard it called that before – a great service.'

He looked uncertain and she had to laugh again.

'Easy doc, don't worry about it. We're adults, we're

young, it's called hooking up and you really should try it more often. You might find there is more to life than Lab Two, Dr Vincent.'

He nodded, but kept distance between them. 'What I was trying to say is that I get more work done with you around.'

'Ah, the person in the other room thing.' She leaned against the counter and studied him. Her body was relaxed, but his stance was uncertain, unwelcoming. 'I get it. I like having someone in the other room as well when I'm working. It's like having company without the work. Makes the hours go by faster.'

'Well, perhaps, but I thought it was more because you didn't pester me with questions about what I was doing, could answer the phone and remind me to eat so I don't pass out from starvation as well as exhaustion.'

Not the most romantic thing, but it would do.

'So, boss,' she said, arching a brow, 'what new position do you want me in?'

His face reddened and he cleared his throat. The man really was too easy to throw off guard. She felt so good and couldn't help the smile that crossed her face. The only thing better would be if he held her in his arms, letting her revel in the feelings of release and closeness. Reaching forwards, she grabbed his arm and pulled him a little closer.

'Um, maybe the office,' he said. She wasn't sure if he meant for her to work in the office, or that he wanted to fuck her in the office. Either way, she was game. Looking at his face, she knew he wasn't sure which he meant either.

'Perfect. I'll start in the office tomorrow,' she said. 'I've been dying to riffle through your notes in there anyway.'

'But –' he began, but she cut him off. She was only messing with him anyway.

'By the way, are you still going out with my sister tonight?'

'Yes.' he nodded. 'Oh, damn, I have to make reservations somewhere else. What do you think? I don't want her getting hives or having some sort of reaction.'

'Oh, yeah, about that.' Kat looked down. She thought about confessing her lie, but she couldn't make the words come out. If she confessed that, most likely everything would come tumbling out of her mouth like a mad rush and she'd admit to being bribed by his parents to be here. No, she needed more time to think about it. 'I'll take care of the reservations.'

'You?'

Kat nodded.

'I'd invite you to come, but you probably already have a date tonight.'

She glanced up. Was he probing? 'Nope, no date.'

'But, I just figured a girl like you...'

'Like me?' She frowned.

'Are you always this argumentative?' He lifted a hand, brushing a strand of hair from her face.

'Probably. Are you always this shy?' She lifted both of her hands and mussed up his hair. It hadn't moved while they had sex and she couldn't stand the sterile hairstyle. Pulling a few strands down around his temples to frame his gorgeous eyes, she smiled. 'There, much better. You should wash the product out of your hair and let it hang loose.'

'I never thought about it,' he said. 'I go to the same barber my father has always gone to and he just cuts it and hands me the stuff. It tames down the curls.'

'Hmm,' was all she said in response, but many thoughts went through her head. 'So, are you going to ask me to come with you tonight, or what?'

'I honestly don't know.'

'Ah, well, let me help you. You say,' she dropped her tone to a lower octave. 'Kat, I'd love it if you'd join me for dinner tonight.'

'And what would you say?' Vincent was adorably shy.

It made her want to kiss him again. She resisted. Even though her body was willing, she wanted to hold back some, make him want her again, make him learn to make the first move. That was her goal, after all, to date train him. Her stomach knotted at the thought.

'That's easy. I'd say, wonderful, I'd love to. And then you would say,' again she dropped her tone, 'I'll pick you up at seven and will never again get all weird and mention the fact I am your employer after we have sex.' Pausing, she threw her voice again, 'Then I say, how very kind of you, good sir. You say, yes it was kind –'

'Did we just turn British?'

'Sorry.' Kat laughed 'Last thing I saw on television was a British sitcom before I sold it to pay for darkroom chemicals.'

'You had to sell your television?' He looked stunned.

'Pawned, actually, but they get to keep it if I don't pick it up.'

'Am I not paying you enough? Did I forget to pay you again? Do you need me to reimburse you for expenses?'

'This was before I started working here, doc, so don't worry about it. To tell you the truth, my old roommate's parents gave it to her and she left it when she moved out. Something about the remote control waves turning channels in her head.'

'Oh, but, you're fine now?' he insisted.

'Why, thank you,' she drawled like a southern belle.

'I mean do you need money, Kat?' He put his hands on his hips and she wasn't sure she liked his authoritarian tone.

'Doc, what I need is for you to pick me up tonight for dinner on time.' She leaned over and grabbed her camera bag. Digging inside, she found one of her photography business cards she'd made by hand one night after too many cappuccinos with the downstairs neighbour, and gave it to him. 'Here's the address.'

'I can do that.' He nodded.

'Good.' Grabbing his lab coat, she pulled him closer, standing on her toes to kiss his firm mouth briefly. It was hard to pull back, but she forced herself to. 'You know, this is the first time we've had a full conversation.'

'It is?'

She nodded.

'Have I been terribly rude?' he asked. She nodded. 'I don't mean to be. It's just that I was behind and I'm slowly getting caught up to where I need to be. Do you think you can forgive my impoliteness?'

She shook her head in denial, but smiled to show him she wasn't serious.

'Even if I tell you my work is very important to a lot of people.'

'OK, but only since you're saving lives.' Her tone was wry. She leaned up to kiss him again, but he pulled back, refusing. She blinked in surprise. He wasn't having doubts already, was he?

'What's happening here?' He searched her face. A moment of panic welled inside her as she thought of his parents and what they wanted her to do. She'd never been wholly comfortable with the idea of deceiving him, especially now, but what could she say? Looking at Vincent, there was something inside her that made her want to be with him. Sure, he was impossible and he could barely take a joke or make one. He spent too much time working and took too little care of himself. If she didn't bring him food and leave it at his door, she was sure he'd starve. Yet, despite how obviously wrong they were for each other, she couldn't stand the idea of not giving them a chance.

'What do you mean?' she asked. His question was loaded, even though he didn't know it. She couldn't answer it for risk of giving herself and his parents' plan away. If she just kept her mouth shut and saw where they could go first, then she could tell him after they got there – metaphorically, of course.

'Well, here? With us? What is going on between us?'

'Why worry about it?' She touched his cheek, letting her palm run over his shadowing of stubble.

'I just don't want to be –'

'Don't worry, you won't be distracted,' she assured him. 'I'm not moving my stuff into your apartment. Don't think everything needs to be defined and named. Some things just are. Can't we just let it go where it goes?'

'But, I'm a scientist. Naming things is what I do. I'm not good at wait and see, at least not without some idea of where I'm heading.'

'Well, it's time you learned not everything can be classified.' She gravitated closer, her mouth within kissing distance of his. 'And I'm going to take off early to go and get ready for a hot date.'

'Hot?' The poor man actually looked shocked. It was all too obvious he didn't give himself that much consideration. 'I'm a hot date?'

'Definitely cool,' she said, using Ella's young hipster tone.

'I don't know that I've ever been hot and cool before.'

'Oh, you poor man.' Kat gave him a pitying look. 'Didn't you at least date in college?'

'Oh, well, not much. I was really busy with classes and internships. Besides, I was the youngest student at Cornell. After testing out of high school early, we felt there was no reason to wait to start college. From there, I was always working and there was never really time to date.'

'We'll just have to change your luck, won't we?' She patted his face. Then, smiling, she said, 'Well, I'm off.'

'It's early yet. It's not time to leave.'

'You just worry about picking me up at seven.' Kat grinned as she walked away, carrying her camera bag. Her heart was beating hard in her chest. Inside she tingled from what they had done. 'I'll take care of everything else, even calling Megan. You just make sure you don't forget and stand me up.'

'Oh, I won't. I promise.'

Kat didn't turn back, but hoped his eyes were on her as she swayed her hips just a little bit more than usual to get his attention.

Finally, Dr Richmond, we're getting somewhere.

Chapter Seven

'Flora, you are an absolute angel!' Kat exclaimed, staring in awe at the vintage dress her downstairs cappuccino buddy held up for inspection. Kat's hair was damp from her shower and she wore a fluffy pink robe over her bra and panties. When she'd told Flora about her date, the woman insisted she had the perfect thing for Kat to wear. Stepping back, Kat let the elderly woman into her apartment. 'You were so right. It's perfect.'

'The last time I wore this more than just sparks were flying. Flora laughed. She had a coarse way about her, from the gravelly tone of her voice to the fact she was often seen with a pipe hanging from her lips. Her face was wrinkled to the extreme and still she dusted her features with make-up as she had in her youth. Even her hair was a pitch-black reminder of what she referred to as her 'better days'. Though, to Kat, the woman was still young and vibrant at heart. 'I believe this dress went flying as well. I had to stitch the hem. That's what took me so long. But, don't worry, it's clean.'

'Flora, you promiscuous woman, you.' Kat winked.

Flora laughed and shook the black crepe material. 'Well, try it on, try it on.'

Kat squealed, still smiling from her earlier encounter with Vincent. Sure, the aftermath of sex hadn't been the ideal cuddling and talking that such an intimate moment would dictate, but at least they'd talked. She took the dress.

Flora's sharp eyes took her in. 'This one's special, isn't he?'

'Who?' Kat tried to feign innocence.

'Don't you "who" me!' Flora demanded, going towards Kat's kitchen to help herself. 'Go get dressed and then I want details.'

Kat ran towards her bedroom to slip the dress on. Circa 1960s, the black crepe and silk-lined evening dress was a true thing of beauty – and definitely much better than anything Kat would have in her closet. It was a little loose at the waist, but it didn't matter. Simple pearl beadwork adorned the bodice, which gathered beneath her breasts and fell in a graceful sweep of elegance down the front. Thick straps and a mid-back plunge finished the simple look.

Since the skirt only fell to her knees, she quickly slipped black pantyhose on underneath. She would've gone for tan, but she didn't have any without runners. Then, going to her closet, she spotted a pair of black and pearl heels. 'This is so my lucky day!'

Everything was coming together brilliantly.

'You're wearing it backwards,' Flora said as Kat walked into the kitchen to show her.

'What?' Kat automatically turned to try and look at the back of the dress, which was impossible since she was wearing it.

'Got ya,' Flora chuckled. 'You look great, doll. Now, about this man. Who is he? And was today the first day you two hooked up, or have you been sleeping with him for a while?'

'Flora!' Kat gasped, though in truth she was hardly shocked.

'Please,' the woman drawled, waving her hand in dismissal as she carried the only food item she could've found in Kat's kitchen – a half eaten bag of baked potato chips. Munching on them as she went towards Kat's bedroom, she said, 'I'm way too old not to know that look on your face. You're grinning like an idiot and your cheeks have been flushed since you walked in the building.'

'Have you been spying on the entrance again?' Kat scolded good-naturedly.

'You bet I have. I don't trust Mills down in security.'

'Mills isn't security,' Kat said. 'He doesn't even work here.'

'Well, I think he's undercover. You know, all that man does is sit down in the lobby all day, staring at the front door like someone's going to come and visit him. The old fool.'

'Why don't you visit him?' Kat suggested.

'Ah, I just use him for sex,' Flora dismissed. 'Old fool keeps trying to get me to marry him, but he did say he'd settle for living together.'

Kat shook her head. 'Flora, darling, you are one of a kind and I love ya for it.'

'Ah, now,' Flora waved her hands and was at a loss for words. She picked up the brush and instantly changed the subject. 'Sit down. I'm going to show you a simple trick we used to do back in my day. They're called pin curls. You know, we didn't have hairdryers like you girls do now and we often slept in our curlers. Damned uncomfortable stupidity just for the sake of fashion if you ask me.'

'It's still your day, Flora.' Kat took a seat in front of her vanity mirror. Picking up her compact, she dusted powder on her nose.

'Oh, bless your heart.' Flora went to work on Kat's damp hair. Her hands were deftly precise as she moulded the locks into several rows of curls, using clips in her apron to pin them to Kat's head so they'd stay. 'So, you never answered. Who is he?'

'Dr Vincent,' Kat said. Just saying his name made a smile cross her features. She picked up her lipstick, a darker red shade that would complement the classiness of the dress.

'*The* Dr Vincent Richmond?' Flora said. 'Mr Bug Man? Mr Never Pays Attention?'

Kat nodded, trying to hide her blush behind her hand.

'Well, do tell. I thought you said he wasn't interested in you.' Flora resumed her administrations. 'I'm going to pin the back of your hair up. It's too long for this style, but don't worry, it'll be the bee's knees.'

'Groovy,' Kat said.

'Now, get to spilling. This look on your face, doll,' Flora touched Kat's cheek, is not the look you had for Jack.'

'No,' Kat agreed, but she was unwilling to go into it further.

'Ah, to be young with so much time to put things off.' Flora chuckled, as if sensing Kat's desire not to delve into what she was feeling. 'Blow dry your hair but don't take it down. I'm going to go to my place and make you something to eat.'

'But I'm going to dinner.' Kat leaned close to the mirror to draw liquid black eyeliner across the top lid. 'He doesn't know it, but I made reservations at Zoe's restaurant. She's been dying to get a look at him and when I called her, she bumped some people to get us in.'

'Yes, but you're going to dinner with a beau. You don't want him to see you eat more than a dainty salad.'

'I honestly don't think he's the kind of man to notice if I have a healthy appetite.' Kat stared into the mirror.

'Trust me, doll. He'll notice. If you make a pig of yourself, he'll notice.'

Kat just laughed as the woman went to make the sandwich.

Kat slipped her hand into Vincent's as she led him into the restaurant. That morning she'd been upset and then, as if by magic, the wall between them was tossed aside in the waves of their passion. No matter how she told herself she was going to hang back and let him make the first moves from now on, she couldn't seem to stop herself. In the cab ride to Sedurre, she'd slid closer to him in the seat. His body had tensed and when he looked at her, a soft, wondering smile was on his face. How could she not kiss him? Things would have gotten heated if not for the cab driver whistling as if they actually wanted him to watch their show.

Glancing at Vincent from under her lashes, she couldn't help but smile. He'd shown up on time, which actually amazed her. She wouldn't have been surprised if he'd forgotten their date altogether. But, the fact that her absentminded scientist indeed valued her enough to come said a lot. Didn't it? Or was it just wishful thinking on her part?

Kat swallowed nervously. She didn't know why, but part of her was scared – scared he'd find out what his parents wanted her to do, scared he would change his mind, scared he would look at her and wonder why in the world he was with a woman like her. These feelings of self-doubt were a new thing for her. She normally didn't care what people thought, but with him she found she cared desperately. His actions, small as they were, said that he liked her. But she wanted to hear him say something. Then, whenever it looked like he might compliment her or say something about them, she cut him off for fear it would be something she'd rather not hear, like, 'I want us to be friends'.

He looked incredible in his dark-blue suit. The classic style of the three button jacket and single pleat trousers complemented her vintage gown. He'd listened to her suggestion and left his hair un-greased. Now it fell in soft waves around his head. Beneath his jacket was a dress shirt in her favourite colour of blue and a subtly striped tie in varying greys. There was just something about being escorted by a man in a suit that made her feel like a princess.

She caught their reflection in the glass door as Vincent reached to open it for her. Her hair was done in perfect, dark waves, just like a movie star from the 1950s. A darker net held the back length up to give it the appropriate bobbed effect and Flora had let her borrow an old silver and pearl hairpin for adornment. The effect must have worked because when Vincent picked her up, he stared at her and not her apartment, as he nodded several times. It wasn't a compliment with words, but she took it nonetheless.

As he led her inside the building, he looked around before turning to her, 'I thought you said your sister was allergic to pasta. This place serves Italian food.'

'Oh, that.' Kat glanced around nervously. Seeing Zoe, she quickly waved at her sister to get her to come over. Zoe didn't come, but pointed towards the back of the room.

Just then, the hostess noticed them and smiled. 'Great to see you again, Ms Matthews.' Kat smiled and nodded, knowing the woman had to call her that when she was on duty or she could lose her job. 'Your sisters have already joined us.'

'Thank you,' Kat said. The woman turned to look at Vincent. Her smile widened and she blinked several times until Kat realised the hostess was batting her eyelashes at her date. Her tone hard, she repeated, 'Thank you, Susan.'

The woman jumped slightly, startled. She gave a forced laugh and motioned for them to follow as she led the way towards the back. Kat tried not to let it bug her. She caught Zoe out of the corner of her eye. Her sister was smoothing out her chef uniform. 'Vincent, I want you to meet my sister, Zoe. She's a chef here and one of the most wonderful people you'll ever come across.'

'Zoe? Another sister?' he asked. 'But I thought you said your other sister was Sasha.'

'I can't believe you remembered that,' she blurted.

Vincent gave a sheepish smile. 'To tell the truth, neither can I.'

'There is Sasha and Ella, Megan, me and Zoe. My parents bred like cockroaches.'

'Well, actually, like in the case of the *gromphadorhina portentosa*, the Madagascar hissing cockroach, they can have up to forty babies after just a few months' gestation. So to breed like a cockroach would mean you have quite a lot more siblings.'

Kat stopped walking, not caring that they stood in the middle of the main aisle of a crowded restaurant. Part of her wanted the women in the place to see that he was definitely there with her. She was like a conqueror, staking her territory. Grabbing his face, she made sure he was looking at her before saying softly, 'Vincent, try to pay attention. You are not allowed to talk about bugs or work tonight. You have to relax and have fun. Got it?'

He started to nod.

'It's so great to meet you, Dr Richmond. Ella has told us all so much about you. In fact, she raves about how you're into milking spiders.'

Kat turned, surprised to see Sasha standing there.

'Am I the only person here who doesn't think bugs are cool?' Kat demanded, though it was more of a rhetorical question.

Sasha lifted a brow, even as she grinned, her dark-blue eyes shining playfully. Her chin length brown hair was all one length with the bangs pulled up at the side with barrettes. The colour matched Megan's, but her eyes were like Zoe and Kat's.

'We were discussing the Madagascar hissing cockroach,' Vincent explained.

'Fascinating,' Sasha grinned.

'You must be Zoe?'

'Sasha.' Sasha corrected. 'It's great to see Kat with a man who knows more than acting.'

Kat frowned at Sasha so Vincent couldn't see. What was with her sisters always taking pot shots at Jack?

'Acting?' he asked, starting to turn to her.

Sasha swept up his arm and began walking with him

towards the back table where Megan sat waiting. 'You were saying something about the hissing cockroach?'

Kat wanted to cringe. Trust one of her sisters to encourage Vincent's oddities. The man hardly needed encouragement to talk about bugs.

'Oh, only that they sometimes produce forty offspring at once.'

Kat wanted to moan. Sasha glanced over her shoulder with a funny look on her face and said, 'Nymphs, right?'

'Right,' he said, smiling.

'What?' Kat asked, more to herself than to them.

'Those are what the roach babies are called,' Sasha said. 'Nymphs.'

'Thanks, College Girl,' Kat drawled, wrinkling her nose. Could the conversation get any more disgusting? Sasha merely laughed.

When they reached the table, Megan stood, holding her hand out to Vincent. When Kat had talked to Megan on the phone earlier, all of her fears as to Megan's intentions with Vincent had been put to rest. The oldest Matthews sister wore her usual black slacks, only she'd opted for a white linen shirt and simple black jacket. Her long dark hair was pulled back to the nape of her neck in a simple bun. 'I hope you don't mind the extra company. When Kat called me to make the change of plans, I just assumed you wouldn't mind if I invited my other sister as well.'

'She likes to multitask us,' Sasha said, grinning.

'Not at all,' Vincent said graciously. 'Any man would find himself lucky to be surrounded by such lovely company.'

'Well, finally Kat brings around a true gentleman,' Zoe said, joining them at the table. She remained standing as the others sat down. Kat grinned. Her sister looked cute in her white chef uniform. 'Hi, I'm Zoe.'

'Vincent,' he answered. 'Will Ella be joining us as well?'

'No,' Megan said, 'she couldn't make it.'

'Vincent's telling us about hissing cockroaches,' Sasha said.

'Um, oh no, not a good subject for a restaurant.' Zoe shook her head, a small grimace on her face. 'How about we talk about the very special dinner I have planned for three out of four of my favourite sisters. It took some bribing, but the head chef has agreed to let me cook your entire meal.'

'Whoo-hoo.' Sasha clapped her hands.

'Very cool,' Kat said.

'So, what are we having?' Megan asked.

'First, I'll start you off with Baked Fleur-de-Lis En Croûte, an artichoke salad and, for the main dish, Maccheroncini del Casale with walnut sauce.'

Vincent frowned, and glanced at Megan at the mention of pasta. Kat caught the look, but none of her sisters seemed to notice. She'd asked Zoe not to make pasta when she'd called.

'Megs, you'll have an olive omelette sans pasta.' Zoe winked at Kat. Megan's wry glance wasn't as enthusiastic. Kat bit her lip. She was going to be in for it later for that one. Megan wouldn't be too happy with an omelette when the rest of them were eating gourmet pasta.

'Mmm, sounds lovely,' Sasha said. 'I love it when you cook for us.'

'You're lucky that Chef Tyrant agreed. He is being his usual despotic self tonight.' Zoe rolled her eyes.

'We'll tell him you're a better cook than he is any day,' Kat said.

'And get myself fired tomorrow?' Zoe shook her head. 'Thanks, but no thanks. I need this gig.' She glanced over her shoulder where one of the waitresses came near. Bowing slightly, Zoe winked and said, 'Enjoy your meal.'

After the waitress offered a wine list, took their drink orders and left, Kat looked at Vincent. He was seated next to her. Megan was across the table for four and

Sasha was on her left. A small vase with a single pink bud and a candle graced the centre of the otherwise unobstructed table. The flower was fake, but a good fake. The restaurant lights were low and the candlelight flickered enchantingly on Vincent's face. His eyes met hers and she trembled all the way to her toes.

'So what field of entomology do you study?' Sasha asked.

'Vincent is going to cure malaria,' Kat said before he could answer, she drew her hands onto her lap, not taking her eyes off him. He looked surprised at her response. 'He's going to develop transgenic specimens and release them into the wild so they can't infect people anymore.'

'Wow,' Sasha said, nodding. 'That's amazing.'

Vincent still looked stunned. Under her breath, Kat said, 'I looked it up online. That is what you're doing, right?'

'Close enough,' he answered. 'I'm actually just one small piece of a much larger project.'

'And it's just you and Kat at the office all day?' Sasha asked. 'You don't work with a team?'

'Internet connections have made laboratory work a lot easier,' he explained. 'We can instantly share information, ask questions, opinions. It's really been great.'

'He does have the occasional intern,' Kat said.

'Yes, I do have the occasional.' Vincent laughed and she wondered if he was thinking of the first day they met. She was.

'I had invited Vincent to dinner to go over case work –' Megan started to say.

'Oh, Megs, not tonight,' Sasha complained. 'I just had a monster of a presentation in class today and just want to unwind.'

'I was going to suggest we do that later,' Megan said.

'Good,' Sasha said, as the waitress came back with drinks. 'I don't see why you'd want to discuss what you do at mealtimes anyway.'

'And what is it you're majoring in?' Vincent asked.

'Political sociology,' Megan said.

'Fine arts,' Kat said at the exact same time. As soon as it was out, she looked at Megan in question before turning to Sasha.

'Actually, its Latin American studies now,' Sasha said.

'You changed it again?' Megan asked in a tone that showed her sisterly concern.

'NYU actually has a great Latin American programme and since I speak moderate Portuguese, they agreed to let me try it out this summer.' Sasha grabbed her glass of red wine and sipped, looking up and to the side to avoid eye contact.

'I think it's wonderful you're trying so many things,' Vincent said diplomatically. He too lifted his wine glass, swirled it, sniffed and then sipped. The gesture was so practised Kat doubted he even realised he did it. When he pulled the wine glass away, he frowned at the liquor.

'Is something wrong?' Kat asked, all three sisters looking at him expectantly.

'The waitress shouldn't have recommended this. It's clear she didn't know what she was talking about.' By the slightly disconcerted aristocratic tone in his voice, she could detect traces of his father in him. Megan gave Kat an impressed look. 'The taste will clash with the walnut of the main course.'

'You know wine,' Kat said. It was more of a question than a statement. Again, all three of them looked at him in expectation.

'I always wanted to meet someone who knew about wine,' Sasha said. 'It's one of those things everyone wishes they knew, but hardly anyone really does.'

'Zoe does,' Megan said, sipping out of her own glass before holding it up to look at it. She shrugged and took a bigger drink.

'My parents are avid collectors,' Vincent said. 'We used to travel Europe extensively when I was a child and I couldn't help but pick up a few things.'

'You drank as a child?' Megan asked, her cop persona coming through.

'Only in Europe,' Vincent assured her. 'Completely legal.'

'Doesn't make underage drinking completely right,' Megan said under her breath.

'Whoa, easy there detective,' Kat said, trying to stop Megan before she scared Vincent off. Kat reached for Vincent's leg under the table before she realised she was going to do it. He tensed as her fingers touched his leg. She started to pull away, but his lips curled up at the side, stopping her retreat. He leaned back, drawing his hands down to his lap. Warm fingers covered hers, holding her hand right where it was.

Vincent tensed as Kat's hand slid over his upper thigh, unable to believe what was happening. He was actually out on a date with Kat, his wildly erotic assistant. Since she'd kissed him in the collection room, her mouth brushing softly to his again and again, he had to keep reminding himself this was real. Even now he could feel her lush mouth against his, her tight body squeezing him as he took her from behind.

That was not how he'd wanted things to go – rough passion in the collection room at work – but it was how it had happened and he could hardly regret something that felt so incredible. He couldn't even remember how long it had been since he'd had sex. There had been occasional hook-ups during conventions and even the rarer girlfriend who ended up leaving him because of his absentminded ways. Sometimes, they'd be gone long before he noticed they'd stopped calling. It wasn't something he was proud of, but it was what it was.

Thus his need to tell Kat that he did indeed see her and he was sorry if he got distracted, as he undoubtedly would continue to do in the future. He knew himself. He would forget special days and dates and those little things important to females – like noticing when she changed hairstyles or bought a new dress.

Part of him was scared he'd mess up with Kat by being such a Neanderthal brute, throwing her sweet body down in front of him so he could fuck her from behind. Damn, but it had been erotic watching that butterfly tattoo as he took her! The point was, he wanted it to work with her. He liked her. She was completely wrong for him, and yet she was right.

Vincent knew his parents wouldn't approve of her. They had grand dreams of him marrying one of their friend's wealthy daughters, Lily La Rue. He didn't care about their wishes, never had. In fact, he'd spurned them more than once causing threats of disinheritance. He did what he wanted and they never lived up to their intimidations. They wouldn't. He was their only child and his mother had taken to hinting for grandchildren. Oddly, Mimi's only argument had something to do about matching pink suits. He really hadn't paid much attention when she called the other day about it. It's not that he hated his parents. He didn't at all. But, Vincent also knew he wasn't like his parents.

Her fingers moved on his leg and his cock twitched in response. The blood rushed from his brain to his lower region. It was all he could do to keep his eyes from closing in ecstasy as he maintained a straight face in front of her watchful sisters. Her pleasing smell drifted around him to delight his senses and tease them at the same time. It was a combination of light perfume, herbal shampoo, lotion, and it was making him crazy with lust.

Vincent tried to smile as Sasha asked him a question. Each sister had a distinct personality and style that was evident from the first moment. They were all strong, confident women who presented themselves with conviction and enthusiasm – but each in their own way. Most subtle was Detective Megan Matthews, but her passion for her job was still there in her eyes. Oddly, Sasha's passion seemed to be school, or perhaps it was learning. When Zoe talked about the meal and cooking it, her eyes had that same sparkle in them that Kat got when she merely mentioned her camera. And Ella, well, she'd been openly eager to state where her passions lie – in saving the world. Vincent had to admit he was completely enamoured with the dynamic of them, of the strong family ties they exuded with each breath. But, for all their original beauty, there was only one Matthews sister that captured his complete attention and kept it. Kat.

He chanced a look in her direction, hoping his arousal wasn't too apparent. He held her hand firm to keep her from rubbing his thigh. At the rate of his oncoming erection, he'd be moaning and begging her to get under the table if he wasn't careful. Then what kind of gentleman would she think him to be?

No, Vincent knew he needed to speak with her first. His mind had been too muddled earlier after sexual release and his thoughts had swum in a sea of mush. But, he had to make his intentions clear. He had to tell her he liked her and that he wanted something serious with her. If anything, as a scientist, he knew to go after what he wanted, to state the facts as best he could before starting something, but always be willing to change the rules as new discoveries were made.

As he thought it, a small fear crept into his brain, making him anxious. What if she didn't want anything serious? Kat was a freer spirit than he was – from the way she talked and dressed, to the way she lived. Her apartment, with its unpolished wood floors and faded paint walls decorated with haphazard canvases and photographs, was a stark contrast to what he was used to in a home.

Was this a fling to her? Would telling her his intentions were noble scare her away? Would they keep her from giving him, giving *them*, an honest chance?

Vincent took a deep breath, trying to pay attention to what Sasha was asking him about. It was impossible. The woman's lips were moving and she was looking at him, but all he heard was the sound of his heart beating in his ears. Kat was touching him and he was lost.

Nerves fluttered in Kat's stomach, but touching Vincent just seemed right. It wasn't like they were complete strangers meeting for the first time. She had been around him every day for a month and a half and knew him through his actions if not so much his words. It was as if some wall broke down between them the moment they kissed and now she was magnetically drawn to him. The pull was so strong, so natural that she couldn't fight it.

His hands stayed on hers, secretly touching her so her sisters couldn't tell. Only when the meal was served, did he pull away. The conversation flowed easily from one subject to another as they dined on Zoe's deliciously planned meal. Vincent was gracious as well as smart, and could even be charming. It was a side she'd never seen of him. The only time she got uncomfortable was when he did something too refined. It reminded her of his father, which only reminded her of why she'd met him in the first place, which only made her feel horrible and deceitful and wrong.

The baked Fleur-de-Lis En Croûte was a little pastry filled with cheese – so good, it was like having dessert served first. Kat didn't care for the artichoke salad and ended up pushing the vile vegetable around on her plate. She even cut up a few to make it look like she tried to eat it so Zoe's feelings wouldn't be hurt.

Vincent ordered the perfect wine to complement the walnut sauce in the Maccheroncini del Casale. Kat refused to tell him she couldn't really taste a difference between the reds, just like she never told Zoe when she didn't understand what food she was talking about.

The main dish was almost too much and Kat felt as if she were going to burst from overeating. It didn't help that Flora had come back with a grilled sandwich demanding she eat before her date. Kat had taken a few bites, but then hid it in her bathroom so Flora wouldn't see it. By the time the waitress offered them a choice between cranberry walnut torte and bittersweet orange chocolate mousse, she couldn't eat another bite and had to decline.

'So, how's the roommate hunt coming?' Sasha asked her, taking a bite of torte. She closed her eyes briefly, savouring the taste.

'Why? You know anyone who needs a roommate?' Kat asked, sipping her after-dinner coffee. 'If so, they can move in immediately, half bills, half rent.'

'Sorry, sis,' Sasha said. 'But I'll keep my ears open.'

'Don't you screen your applicants?' Vincent asked, appalled.

'Sure,' Kat chuckled, 'on a good day. But, I need to make rent too. If they come with cash, I'll give them a shot. Besides, my sister's a cop. Anyone messes with me, she'll make them disappear.'

'That's the mafia,' Megan corrected.

'Oh, sorry, my mistake.' Kat giggled, lifting her glass of wine to toast Megan before taking a sip.

Vincent leaned towards her. 'This isn't . . .' He hesitated and then sat back in his chair, not saying another thing about it.

The waitress brought the bill and set it next to Vincent. Without pause, he reached for his wallet to take care of it. Kat's stomach knotted and she almost offered to buy dinner for everyone. Problem was, she didn't have the money to pay for it. When she planned this outing, she didn't think about who would pick up the bill. She'd been too excited to finally get her date with Vincent.

'That's very kind of you,' Megan said and Sasha readily agreed as they both thanked him. Kat simply slipped her hand back onto Vincent's upper thigh. He glanced at her, but didn't move to take her hand in his this time. However, he did angle his leg towards her to give her better access.

As they left the restaurant, the hostess stopped Vincent to hand him a receipt. He thanked her and slipped it into his pocket. Kat glared at the woman behind his back as he opened Sedurre's front door. When they were outside, Kat stood apart from him as they said their goodbyes to her sisters. Megan offered to give Sasha a ride home. As they walked off, Vincent asked, 'Did something happen? You seem tense.'

'Do you always take other women's phone numbers when out on a date?'

'Other women's numbers?' He blinked, looking at her as if she'd suddenly sprouted two heads. 'What do you mean?'

Kat frowned, lifted his jacket and stuck her hand into his pocket to find the receipt the hostess gave him. Pulling it out, she lifted it up without even looking at it. Vincent took it and unfolded the paper. Sure enough, there was a number written on it next to a bunch of little hearts and the name Susan.

'Wh-what?' He glanced back at the glass door. 'But, I –'

Kat didn't give him a chance to finish. His innocence was adorable. Throwing her arms around his neck, she staked claim to him, hoping the hostess was peeking out on them to see the show. His body pressed tightly into her, until she felt every subtle shift of him next to hers. The mass between his thighs lifted, becoming slowly erect as she rolled her tongue into his mouth, tasting a potently erotic combination of just a hint of red wine and bittersweet orange chocolate mousse.

Sighing, she pulled back, but didn't unwind her arms from his neck.

'What was that for?' he asked, holding her about the waist.

'I don't know for sure. I just wanted to kiss you all night,' she said.

'Really?'

'Who knew you'd spruce up so nicely, or that you'd be so utterly charming out of the office?' She laughed, moving to twirl a piece of wavy hair around her finger. 'Ask me back to your place.'

'Yes,' he said without missing a beat.

'Oh, well,' Kat batted her eyelashes, playfully slipping away from him. 'That wasn't very convincing of you.'

As her arm glided down his, he grabbed her wrist and pulled her back into his chest. The gesture was surprisingly forceful for Vincent and instantly her body met with the hard outline of his arousal. 'Come back to my place, Kat.'

Kat glanced down meaningfully to where his cock strained between them. 'Well, if you put it like that, Dr Richmond.'

'Kat, I . . .' he paused, pushing back a lock of her hair. 'I've never met a woman like you. I'm sorry if I didn't . . . If I was . . .'

Kat lifted up, silencing his words with her mouth.

'Mmm.' Vincent pulled back, lifting his arm to a cab that was passing by. The car stopped and he led her by the arm to the kerb side. As he opened the door, Kat glanced down the sidewalk, seeing the receipt with the hostess' number rolling away in the breeze. Vincent helped her into the car and slid in next to her. Instantly his hands were on her waist, holding her firmly against his side. To the driver, he said, 'East Seventy-Eighth, and step on it.'

Chapter Eight

Kat stared in open-mouthed awe at Vincent's home. Located on the beautiful Seventy-Eighth Street lined with shrubs and trees, his was the top apartment in the old pre-war building. The place was clean and she knew he hardly spent anytime at home, which would account for the unlived-in look. He had said he lived on the Upper East Side and she knew he came from a rich family, but she still wasn't prepared for the sheer size of his home.

The living room was nearly thirty feet long and eighteen feet wide, with towering ceilings much taller than her apartment's. The pristine white walls and polished wood floors were tastefully accented with sweeping floor to ceiling dark curtains and minimal furniture. Large casement windows looked southward over the city. A wood-burning fireplace dominated one wall, centred between two built-in bookcases.

Walking across the large living room, Kat ran her hand over the back of his white sofa. The wooden legs were a little darker than the floor. Somehow the furniture, though elegant, reminded her of Mimi Richmond's style and made Kat not like it as much.

'Would you like a tour?' Vincent asked, coming up behind her. His hand slipped from the small of her back around her waist, resting on her stomach. Holding her, he brushed her hair aside. A little chill worked down her spine as his breath fell against her flesh.

'I'd love one.'

'This is the living room.' He kissed the nape of her neck. Fingers trailed down her shoulder, over her exposed back to dip just beneath the edge of the silk and crepe gown.

'I see that.' Kat again glanced around. There were no pictures on the walls and no television. But, there were some books on the built-in bookshelves.

'And –' Vincent leaned over, sweeping her up into his arms. Kat laughed in surprise as she held onto his shoulders. Walking quickly, he carried her to an archway that led to a long white hall. The lights from the living room shone behind him to light the way. '– here's the hallway.'

'Interesting.' Kat giggled, kicking her feet in the air as he easily carried her to the nearest door instead of down the barren hall. If it had been her home, she'd have put photographs down each side like a small gallery. The door he carried her through led into his kitchen. He manoeuvred her in his arms to flip the switch while still holding on. The kitchen too was white from the walls to the appliances, even the floor. Though she had little use for a kitchen, she could appreciate the magnificence of it. Zoe would've been in heaven.

'Kitchen.' Vincent then rushed through the kitchen leaving on the opposite side from where they entered. He didn't bother to turn off the light and used it to guide the way through the next dark room. Instead of back to the hallway, the door led into a dining room. She saw hints of a scrolled ironwork chandelier as he walked her around the long wooden table, curving around a beautifully carved armchair. As he carried her towards a door on the opposite side of the room, he said in a rush, 'dining room'.

The hallway had curved around and they again entered it from the dining room. Hitting a door open with his shoulder, he let her have the briefest look into darkness and said, 'office', before continuing down the hallway. 'And the last stop. Bedroom.'

'I think you missed a door.' Kat giggled, winding her arms tighter around his neck. The room was dark, but he moved easily through it, not running them into anything. She kissed his jaw, dragging her parted lips over his smooth, shaved flesh to nip at his earlobe.

'Bathroom,' he answered. 'Terribly dull. Not worth seeing.'

Suddenly, he stopped, letting go of her legs so she stood before him. Kat reached for his chest, unbuttoning his jacket as Vincent set to work on her gown. As he cupped her face in both palms, the gown slithered to the floor, leaving her in her underclothes.

His tongue edged her lips, parting her mouth in a delicate sweep. Vincent hummed softly, it was a faint sound but one she recognised him making earlier when they had come together. Most likely, it was an unconscious sound, but she found it incredibly endearing of him.

'I've thought about you all day,' he said, his words hushed against her moist lips. 'I wish I could take back what happened earlier between us.'

Kat blinked, tensing as the words started to sink into her brain.

'It was too fast. It was not how I imagined it should be.'

She smiled, feeling a rush of girlish pleasure. Untucking his linen dress shirt from his pants, she slowly pulled on the buttons. 'That has to be the sweetest thing I've ever been told. So, you've been imagining me, have you?'

A small gasp of air left him, as if he were struggling with his words. Was he embarrassed?

'When?' She pushed his shirt off his shoulders and pulled it off.

'Excuse me?'

'When did you start having these wicked thoughts about me?' She pulled his undershirt over his head.

'I wouldn't call them wicked,' he defended. Kat wished she could see his expression. It was hard to tell what he was thinking from just the tone of his soft voice.

'Pity.' She tossed the shirt aside. Taking a step back, her knees hit the end of a bed. There was no footboard, only soft material covering the mattress. As her eyes adjusted to the dark, she saw a thin line of light and knew from the direction of it that it had to be from a window.

Crossing over to it, she realised she still wore her heels. She felt her way to a cord along the side and pulled it just enough to cast a subtle blue light into the room. The cityscape lay beyond the window.

'Don't move,' Vincent said, his voice hoarse.

Kat looked down. The light from outside had silhouetted her against the darkness, giving off every intimate line of her body as she stood to the side of it. She'd hoped for this to happen between them again and had chosen her bra and panties carefully. Though hardly made for comfort, the black lace thong and the skimpy push up bra made her feel sexy. Catching the back of her heel on her toe, she kicked off her shoes before moving to push off her pantyhose, all the while keeping her profile to him.

Vincent's breathing was audible, almost as much as the hard beat of her heart in her ears. For some reason, she was still nervous with him. Was it guilt over why they met? Was it knowing that even though she wanted to be here with him, she was still using him for an art show? Or was it something else? Was it that, for the first time in her life, she wanted a man to be pleased with her, to like her, to want her and desire her above all others? When the hostess had given him her number, Kat had been jealous to the point she wanted to beat the woman up. If it had happened to Jack, she would've laughed it off.

Slowly, she turned to face Vincent so the light would

outline her hips and inner thighs. She felt more than saw his gaze on her, looking at her body. His shoes and pants were gone and he wore only boxer shorts. Her gaze travelled down, enjoying the look of him. If he worked out, she had no idea when he fitted it into his schedule. Not a measure of fat marred his thick frame, at least from what she saw in the dim light.

Her hands shook as she waited for him to make a move. When he didn't, she said softly, 'Come here, Vincent.'

He obeyed, closing the distance between them. His hands glided over her hips, moving around to cup the exposed cheeks of her ass. He squeezed, drawing her to his hips. Silk rubbed her stomach, heated by the unmistakable bulge of his desire for her. When he kissed her, her knees weakened and she fell back against the curtain. His body was right there with hers, pressing her into the window frame padded by dark velvet. The city light contrasted his body, making his features more pronounced and his muscles more defined.

'Kat,' he whispered.

'Vincent,' she said, just as softly.

'What is it short for? Kat?'

'Katarina.'

'I did see you, Katarina.' Vincent pressed a kiss to the tip of her nose and then each cheek. 'No matter what I did or said, I did see you. And I thought you beautiful from the first moment. That's when I had my first wicked thoughts of you.'

She smiled, touched by his words. He sounded so sincere.

'I am a man preoccupied by work. I –'

'Vincent,' she laughed softly, cupping his cheek. 'You don't have to explain. I'm obsessed with my work too. It's all right. I don't mind.'

'But, I want to explain. I don't want you to –'

Kat kissed him, turning him towards the window. She

explored his chest and sides, rubbing her hands over his nipples until they were warm, erect peaks. Vincent rocked his hips into her and the silk of his boxers seemed to melt away. Licking and biting a path from his lips to his chest, she sucked one nipple between her teeth and then the other.

Slowly, she kneeled, using her mouth and hands to tease and explore. When she bit his hip, his body jerked and he groaned. Lifting a hand above his head, he grabbed onto the curtain. Kat bit him again and his whole body strained, becoming taut. Could it be Mr Distracted Scientist liked it a little rough? After the way he took her in the collection room, she should've suspected. Though really at the time she'd thought it had been a long time since he'd had sex and he'd been over eager in his excitement.

Kat raked her nails down his chest. Vincent bucked his hips, groaning softly in approval. Alternating between licks, nibbles and bites, she covered his flat stomach while pulling the silk boxers off. She was surprised to find he was well groomed, as if he'd prepared for this by shaving earlier. Try as she might, she couldn't remember if he was shaved clean earlier in the collection room. She'd been too impatient after a month and a half of erotic dreams to notice those things at the time.

Vincent thrust towards her face, gasping for breath as she lightly blew along his shaft. His lips parted and his eyes pierced her with their intensity. It was a breathtakingly handsome look.

All the blood in her body seemed to pool between her thighs, stinging her sex with the need for direct stimulation. Kat wiggled slightly, wishing the friction of lace against her clit was stronger. She couldn't resist a little selfishness as she reached between her legs to rub against her slit. She ached for him, was wet and so very ready for him, but didn't seek to rush things. Thoughts of her deceit tried to surface in her mind, but she pushed them away, refusing to think about anything but Vincent and this enchantingly erotic moment.

His erection stood tall from his narrow hips, but she took her time, torturing him with teasing pleasures as she watched his reaction to each nip of her teeth. Kat mapped out his thighs, his hips, even going so far as to lick around his navel. In all her tormenting, she didn't touch his cock, except when she occasionally bumped it. One of his hands still gripped the curtains as the other took hold of her hair. Every nerve focused on him until she was unaware of anything but the man before her. He petted her, stroked her, gently urged her towards his ready shaft.

Kat was on fire, her entire length shivering with need and still she denied her own body, savouring the anticipation. Her bra felt tight, but she didn't mind it as she brushed her arm purposefully against her nipples to give the tiniest bit of pleasure to the aching tips. Soft noises left her throat, telling him how much she wanted to be with him and he answered in kind with primitive moaning and grunting.

The soft glow from outside caressed them, but they were high enough so that no one should be able to spy on what they were doing. She parted her lips as he again urged her to take his cock into her mouth by thrusting his hips towards her face. Her tongue darted out, lightly licking at the tip, twirling around the ridge, before she sucked him into her mouth. His groans became louder. She pulled back, teasing him as she nibbled up and down the sides before latching onto him once more. Gently, she sucked his penis deep into her mouth, puckering her lips around the smooth shaft.

There was something about the first intimate taste, an excitement and anticipation which welled inside her, making her desperate for more. With each pull of her lips, he tensed and flexed magnificently, and she knew he was under her control. His arousal was thick and long and she took it deeper into her mouth, bringing her hands to help pleasure the length she couldn't comfortably suck between her teeth. She liked the smell of him, the feel, as she took her time teasing him into complete submission. Cupping his balls, she pulled lightly, rolling them in her palm. Then, finding the tender bit of flesh buried beneath the soft globes, she rubbed him there as well. With the other hand, she grabbed the base of his shaft, working in rhythm with her mouth.

She watched his reaction, learning his body's responses. With each stroke, her grip tightened, and when she scraped her teeth lightly along his shaft, she was rewarded with hard jerks of his body.

Vincent gripped her hair, pulling her locks. Kat groaned at the idea of him coming inside her and sucked harder. She liked the primal sounds he made in the back of his throat. He pulled at the curtains, staying upright even as he swayed his hips back and forth in a building rhythm.

Suddenly, he groaned, jerking her roughly back by the hair. Just as her lips slipped off the end, he came. Hot moisture hit her shoulder seconds before a loud popping noise sounded over the room. He had pulled the curtain too hard and it fell around them, covering her head. Surprised as it encased her, she fought to be free of it.

'Oh, sorry,' she heard Vincent's muffled, out of breath words. 'Katarina, I'm sorry. Are you all right?'

He managed to help her out and she laughed, using his silk boxers to wipe off the evidence of his release from her shoulder. Vincent leaned over, pulling her up. She laughed weakly as he brushed his mouth against hers. He walked her in the direction of the bed, his steps unsure in the aftermath of his release.

He might have met his climax, but her body was still tight with arousal. Vincent urged her to lie down on her stomach. The soft mattress pressed against her breasts. His hands ran along her spine in a small massage, stopping briefly to unhook her bra. Next, he rubbed his way down, pulling off her thong panties.

Vincent touched everywhere, running his strong fingers over her feet, her calves, her hips. Soon, his mouth joined in the exploration, kissing a fiery trail over her flesh. Kat gasped, squirming as she became almost desperate for release. The tension had built to a fevered pitch and she was sure if she didn't come soon she'd die from need. She grabbed handfuls of the soft comforter as she wildly thrust her hips against the mattress.

Biting the comforter, she groaned. As she wiggled for more, her nipples rubbed against the bed. Kat spread her thighs wide in mindless invitation. 'Vincent, please, please.'

Answering her plea, he thrust a finger in her from behind. It slid within her moist sex and she rocked back against his hand. Soon more fingers joined the first and he exerted pressure against the sweet spot inside her pussy. Kat arched her head back in surprise at the expert way he fucked her with his hand, shaking and wiggling violently inside her.

'Oh, oh, oh,' she panted, shaking as a hard climax racked over her. Her fists tightened and she pulled so hard the fitted sheet snapped off the bed.

Vincent removed his fingers from within her and slowly crawled so he lay alongside her body. She was too weak to do more than moan as she turned her face towards him.

'You are so beautiful,' he whispered, brushing kisses along her cheek and shoulder. Fingers skated up and down along her spine and she shivered. Goosebumps formed on her arms as he reached the back of her neck.

'This is so embarrassing, but I have to ask,' Kat lowered her lashes so she wasn't looking at him. 'Where did you learn to do that?'

'What?'

'You know,' she giggled, 'that.'

'Oh.' he laughed, skating his fingers in a haphazard pattern down to her ass. The light caress tickled. *'That.'*

'Well?'

'In college.'

'You took a class in mutual masturbation?'

'No, I roomed with a future gynaecologist. He had books and I read.' Vincent chuckled.

'And did you practise your newfound skills a lot in college?' Kat felt the tiniest twinge of jealousy, though she knew it was completely unfounded. Everyone had a past, or at least in her opinion they should have. If you didn't have a past, how could you understand and appreciate what you have in the future?

Vincent's brow lifted slightly. 'You're asking about my past?'

'Why? Is it sordid? Dark? Very naughty?'

'I wouldn't say all that.' He cleared his throat. 'I dated a few times in college, nothing major. I was younger than a lot of the students so it was hard. Then, afterwards, there were a few scientists. Nothing really to talk about. How about you?'

'Uh.' Kat hid her face in the mattress. How in the world did she admit her experience compared to that? The man was practically a saint. Then, still feeling the after effects of his very un-saintly-like behaviour, she laughed. 'I dated, ah, men.'

He pulled his hand away. 'Men?'

'Several men.'

'Several men,' he repeated. Was there censure in his tone?

She peeked up at him. His expression wasn't judging at all. Maybe she was just being sensitive. 'Well, there were several guys in high school, but nothing lasted past a few months and nothing really happened. Then, I dated a photographer I assisted after graduation. And for the last four years, I've been kind of dating this guy, Jack. We ended it –'

'You're coming out of a four-year relationship?' he asked in surprise.

'It's not like that. We were together for lack of anything better. The break up was mutual and we parted as friends, no mess, no strings.'

'What caused the break up?'

'I saw something I wanted more.'

'Something?' He kissed her shoulder.

'Someone,' she corrected herself.

'Someone?' He nipped at the tender flesh at the curve of her neck.

'You,' she admitted, not knowing what made her say it. Being with him felt wonderful and she wanted to share everything with him. But, as any prudent woman of the world knew, sharing too much too soon was the surest way to scare a man away.

'Me,' he said. 'You broke up with him when you met me?'

'It was time to end it. The relationship hadn't been going anywhere since it started.' Kat bit her lip. That probably wasn't the best thing to say. It sounded like she was already making long-term plans, which was ridiculous considering they'd only been dating less than a day. Oh, and the little fact she was being compensated to go out with him.

Just like a prostitute.

Kat closed her eyes as she thought it. Of all she'd done in her life, this was the only thing she was ashamed of. But it wasn't too late. She could turn things around with his parents. All she would have to do is tell them the deal was off. 'I have a confession.'

And she could say goodbye to Faux Pas.

No Faux Pas?! Was she serious? Was this man really worth giving up her dreams for? Kat took a deep breath, confused. She felt guilty about what brought them to this moment, but the moment itself didn't feel wrong. Why couldn't she have both? She knew what the high road was. She knew she should tell his parents to shove it if she wanted to have a real chance at dating Vincent. But, if she did then wouldn't she just end up resenting him? Would the attraction to him disappear if the power he had over her dreams was gone? It's not like they were in love.

We're not in love, she told herself. No reason to make any rash decisions. Maybe he won't care how we got to this point.

'Confession?'

Kat took a deep breath. Crap! Had she said that out loud? 'Ah, yeah, I have a small confession and I hope you won't hate me for it.'

He pulled back.

'I lied about Megan being allergic to pasta. I was jealous and I panicked and tonight she ate that omelette because I asked Zoe to make it and her to eat it and –'

Vincent chuckled. 'Is that it? That's your big confession?'

'Well –' she shrugged, embarrassed. '– part of it.'

'What's the other part?' he asked, kissing her shoulder in such a way that made her gasp for breath. He kept the contact light, as he drew his tongue over her flesh.

His hand was restless along her body and as she heated anew to him, it became hard to concentrate. Why couldn't she just shut up and have sex with him? Soon she'd be telling him everything. She really needed to think and he was making it very difficult.

'Megan's not engaged,' she whispered, barely able to hear her own words as she said them.

'Why did you lie?' His breath whispered against her flesh and she rolled onto her back to give him better access. He took it, moving the torturous kiss down her collarbone to her breast.

'I was jealous of you going out with my sister when I wanted you to ask me out.'

Vincent opened his mouth to speak and she quietened

him by surging forwards to press her lips against his. She didn't want to talk now. Talking was dangerous. When she was with him, she was either trying to impress him or trying to confess her secrets. Her thoughts were too uncertain right now and she couldn't trust herself. Her soul told her to confess, but her mind held her quiet.

Rolling her tongue into his mouth, she moaned, letting him hear her passion for him as she drank in his sweet taste. Ravishing him with her tongue, she said into his mouth, 'Condom.'

Vincent pulled back and she saw the sexy hint of his naked body in the dim light coming from the window as he crossed the room. Disappearing out the bedroom door, he was only gone a few seconds. Kat ran her hands over her body, tweaking her nipples and massaging her clit to keep her body stimulated. Slipping a finger inside her sex, she tried to stroke herself the same way Vincent had. It wasn't the same.

'Damn,' he groaned, and she could tell by his tone he was watching her touch herself. 'That has to be the sexiest damned thing . . .'

Vincent hurried through the room and jumped on the bed. He landed next to her, automatically reaching to grab her breasts. She smiled as he sucked a taut nipple between his teeth, biting it lightly. Kat drew her leg over his and thrust her hips against him. Her pussy was wet as she sought to relieve some of the tension by rubbing against him. The thrill of Vincent was in her blood, causing her heart to race in excitement.

Vincent groaned, rolling over onto his back as he lifted her on top of him, so her legs were forced astride his. She squirmed against him in longing, liking the feel of his semi-erect cock. Desire wove its way into her, until heat seemed to radiate over her nipples and clit, racking her body in continual waves of passion. He was partially aroused and she stroked his penis to help him along the rest of the way.

Vincent pulled her face down, before trailing his lips over her neck, causing her to shiver as he nibbled on her earlobe. His hands were on her body, massaging and stroking, grabbing and squeezing. Animalistic noises escaped the back of his throat. Urgently, she tried to touch him everywhere at once. Her pussy ached to be filled, to have his stiff cock thrusting into her once more. Lifting up, she took the condom and tore the wrapper. She ran her hands down his flat stomach, pumped her fist over his penis several times only to grab the turgid shaft firmly to work the rubber on.

'Vincent,' she whispered. He shifted his hips until his cock wedged along her soaked sex, hot and so very stiff. Eagerly, she adjusted her body over his, slipping his erection along her slick folds, finding aim so she could take him deep. 'Vincent. Mmm, Vincent.'

Kat lowered herself slowly, savouring the feel of him. She scratched at his chest, raking her nails so they left little red trails. Vincent gasped, arching into her, burying himself to the hilt.

She liked watching him. His face was no longer lost in its usual sea of confusion. Now he was focused, driven by their single purpose. Vincent stared at her breasts, his eyes glinting in the soft light.

'Ah, yeah,' he said, stroking her clit in small circles as she rode him in shallow thrusts. All she could do was moan in breathy response. 'That's it, my butterfly. Just like that.'

The strange endearment made her giddy with pleasure. They said nothing about their feelings, but when he looked at her, there was something in his eyes that touched her on a deep level. He grabbed her hips, rocking into her as if savouring each movement. She wanted this, loved the feel of his body inside of hers.

'Vincent,' she whispered, over and over, unable to think beyond that one word.

Suddenly, her pussy clenched as she orgasmed. Vincent kept going, grunting softly towards the primal moment of completion. Trembling, she dug her nails into his flesh. His hips jerked and he came, gripping her waist tightly. She'd never felt anything like it. Maybe it was fanciful, metaphorical nonsense, but she felt as if she were flying.

'Vincent,' she gasped, awed by the man. He took her breath away. Shaking her head in wonder, she dropped onto his chest. A light sheen of sweat covered her flesh, but she didn't care. 'Wow.'

Her hair had come undone and strands of it stuck to her back. He pulled them aside, as he urged her next to him on the bed. Kat snuggled against the length of him. With Jack she'd always been ready for space after sex, but with Vincent, she didn't want to move.

'Don't leave, butterfly,' he said, his voice so soft she barely heard the words.

'No.' She rested her hand next to his heart. The steady thud of it was comforting. 'I won't leave.'

Chapter Nine

Kat smiled at Zoe. In fact, she smiled at everyone who passed by them, but she couldn't stop. The last few blissful days with Vincent were like the happy ending to a movie. Their lips locked, their eyes met and she heard violins playing in the background. OK, no violins, but once when he kissed her, a drunk had been screaming at the top of his lungs about aliens and that was close enough for her.

It was Sunday and the afternoon was beautifully warm. A light breeze swept over the outdoor seating area of the small coffee shop. About a block away was a major chain store, but the privately owned business had a uniqueness that kept its doors open despite the corporate competition. Bright orange and red punctuated the beatnik artwork and round metal tables. Wrought iron fencing blocked in the dining area from the rest of the sidewalk. Plants hung from the awning, bright flowers in dark-red pots, and around the side of the building was an old balcony supported by a stone base. In the spring, an acting troupe did the famous balcony scene from *Romeo and Juliet* on it to entertain those who passed by.

'What is with you?' Zoe demanded, taking a sip of cappuccino.

Instead of answering, Kat toyed with the thin overlay material on her skirt, lifting it up to examine the hem. The brick-red dress had a thick see-through strip along the waist, knitted halter-style top and a flowing print chiffon skirt. They were alone. Sasha was supposed to join them, but she had called at the last minute saying she couldn't make it.

'Kat?' Zoe asked, insistent.

'You know, sis, I could see you owning a place like this. We could call it Glowy Zoe's. Then you could cook your own menu and drink coffee all day with –'

'My famous photographer sister who comes to drink away my profits?' Zoe broke in, teasingly.

'Yeah,' Kat said under her breath, her smile faltering.

'What?' Zoe asked. Her face fell as she reached across the metal table. 'Oh, Kat, no I'm sorry. I didn't intend for it to sound mean. I really don't mind feeding you. You're my sis. I like being able to help you out. I hope you know that.'

'Oh, I know, it's just the famous part,' Kat said. 'I think it might be time to give up that dream.'

'Oh, honey, no. Don't think like that. I know you're going to make it.' Zoe patted her hand. 'I saw you with Mr Bug Man –'

'Vincent,' Kat corrected automatically.

'Yeah, I saw you with Vincent,' Zoe said, not missing a beat. 'I think it's going great. You should definitely keep up the friend date thing. The sisters don't mind him at all and I'm free from the restaurant next weekend. Chef Tyrant is doing a live cooking show and I'm not allowed to be there.'

'That's bullshit!' Kat exclaimed.

'It is what it is.' Zoe shrugged, but Kat could tell she was frustrated. 'Now, about Vincent, I was thinking we could all go out. It'd be nice to see what Ella and Sasha keep raving about.'

'Ella and Sasha rave about Vincent?'

'Uh-huh.' Zoe nodded enthusiastically, picking up her drink. 'Ella especially. In fact, I think she might have a little crush on him. Even Megan said it was too bad you weren't serious about the man. We all like him better than Jack.'

Kat looked down at her espresso. 'I don't think I can do it.'

'What do you mean?'

'It seems wrong.' Kat shrugged, taking too quick a drink. Choking on the hot liquid, she fanned her mouth as pain seared her tongue.

'Oh, Kat, oh!' Zoe fanned at her face before grabbing her ice water and handing it over. 'Drink this.'

Kat did, letting an ice cube sit in her mouth. Mumbling around it, she said, '*I muprfh mifth I camfuet.*'

'Sure you can,' Zoe assured her.

'No, *mitz no meam.*'

'It's mean?' Zoe repeated.

Kat nodded, glad Zoe could translate her.

'Using him to further your career?' Zoe asked.

Kat nodded again.

'You had sex with him, didn't you?'

Kat nodded, dropping her head on her arms. She stared at the metal table and swallowed the rest of the ice cube. Her mouth was still sore, but she ignored it. 'The same day you saw us at Sedurre and several times since then.'

'Let me guess, you think because you were hired to help him learn to date in exchange for a shot at Faux Pas, you're a bad person. And, since we both know you're not a bad person, you think your only option is to either break it off with him thus ending your chance at Faux Pas, or to tell his meddling parents to shove it where the sun doesn't shine so you can date him guilt free thus ending your chance at Faux Pas.'

Kat nodded, moaning, 'Mmm-hmm.'

'That is a tough one,' Zoe said, getting quiet for a long time.

Kat peeked up at her and saw a thoughtful look on her face. She knew Zoe would come up with a solution.

'Well,' Zoe said at last. 'You could look at it this way. Technically, you've only been dating him for a few days, and then only if one of you has verbally said this is more than just sex for fun. No one is expected to tell everything about themselves until at least three months have passed in a relationship. So, I see no reason why you have to decide anything today. If you and Vincent's relationship does go somewhere, you can tell him when the relationship is more secure and his feelings for you are cemented. If you don't work out, you have fun with him and you don't give up your dreams for no reason. It's not like you're the only one getting pleasure out of the relationship. Besides, if it goes the first way and you two do work out, then you will have given him time to discover for himself how wonderful you are and most likely he won't think it's a big deal. At that point, if he really cares for you, he'll be happy for you as your career is advanced. His parents will be happy he's dating, for they did pick you for him after all. Everyone will be happy.'

Zoe smiled. Kat was slower to follow, but soon she was beaming. Jumping out of her seat, she ran around the table and hugged Zoe. 'Thank you. Thank you. Thank you. You are the best sister ever. I love you.'

Zoe laughed, returning the hug before pushing Kat gently away. 'You're welcome. So, how did it happen? Tell me everything.'

'He's just so lost all the time. It's adorable. He calls me his butterfly,' Kat said, still smiling brightly as she became lost in thoughts of Vincent. 'And when he touches me, I feel as fluttery as one. When he doesn't touch me, I'm fluttery just thinking about him touching me.' Kat lifted her hands, letting her sister see the subtle shake in them. 'See, even now. I don't know what that means. Is it weird? Me and the bug guy? I mean I still hate bugs, but I really like him.'

'Yes, it is strange,' Zoe said, giggling as she nodded. 'But, then again, Kat, you've never done anything that could be considered completely normal.'

* * *

Kat paced outside Lab Two's door, running her fingers over the wood, tapping them as she passed. The light thumping noise she made was soft, but she knew Vincent could hear her. She refused to go inside with the live insects, so her only choice was to draw him out.

There was sound from within. The door opened and Vincent poked his head out. Very sternly, he said, 'Katarina, I told you I have to work.'

She pouted her bottom lip and answered, 'But I'm bored and you said you were caught up. Can't you take a break?'

A small smile of feigned exasperation crossed over his features and she knew he was trying really hard not to grin at her. His gaze dipped down over her light-pink tank top and casual dark-pink terry cloth skirt. It was short, falling to upper-mid-thigh.

Vincent groaned lightly. 'I have to do this.'

'OK,' Kat agreed, widening her stance.

'There's so much work that still needs to be ...' His voice tapered off into a suppressed groan as he looked at her breasts. She'd rubbed the nipples into erect peaks before he'd opened the door.

'I understand.' Kat flipped her hair over her shoulder, purposefully knocking a pen out from behind her ear. 'I don't want to be in the way.'

Impishly, she turned her back towards him. Kat didn't bend her knees as she leaned over to pick the pen up. Vincent's low growl turned into a loud moan. Coming up behind her, he grabbed her hips and pulled her into his erection.

'You did that on purpose,' he said.

Kat stood back up and laughed. 'Yes, I did. How else is a girl to get any attention around here? It's not like I can compete with your insects.'

'There is no reason to be jealous of the mosquitoes, sweet butterfly.' He chuckled, walking her along with his erection firmly against her backside. 'You're much prettier than they are.'

'Ah, but I still bite,' she said.

Vincent closed his eyes briefly at that. 'Yes, you do.'

When she hit the hallway wall, he pressed his length along her backside. Grabbing her hands, he drew them up over her head, pinning them with one of his larger hands so she was trapped. Kat's cheek pressed into the old wood. When she breathed, the tank top didn't protect her from its grainy texture and the feel of it against her nipples was highly erotic.

Vincent rocked against her before pulling away. She could feel him moving behind her, but she couldn't see what he was doing. The sound of material falling caught her attention and she imagined his pants falling to the floor.

'Should we do this here?' she asked, moving to look at the door. Her other cheek pressed into the wood as the first had. As she stared at the door, she felt a rush of excitement. The thrill of being seen pumped through her veins, arousing her as Vincent held her trapped.

'Why not?' He ran his hand boldly down her side.

'Your job,' she breathed heavily.

'What about it?' Vincent grabbed at her hip, working her skirt up. Kat purred in the back of her throat. He exposed her ass to him, barely covered by the thong she wore. His hot breath fanned over her neck, causing her to shiver. 'No one ever comes to the office.'

Reason told her to argue, but as he found the delicate lace side of her panties, all words left her. Keeping his fingers on the outside of the material, he ran his hand over the front. Then pulling the crotch aside, he exposed her sex without undressing her. Bold fingers dipped along her slit, parting her folds as he wedged his cock along the cheeks of her ass. The slick, cool feel of the condom soon heated against her flesh. An animalistic sound left him as he let go of her wrists. Her arms fell slightly, but she was still trapped.

'Do you do this to all of your assistants, Dr Richmond?' she asked playfully. A popping noise sounded and the crotch of her panties fell forward. He had torn the delicate material. The man never failed to surprise her when it came to sex.

What had become a near marathon of orgasms the night they'd gone to Sedurre had grown into a whipped cream-covered breakfast in which she was the main course. They'd had sex on his desk in the office, throwing aside the mess of papers as they lay on top. There was the blow job she'd given him in the collection room, the returned favour he did for her in the same place. The man had great hands and as he brought her release using both his fingers and his mouth, she'd been as close to heaven as any woman could get.

Dragging his cock up and down the cleft of her ass, he brought the tip to her pussy. Naturally, she parted her thighs, waiting for that first solid thrust. It didn't take much to make her wet for him and Vincent came to her as if insatiable. She guessed it was due to a combination of stress and the fact he hadn't had sex for a while before her. Whatever the reason, she was reaping the benefits.

Vincent pushed into her, groaning as he propelled his hips back and forth. The position made for a tighter fit. Usually she wasn't one for feeling helpless, but she didn't mind being trapped to his whim. Whatever book he'd borrowed from his gynaecologist friend in college, it should be mandatory for all males over eighteen.

Her nipples stung as she was pushed hard with each thrust. He placed a hand over her sex, so each plunge rocked her into his hand, stimulating the hard bud of her clit. Kat stared at the door, imagining it might open at any second.

'Come for me, butterfly,' he urged.

Kat closed her eyes, gasping for air as she did just that. She climaxed, her fingers gripping onto the wall. Vincent grunted, jerking as he too met his release.

Suddenly, she heard a noise coming from the front. What were the odds that someone was going to come inside the building at that moment?

'The door,' she gasped, pushing away from the wall as she was propelled into action. Kat brushed her skirt down around her hips. She was breathing hard. Vincent grabbed his pants around his ankles and pulled them up.

'Here,' said Vincent, starting to pull her towards Lab Two.

'No, this way,' she demanded, refusing to go in with the live specimens. She pulled in the opposite direction, leading him towards the collection room. Opening the door, she shoved him inside, just as she heard the squeaky hinges of the front door to the building.

Vincent pulled off the condom, looked around frantically and finally flung it into a trash can, before setting to work on his waistband. Kat pulled off her underwear. They were ruined, hanging about her waist, crotchless. She tossed them in the trash.

'Dr Richmond?' a male voice asked, seconds before he mumbled, 'We really need to hire that man a secretary. Maybe then his phone will get answered. None of his interns can seem to manage it.'

Kat combed her fingers through her hair, only to see Vincent was doing the same. Seeing that he looked presentable, she nodded her head. The sound of footsteps passed the collection room door.

'Wait here,' he whispered. 'Fix your, ah . . .' He circled his finger around his face before pointing at hers, signifying her make-up.

'Can't. My bag is in the office,' she whispered back.

He licked his fingers, swiping it under one of her eyes. 'There. It's still a little black, but that'll do.'

Kat giggled, brushing a lock of hair off his forehead.

'Wait here.' Vincent kissed the tip of her nose. Within seconds he was gone.

Kat watched him close the door, a smile on her face. Sighing heavily, she laughed, saying to herself. 'Damn, that was close.'

Vincent couldn't believe how close he'd been to getting caught in a very unprofessional position, and by the head of his department no less. Dr Huxley was a sober man, with little tolerance for any sort of monkey business. Getting caught screwing his very sexy assistant against the hallway wall would definitely fall into that category.

'Dr Huxley,' Vincent said as the grey-haired scientist came out of his laboratory. He was followed by two colleagues, Mr Martens from Australia and a woman he'd never met. She wore a drab brown business suit and a no-nonsense expression.

'Ah, here he is,' Huxley said, nodding. 'Dr Richmond.'

Vincent returned the greeting before turning to acknowledge Martens.

'This is Dr Sylvia Waters,' Huxley said, motioning to the woman with flawless dark skin at his side. 'She's visiting from London.'

'Dr Waters,' Vincent said.

'Doctor,' the woman returned the greeting, her tone clipped and very enunciated. 'I understand you are in the process of cataloguing the museum's extensive display of desert insects.'

'Yes, I've hired an assistant to photograph the specimens. In fact, we were just going over some of the last details. You see, the old catalogues were ruined some time ago,' Vincent said.

'Fire?' asked Dr Waters.

'A pipe burst,' Huxley said, 'at the old building.'

'It's lucky your specimens weren't lost,' said Martens.

'Was there no computer backup of the information?' Waters asked, her brow drawn in a severe frown.

'No, unfortunately not.' Vincent tried to keep his breathing level, though his body was still a little numb from release. 'They had yet to be scanned into any database.'

As Dr Waters suggested the importance of computer backups and digital filing being a priority, Vincent studied her. She was pretty, in an academically serious way, with dark-brown skin and short, tight curly hair. Her rounded brown eyes had flecks of green in them. The woman was hardly a supermodel, but then so few people were, but she was slender and refined, with an intelligence that showed in each word. Vincent said all the right things, asked all the right polite questions, as he'd been raised from birth to do. Being the son of wealthy parents had trained him early in the art of refined conversation and it was second nature.

He offered to give them a tour of his project. In truth, he hated having them in his laboratory, but what else could he do? It wasn't long before Waters launched into her own personal interest in the lifecycle of the Namib Desert beetle and its importance to its ecosystem.

Vincent listened, nodding his head, but not really hearing what she was saying. Then it hit him. He was bored out of his mind. All his life, he'd been raised to civil conversations and academic pursuits. Before he met Kat, Dr Waters was exactly the woman he would've pursued. She was serious, work oriented and she had passion. But the passion in Dr Waters was for her job. When he looked into Kat's big blue eyes, he saw a different kind of passion – a passion for life, for him, for sex. She loved her work, but perhaps it was the nature of her work that made what she felt different. He was science. She was art and everything such a pursuit would entail.

Katarina Matthews was everything he'd never looked

for in a woman. She hadn't gone to college, her hair had been pink when he met her and she dressed in trendy little outfits no woman of scientific pursuits would dare be caught in. Oh, but damn those outfits were cute – like the little pink one she wore today. Even now he could picture her pert ass as she bent over to pick up her pen. Once, he'd wanted to tell her not to be offended if he didn't notice things like her hair or her clothes, but the truth was, he did notice those things with her. How could he not? She was just such fun to look at.

He glanced at the hall floor as he led them towards the collection room. The pen was still there. His cock shifted, as if offering to rise if it should need to be called into action, and Vincent was again glad for the lab coat as it hid his lust from his visitors.

'Dr Richmond?' Huxley asked, his tone insistent.

'Yes, sorry,' Vincent said, realising they were waiting for him to lead the way. Then, raising his voice so Kat would hear him, he reached for the door. 'I believe my assistant, Ms Matthews, is just cleaning up.'

He pushed open the door. Seeing Kat was like a kick to the gut. She looked adorable. A light flush still spread over her cheeks, but he assured himself no one else would know what had happened between them – so long as he didn't stare too long and hard at her.

'Ms Matthews,' Vincent said, keeping his tone professional. She blinked in surprise, but nodded her head slowly as he introduced her to his visitors. He made a point of not looking at her for too long, so as not to arouse any suspicion as to why he had a young, pretty thing in a short skirt working alone with him in his office. To his colleagues, he said, 'Ms Matthews has just finished the photographic catalogues.'

'Ah,' Dr Waters said, eyeing first Kat then the long row of drawers. 'Then perhaps you can tell me where I might find the Namib Desert beetle.'

Kat bit her lip and stepped around the table to the

drawers. Dr Waters smiled, but it wasn't a very pleasant expression. Vincent cringed, even as he wondered if he'd have noticed the look before meeting Kat. How many times had he looked down his nose at someone, thinking them less intelligent? He'd like to think never, but somehow he wasn't so sure.

There was no way Kat would know which of the drawers held the beetle. She couldn't possibly decipher the coding system. Slowly she reached for a drawer and pulled it open. Vincent watched intently, to see what she would do. He had to admit a part of him was curious as to how she would handle this.

'That's the one with the legs, right,' Kat said softly. She shut the drawer and opened another. Repeating the process several times, she continued, 'So that its body is kept off the sand.'

'That is correct,' Dr Waters said, not looking very pleased with the oversimplified explanation Kat gave.

Vincent glanced at Mr Martens, feeling a pang of jealousy as he saw the man's eyes glancing over Kat's ass. He balled his hand into a fist.

'Ah, here, I think this is it,' Kat said, stopping him from acting impulsively. She pulled the long drawer out and set it on the counter.

Kat stood back as all of them leaned over the case. Slowly, standing back up, Dr Waters quipped, 'Very nice specimen, Dr Huxley.'

Vincent hid his smile. Kat had found it.

'I actually think this stag beetle here is cooler to look at,' Kat said.

Vincent wanted to cringe. Cooler?

'Mmm, that is a rhinoceros beetle,' Waters said, her tone dismissing.

'If you ask me, mate, I don't see what all the fuss is about these bugs,' Mr Martens said, coming to Kat's rescue.

'I hired Ms Matthews for her photography and she's

done a very good job of it. If the board is interested in publishing the collection, I'm sure she'd be willing to prepare the necessary materials. I'll need an extra couple of interns for the project and I'd sign off on the classifications . . .' He let his voice trail off as Huxley considered it.

Vincent wondered why he offered when he had so much to do already. He really didn't want more interns in his laboratories, but on the other hand he didn't want Kat to leave. It was apparent she was bored during the day and he was afraid she might quit if she no longer thought she was of use to him. Already, he'd offered her money to get her television back and she'd refused. She was a proud woman and she would hardly allow him to continue to pay her for sitting around the office just to have sex with him whenever he took a break from work. Though, he'd gladly pay to have her stay with him. The sex was actually a great stress reliever and he'd been getting so much done. What man wouldn't be energised with a willing partner in the other room, always eager to suck his cock or be fucked up against whichever wall was closest? However, it wasn't a proposal he could put forth without insulting her and implying she was a whore, even if that wasn't how he looked at it. The truth was, he enjoyed her company, enjoyed knowing she was near.

'Prepare some samples of what you had in mind and I'll present it to the board,' Huxley said at last, nodding at him then at Kat. 'Mr Martens, Dr Waters, shall we?'

'What was that all about?' Kat asked him when they were alone. She put the drawer back into its slot.

'Tour. They come through every once in a while when visiting scientists are in town.'

She turned and he automatically looked at her breasts. His cock was still partly aroused from his earlier thought in the hall and he had the strongest urge to lay her naked body down on the countertop.

'Thank you for recommending me for the project,' Kat said.

'Why wouldn't I? You did all the work to date.' Vincent forced his gaze up to hers. To his surprise, she didn't look overly excited. 'Did you not want to do it? I just assumed...'

'No, no, the job is fine. It's a great opportunity for me, really, and a wonderful credit for the resume.'

'Is this about Dr Waters? Don't pay any attention to her,' he said. 'She's just an elitist snob.'

'She's not the only one,' Kat mumbled.

'What?' Vincent asked, wondering if he'd heard her right.

'Nothing,' she said without missing a beat. Giving a nervous laugh, she said, 'So, that was close, huh?'

'Yeah, how did you figure out the answer, anyway? I mean it took a few tries at the drawers, but you got the Namib Desert beetle right.'

Kat arched a brow. 'I meant about us almost getting caught with our pants down. Well, yours down. Mine are...' She glanced at the trashcan. 'Listen, I'm going to take off early and see my sister. You don't really need me here, do you?'

Vincent wanted to say yes, but he didn't really have anything for her to do. 'Sure, fine. Which sister?'

'Um –' she paused and he wondered why she was thinking about it so hard. '– Sa-Zoe. Zoe.'

'All right.'

'See ya later, doc,' Kat said, patting his arm.

Vincent leaned down, waiting for a kiss, but instead got a forced smile as she grabbed her bags and left. Staring at the door, he frowned. What was that all about? Was she mad? Embarrassed? Using him?

To himself, he whispered his goodbye, 'I'll see you later, butterfly.'

After he knew she would be gone, he left the collection room for his lab, still confused about what was happening between them.

Chapter Ten

Kat might have smiled and said goodbye, but inside she was irritated with Vincent. First he treats her like some distant employee because he's embarrassed to be seen with her in front of his snooty friends. The man didn't even look at her in passing tenderness or friendship when they were around. And couldn't he have tried to come to her rescue when Dr Waters was being a bitch? He'd just stood there calling her Ms Matthews.

'Ms Matthews, my ass!' she grumbled.

If that wasn't insulting enough, he then acted surprised because she could pick out some stupid beetle – well one of them at least. So what if she hadn't known what it was a couple months ago, she did now. After spending so much time staring at the bugs through her lens, she had thought to impress Vincent with a basic knowledge of them. One non-fiction children's book later and she was on her way to memorising bug names. The common ones anyway, Latin names were too hard.

'Um, that is a rhinoceros beetle,' Kat sarcastically mimicked Dr Waters before ranting, 'Pretentious jerks. I have news for you idiots, no one cares about your stupid beetles! You're the freaks. Not me!'

'Kat?'

Kat blinked, seeing Jack. She'd marched in anger all the way to the front door of Sedurre without even paying attention to where she was going. All she knew was she had to get away from Vincent. The man obviously thought of her as nothing more than an office screw.

'Jack,' Kat said in surprise, seeing the man. She glanced

at the restaurant's front door in surprise. 'What are you doing here?'

'Just eating,' he said, almost nervously.

Kat studied him. Before she could stop herself, she asked, 'With someone?'

'What? Oh, no, nothing like that. I'm not with anyone, I just stopped in for a late lunch.' He looked as if he was going to lean forwards, but held back. Running his hands through his hair, he gave a small laugh. 'This is weird, huh?'

'A little.' Kat nodded. 'But it shouldn't be. Nothing has really changed. We're still friends.'

'Right,' he drawled. 'Friends.'

'Jack, are you . . . ?'

'Fine. I'm fine.'

Kat nodded and smiled, though she didn't believe him. He didn't look fine. Dark circles fanned under his blood-shot eyes. Had he been drinking? A lot? He was still as handsome as ever, but there was a pale undertone to his skin that normally wasn't there.

'And you? Seeing anyone?' he asked.

Kat thought of Vincent. Well, if he was going to be too embarrassed to introduce her as more than just Ms Matthews, she wasn't going to admit to him either. 'Nope, no one at all. I've just been concentrating on work.'

'That's right. You got a new job. What do they have you doing?' Jack stood back from her. In the past, he would've slung his arm around her shoulders and held her to his side, before making some wickedly improper remark about wanting to sleep with her.

'Yes, I do and it's a great job. Photographing and cataloguing an important collection. I might even get a book published out of the deal.' Kat swallowed. It was only a slight exaggeration, but it sounded more impressive than, 'I take pictures of bugs'.

'Wonderful. And your boss? Is he treating you nice?' Jack's head tilted to the side as he studied her. Did Jack know about Vincent? How could he? She'd only told her sisters about the deal and she highly doubted Mr and Mrs Richmond were spreading the news of what they'd hired her to do.

'Yeah, I guess so. I really don't see him too much. He's just this old man who sits in his laboratory all day as I do my work in the collection room. It gets a little boring without company, but a job's a job and I'm doing what I love.' Kat patted her camera bag.

'Good for you. Congratulations.' Jack again looked as if he would touch her, but stopped himself from the familiarity. Kat pretended not to notice. 'My play was cancelled.'

'Oh, sorry to hear that,' Kat said. She reached forwards and patted his arm. It wasn't the first time it had happened and it wouldn't be the last. 'What happened this time?'

'Artistic differences between the director and the rest of the world. He quit the show, which caused the investors to pull out.'

'That sucks.'

'Tell me about it.' Jack didn't pull away from her hand. His voice lowered, and he gave her a ghost of a smile. 'So, you want to come back to my place? Maybe watch a movie? My guess is you didn't get your TV back yet.'

Kat laughed. He was right. 'No, I haven't.'

'So, you want to come over?'

Kat knew that tone in his voice, knew what he was asking. She thought of Vincent, of how it would be the perfect slap in the face if she were to go off and screw Jack. But, she couldn't do it – not to Jack, or Vincent, or herself. 'I'm sorry, Jack.'

She wanted to explain more, but she didn't have to. Jack nodded in understanding. 'Take care of yourself, Princess Katarina.'

'Call me if you need to talk,' Kat said. 'You look like you've been doing everything but sleeping.'

'I will.' Jack patted her hand on his arm before walking down the sidewalk. Kat sighed, turning to go into Sedurre.

'That was tense,' Zoe said. Her sister was leaning against the hostess station, making no effort to hide the fact that she'd been watching Kat talk to Jack. Her sister wore her cute little chef uniform and looked as adorable as always. Too bad Zoe seemed to be picky when it came to dates, otherwise she'd have them knocking down her door.

'It's nothing,' Kat said. 'What was he doing here?'

'Had dinner with some strange man,' Zoe said. He didn't look too comfortable about it.

'What guy?' Kat asked.

'Don't know. He left about twenty minutes ago. Jack just sat there drinking wine. I didn't really talk to him much.'

'They just cancelled his show. I'm sure that was it,' Kat said. She knew her sisters didn't like Jack so much and didn't feel like talking about it. Even though she knew they weren't going anywhere, a part of her still missed him. They had been close friends for four years. She'd always told herself that when they broke it off nothing would change. What a fool's dream. Of course things had to change. They'd been sleeping together and now they weren't. All she could do was hope time would reinvent their friendship for them. She wasn't ready to give up on that.

'I thought you'd be at work,' Zoe said.

'I was. I took off early.'

'Uh-oh. What happened?'

Kat glanced around the restaurant. It was in between rushes and not too busy. 'Vincent's ashamed of me.'

'What?' Zoe said, a little too loudly. The few patrons there turned to look at her. 'Here, come with me.'

Zoe led the way towards the cook's area. The pristine kitchen looked as if it had been freshly polished. The silver countertops and appliances gleamed. They were cluttered together to make the most of the tight space. The red stone tiles on the floor had been swept, though there were places that looked as if they needed to be mopped.

'I don't know how you all do it. I can't even get my kitchen this clean and I never even use it.' Kat shook her head in amazement.

'Chef Tyrant is a stickler for details,' Zoe dismissed. 'Now spill. What's this about Vincent?'

Kat quickly told her sister what happened, skipping over the more intimate details by just saying, 'We fooled around and were almost caught by his department head.'

When she finished, Zoe bit her lip in thought. 'I don't know, Kat. It could go either way. He could be embarrassed of you like you think, or he could merely not know how to introduce you. Have you had the "you are my boyfriend, we are exclusive" talk yet?'

'That is so high school, Zoe.' Kat cringed.

'Mmm, and yet still necessary I'm afraid.' Zoe laughed. 'Actually, I'm compelled to like the man. He's polite, smart –'

'You barely talked to him the other night.'

'Well,' her sister rolled her eyes. 'OK, I'm biased. I don't know exactly what he said, but Vincent made a call to the restaurant owner, Mr Gregor. All I know is he sang my praises to the point the stingy bastard gave me a raise and a small promotion this morning before the lunch rush. Nothing huge, but it's a step up the culinary ladder. Chef Tyrant is pissed, but he can't say anything because rumour has it the owner has him by the balls.'

'Vincent did that?' Kat gasped in surprise. 'You're sure it was him? Not one of your other customers?'

Why hadn't he told her?

'Oh, yeah, I'm sure.' Zoe nodded excitedly. 'Mr Gregor mentioned potentially booking several museum functions because of me and my patron. When, in my obvious surprise, I asked if it was Dr Richmond, Mr Gregor said yes. I thought maybe you'd put him up to it.'

'No, I didn't and he didn't say a thing to me about it,' Kat said.

'Well, I don't know if he realises how much he helped my career with that one, but I'm inclined to tell you to give him the benefit of the doubt on this not introducing you to the boss thing.'

Kat smiled, really touched by what Vincent had done for her sister. Maybe Zoe was right, maybe she was overreacting about how he introduced her to his colleagues. There could be things happening she didn't know about. Or, perhaps he just didn't know how she wanted to be introduced.

'You're right, Zoe,' Kat said. 'I'm probably just overreacting. Now, what "thing" does Gregor have on Chef Tyrant? Spill all the juicy details.'

'I have no idea, but all it takes is one look of warning and the man shuts up. It sucks, because Tyrant takes it out on us later, but it's also pretty amusing.'

'What do the rumours say is going on?' Kat put her camera bag down on the floor.

Zoe laughed. 'That he was caught with one of the line cooks in a compromising position and that Mr Gregor has it on tape.'

'Chef Tyrant is banging one of the women here?' Kat giggled.

'Um, rumour has it he's banging one of the men.'

'Oh my gawd! You're kidding!' Kat threw back her head and laughed. 'I didn't take him for that type.'

'I know, he acts all prim and proper and sophisticated and a scandal like that would undoubtedly mar the "Chef Savvy" thing he has going with the older rich ladies who come by to drop presents on him like sugar mamas.'

'They should make a soap opera about what happens here behind closed kitchen doors.' Kat smiled, feeling a lot better now about Vincent. Guiltily, she thought of what she told Jack, but quickly shrugged it off. The man was obviously going through a rough time and there was no need for her to add her new sex life onto the heap of stuff he had to pine over – especially since he didn't have one of his own right now.

'OK, Miss, what will it be today?' Zoe asked, stepping towards the refrigerator. 'Chicken sandwich? Roast beef? Ham and cheese?'

'Yummy. I'll take the roast beef with some of that ranch stuff you invented.' Kat automatically felt hungry at the thought of Zoe's food.

'Then roast beef it will be. Just go find a seat and I'll bring it out in a minute.'

Kat pulled at the front of her plush robe, hiding the cropped black with pink overlaid lace camisole. The matching boy shorts were low enough on her hips to show off her stomach. Her legs were bare. She'd just finished shaving them by sitting on the side of her tub instead of taking a full shower. On her feet, two kitty slippers stared up at her, their orange furry heads almost lifelike.

Opening the door, she was surprised to see Vincent. It was still early evening and he usually worked. He'd changed out of his work slacks and lab coat into a dark coffee-coloured button-down linen shirt and a pair of khaki cotton twill pants. The shirt was untucked, which was a new fashion statement for him. She had no idea why she noticed it, but she did. Kat opened her mouth to say something, but he stopped her by holding up his hand.

'I'm sorry. I don't know why you're mad at me, but I didn't mean to do whatever it was I did or didn't do.' He held out a box. 'I got you this.'

Kat scrunched her brow in confusion, as she looked at the box of blue hair colour. 'Hair dye?'

'I thought you might like it. You know, because you

had that pink colour in it when we first met. Never mind, it's . . .' He started to reach for the box to take it back, but she pulled it away and kept it. The shade wasn't one she would've picked as it was too light a blue and the brand was one she'd never heard of, but the thought was sweet. The man was trying.

'Thank you,' she said.

He nodded and reached to the side. 'If that doesn't do it for an apology, I did get you these.' Vincent's hand came back into view holding a dozen multicoloured roses. I just thought that even though it is a more traditional choice than a woman like you might like, maybe the bright, mismatched colours would make you happy.'

'A woman like me?' she repeated, struck by the way he said it. Kat was sure he didn't realise how pompous he sounded when he made offhand comments like that.

'OK, I see you don't like them.' He started to put them back when she swiped forwards and grabbed them away from him.

'I'll take them.' Kat sniffed a purple blossom and smiled. 'I happen to love roses and, for future reference, I like the purple and white ones.'

'You do?' The expression on his face, a mix of fascination and self-pride, was too much. Kat giggled as she stepped back to motion him in.

'Oh, I'm not done yet,' he said, gesturing to the side. 'I have more.'

Kat raised a brow and leaned forwards to peek around the corner. In the hall, sitting on the floor were several unwrapped gifts. There was an orange scarf with blue stripes, a giant heart filled with chocolates, a teddy bear even bigger than the red heart, and several individually wrapped bunches of flowers from daisies to lilies.

Vincent brushed her hair back over her shoulder, prompting her to look at him as his hand settled close to her neck. The warmth of him radiated through the plush robe. His lids were lowered over his eyes as he said quietly, 'I can be a little slow to pick up on things, but you were upset with me when you left, weren't you?'

Kat gave him a small smile. He really was thoughtful.

'And, although I'm not sure why you were upset, I can guess it had to do with Dr Waters being a . . .'

He hesitated so she said, 'Bitch?'

'Yes.' he nodded.

'Chocolates,' Kat said.

'What?' he blinked, not following her.

Kat pointed down towards the gift pile. 'Bring in the chocolates.'

'Oh, all right.' He hurriedly did as she bid, looking all too excited by the request. 'So you're better now? You're not mad at me?'

'If you must know, my period started,' Kat said. Not only was it true, but it was better than having to admit that in some bizarre way she'd gotten jealous over a woman like Dr Waters.

'Oh. Ooooh.' He nodded and his expression became very male with a sort of irritating acceptance and understanding to it. What was it about referring to menstruation that made men automatically think it was the sole root of all feminine tempers? Like anything they did couldn't have contributed to the foul mood because the woman's body was obviously taken over by irrational hormones. Stepping forwards, he gingerly handed her the heart as if the chocolates inside were some medicine she desperately needed. 'Are you all right?'

Kat wanted to laugh. There were about a billion smartass comments she could answer that with, but she chose to say, 'Yes. I'm better now that you came bearing chocolates.'

OK, so maybe they were a sort of period medicine. All she knew is that she felt better when she ate them.

'You sit down. I'll get the door.' Vincent busied himself by gathering up the presents and shutting her door. Kat sat on the couch, struggling to get the box of chocolates opened. He disappeared into the kitchen, only to ask, 'Do you care which vase I use for the flowers?'

'I don't have vases, just put them in cups.' Kat bit at the plastic, mumbling, 'Damn it. Do they have to wrap these up like there are diamonds hidden inside?'

Finally, nibbling a corner to the point the plastic broke enough so she could slip her nail along the edge, she opened it. The sound of running water came from the kitchen, along with that of Vincent unwrapping the flowers. When he came out, he was carrying two cups crammed with blossoms. He set one near her drafting table and another on the windowsill.

'Mmm,' she moaned, blindly lifting the first chocolate her fingers touched. She didn't care what flavour it was as she brought it to her mouth and popped it inside. The sweet had a bit of tang to it, not unpleasant but definitely not her favourite. Still chewing as she talked, she said, 'They're beautiful, thank you.'

He nodded, his way of saying 'you're welcome'.

'Can I get you anything else?' he asked, sounding concerned.

'I'm menstruating,' Kat laughed, popping another chocolate in her mouth, 'not sick.'

His look said he didn't really get the difference. 'Sorry, my mother always shut herself up in her room during her ... Well, *that* time.'

Kat stood, giving him a bemused look. 'You're technically a doctor and I know from firsthand experience you have a pretty extensive knowledge of the female genitals but you can't say the word menstruation?'

He laughed. 'I may be a scientist, but I'm still male.'

'I noticed.' Kat winked. Then, amazed, she watched as a blush crept over his face. 'Why, Dr Richmond, are you embarrassed?'

'What? No. No.' He tried to keep a straight face, but failed.

Then, deciding she'd like to change the subject from her ovaries, she asked, 'So, what are you up to tonight?'

'Ah, I was just hoping you wouldn't kick me out before I got through the door. Beyond that, I didn't make plans.'

'Vincent...' she hesitated. They had been going at it like rabbits and the way she was fighting cramps and bloating didn't make her feel too sexy. Jack always disappeared during this time, like she was contagious. '...I'm not really feeling up to –'

'I didn't come over here just for sex,' he interrupted, as if reading her mind. She liked it when he smiled. His mouth curled in a way that was too adorable for words. His dark eyes were framed by his dark bangs, a stunningly attractive look, and they were only made darker by his brown shirt. 'I thought maybe we could spend some time together.'

'OK.' she smiled. 'I'd like that. I'll just grab some clothes.'

'You look fine.' Vincent crossed over to the couch to stand beside her. 'Beautiful.'

Kat glanced down over her attire.

'I like the slippers,' he said, reaching for the front of her robe. He ran his finger down the front, loosening the flap. Seeing her breasts beneath the camisole, he said, his voice suddenly hoarse, 'And I like your T-shirt.'

'Camisole,' she corrected.

'And I like your camisole,' he repeated, in the exact same tone as before. Kat giggled. Vincent groaned softly and pulled her robe back together to hide her sexy lingerie. 'We'll just cover that back up.' Then, suddenly, he stopped, turning serious. 'You weren't expecting someone were you?'

'Well, I was about to call the delivery boy down at Chang's Chinese Restaurant,' she teased. 'You hungry?'

He glanced over her. 'Oh, yeah, I could definitely eat.'

'I'll get the menu.'

After a brief discussion, Vincent called the restaurant

and ordered fried cheese wontons, chicken lo mein, General Tso's chicken, shrimp with lobster sauce and Chinese vegetables, Szechuan Beef, fried rice and, Kat's personal favourite, egg drop soup.

'Do you think you got enough?' Kat asked, laughing.

'Why, you want me to call them back?'

'Um, no, I think we're good. I'll be eating leftovers for a week.'

'I didn't see this last time I was here,' he said, pointing at the wall. Kat turned, looking at the collage of her and her sisters. When he had picked her up for their date, she hadn't invited him that far into her home. Besides, his eyes hadn't been looking at her walls. 'It looks like you spent a lot of time on it.'

'My whole life,' she said.

'I like it.'

It was hardly the glowing compliment an artist liked to hear in regard to their work.

'May I see your other pieces?' he asked. 'Didn't you say you had a darkroom?'

'Oh, yeah, over here.' She led the way to a small closet she'd converted into her darkroom. It was a pain because she had to haul tubs of water back and forth to make it work. Opening the door, she flipped on the light. Red shone from above from her photo bulb. Several prints hung from clothespegs attached to hangers. The hangers were on the bar intended to hang coats from. The space was small and they crowded inside.

Vincent leaned over to study a print. 'Where was this taken?'

'Colorado,' she said. Then, panicking as she realised what she had up, she glanced down the line of hanging black and white photographs. There, at the end was a picture she'd snapped of his parents getting into their limo. She unclipped a mountain scene with some flowers and thrust it at him. 'This one is my favourite.'

Vincent took it from her and moved closer to the door to use the white light from the other room. Kat reached over, grabbed the picture of Mr and Mrs Richmond and yanked it off the hanger before dropping it on the floor – all before he turned back around.

'It's nice.'

Kat frowned. Nice? That's all he had for her was 'I like it' and 'it's nice'?

'You favour black and white?'

'There's something nostalgic about it. Plus the chemicals used to process colour prints are much more toxic and require better ventilation than I have.'

'Ah, now this,' he said, pointing at a photo she'd taken of a little girl playing on a street kerb. 'This is an excellent photograph.'

'Why?' she asked automatically.

'Because of her face. She's sitting in filth on – if the guys sweating miserably in the background are any indication – an unbearably hot day, yet she's perfectly happy in her own little daydreaming world.'

'You like kids?' she asked.

Vincent shrugged. 'The last time I talked to my mother she was begging for grandkids.'

'That doesn't answer the question.'

'I guess I haven't thought about it too much. I like their innocence.'

'I haven't thought much about it either.' Kat stepped for the darkroom door, prompting him to get out of the small room. 'I think I could be happy both ways. If I met the right person and we had children, I'd be fine with it. Or, if I never met anyone and never had kids, I think I'd be fine with that as well.'

The front door opened and they both turned towards it.

'Kat,' Flora called. 'You home?'

'Here,' Kat said.

Flora smiled. Then, as her eyes found them, the look

faltered. She sized Vincent up. 'You're the man who came here the other night to take my Katarina out on a date, aren't you?'

'Yes, ma'am,' he said.

'And kept her out all night, didn't you?'

Vincent looked stunned.

'Flora,' Kat scolded.

'What?' the old woman laughed. 'I'm just bustin' his balls.' Hitting Vincent on the arm, she said, 'You should've seen the look on your face.'

'Flora, this is Vincent, my –' Kat hesitated, not knowing what to call him. His dark eyes met hers. 'My date. Vincent, this is Flora. She lives in the building and makes the best cappuccinos in all the city.'

'She only thinks that because they're free,' Flora told him.

'Come look what Vincent brought me,' Kat said, directing the woman's attention towards the flowers and chocolates.

'Now there's a good boy,' Flora said. 'Glad to see you found a man who knows how to treat a woman and buys you flowers.'

'You know, Mills would buy you flowers in a heartbeat if you'd give him just a little encouragement,' said Kat.

'You really think so?' Flora asked.

'Want me to ask him?' Kat grinned. 'Vincent wouldn't mind me inviting him up for a little double date tonight. We ordered enough food.'

'What kind of food?' Flora asked, as if that was the most important factor.

'Chinese,' said Vincent.

'I'll go get the old codger.' Flora walked out of the door, leaving it hanging open.

'You don't mind, do you?' Kat asked when they were alone.

'Not at all. I think having a chaperone here is a great idea,' he teased. 'But, you might want to put some clothes on. If this Mills character starts staring at my girl, I might get jealous.'

Kat laughed, but pleasure rippled through her at the comment. She went to her bedroom, half expecting Vincent to follow behind her to watch her change. He didn't. By the time she put on a pair of black and navy track pants and a matching T-shirt, Flora was back with Mills in tow. The delivery boy was a few seconds behind them with the food.

Mills was as wrinkled as Flora and half as lively. He wore an old sailor's cap, a navy jacket with a white shirt underneath. Kat almost felt sorry for the man. It was clear he was smitten with Flora and Flora acted as coy and as hard to get as the best of them.

Dinner was eaten in the living room with Kat and Vincent on the couch and the other couple in her two chairs. They fell into easy conversation, laughing and telling funny stories. Mills had a surprising number of misadventures from when he was young – from run-ins with the law to nearly being shanghaied into the Navy, which he'd later joined anyway.

Vincent's hands stayed possessively on her as they sat together on the couch. After dinner, Kat put on a mix CD she'd gotten from Flora. It had all the classics from the best of the Rat Pack – namely Frank Sinatra, Dean Martin and Sammy Davis Jr.

Mills asked Flora to dance as 'Ain't That A Kick In The Head' started to play. Kat smiled, watching as the man artfully led Flora about the wood floor.

'Dance with me,' Vincent said, standing.

Kat slipped her hand into his and he pulled her forwards. It felt natural being in his arms and she relaxed against him as he took the lead. The man could dance, but she really wasn't surprised. He twirled her one way and then the other, gracefully moving her about with ease. Kat never danced like this and yet, with Vincent leading the way, it was like she was born to it.

By the time 'Fly Me To The Moon' and 'I've Got You Under My Skin' played, she was completely under Vincent's spell. And that night, she did something with Vincent she'd never done with a man before. She slept next to him all night without having sex.

Chapter Eleven

Marred perfection.

That was the only way to describe how she felt when she was with Vincent. Kat wasn't stupid. She knew this was the honeymoon period – the euphoric beginning of a relationship that blinded both participants to the other's faults, the time when the sex was still explosively hot and everyone was always on their best behaviour, the part where both sides were thoughtful and yet mildly deceitful at the same time.

It was the deceitful part that spoiled the relationship's perfection. Every new couple lied, she was well aware of that. They lied by omission – by pretending to be incapable of flatulence or belching, by hiding any number of little faults from the other. But Kat felt her lie was much worse. It weighed heavily on her mind and was never far from her thoughts when she was with Vincent. Luckily, Vincent was usually preoccupied to a fault and never noticed her distraction. Or, if he did, he never let on.

For the two weeks after they danced around her apartment and slept in each other's arms, Kat had tried to pretend the Faux Pas thing didn't exist, applying the out-of-sight, out-of-mind philosophy. She told herself the possibility of meeting Howard Faustino was just a random opportunity that would show up sometime in the future, like a happy accident. When lying to herself had stopped working, she promised herself she'd wait a few months and see where this thing with Vincent was going. There was no reason to throw away opportunities if the relationship didn't work out, was there? In which case, confessing she was hired help was just stupid.

Besides, it's quite possible he won't even care, she often thought. Even so, she didn't tell him the truth.

Kat took a deep breath, glancing up from Vincent's desk to the office door. The room was clean, as was every other inch of the building. Vincent was working in the lab again. Aside from luring him out of the laboratory with a cup of coffee and a doughnut that morning, she hadn't seen him all day and it was almost quitting time.

Over the weeks, Vincent had invited her into his laboratory a few times, but she'd declined. No matter how often she looked at the little critters, she couldn't muster his level of appreciation for his creepy crawly friends. In that, her opinion hadn't changed. Girls and bugs didn't mix. Sure it was stupid to avoid a whole room just because one bug might escape, but she didn't really go into basements or the crawl space under a house for the same reason.

Turning back to stare at the desk, her eyes bore into the piles of pictures she had set around her. She was supposed to be making progress on the page layouts for the insect catalogue the museum was commissioning – a commission and opportunity only made possible because of Vincent's kindness. The task at hand was to put together a few layout proposals before they hired the writers, but she couldn't concentrate on what she was doing.

Vincent's kindness didn't stop with her. He'd given Ella the graduation gift, which ended up being a beautiful set of engraved dog tags – the perfect thing for the youngest Matthews sister. He'd helped Meg on a case, giving her his time and expertise. It was something that ultimately helped the oldest Matthews catch a killer. Megan's picture had been posted all over the papers and on national news because of it. He'd called the restaurant and got Zoe promoted at her job. Kat had once started to thank him for it, but he'd cut her off in embarrassment. So, instead of thanking him in words she'd thanked him with her body. It was a night filled with ice cubes and strawberries they would never forget. As far as she knew he hadn't done anything for Sasha, but she was sure if the opportunity ever came up he'd be most willing to help out that Matthews sister as well.

Kat sighed heavily, feeling sick to her stomach. It was time to make a decision about what to do. But, it was just so hard. She was torn, held by the fear of losing Vincent and the fear of losing the only chance she may ever get to make all her dreams come true. Those fears kept her from telling the truth.

Slowly, she reached down into her camera bag and pulled out a stiff piece of parchment. Mimi Richmond's stoic butler had delivered the note to Kat's house early that morning. Her hands shook as she held it up, to again read what the woman had sent.

Please be informed that Mr and Mrs Vincent Richmond require your attendance at dinner on Sunday with their son. Mrs Richmond will be calling at the office during your working hours. It is requisite you secure a personal invitation through their son, Dr Vincent Richmond, or the aforementioned agreement between both parties will be terminated.

Who wrote notes like that?

Please be informed? It is requisite? Aforementioned agreement?

If the feminine script was any indication, it was from Mimi Richmond. But why refer to herself in the third person?

'Rich people,' Kat said derisively under her breath. Vincent was working and she wasn't worried about him overhearing her muttering. 'Always acting like they're about to be sued.'

It was Friday, which meant she had only a couple of days. Would Vincent invite her along with him? If he didn't, she could hardly blame him. He didn't know it, but she'd met his parents and could see why they'd be an embarrassment to him.

She glanced at the phone. How in the world did Mimi expect her to 'secure a personal invitation' from Vincent? It's not like she could say, 'Hey, take me to your parents' house', could she?

'Yeah, nothing says desperation like begging an invitation to meet mom and dad.' Kat made a sour face at the note. Groaning, she stuffed the parchment back into her camera bag and stood. She frowned as she put her head down on the desk, hitting her forehead lightly against the hard, photo-covered surface as she spoke, 'What am I going to do?'

'Kat? Katarina Matthews?'

Kat whipped her head up and gasped, 'Jack?'

A photograph stuck to her forehead and she pulled it off. It was a close-up of a pinned beetle. She threw it on the table, shivering in disgust even though it was just a picture.

'Kat?' Jack called, his voice sounding closer.

'Oh, gawd!' Kat stood up too fast and hit her knee on the side of the desk. 'Ow! Shit!'

What in the world was Jack doing there? Could this day get any worse? Groaning, she remembered their last meeting – outside Sedurre. She had tried calling him one night, but he didn't answer and he never called her back.

'Is there a Kat Matthews working here?'

Hopping and rubbing her bare knee, she looked around the office in a panic. It was a useless task because there was nothing there that would help her. Glancing down, she examined her outfit. Spearmint-green pleated sheer organza was accented by rose-coloured ribbon and beadwork on the neckline. The camisole dress was cute, with a baby doll waistline, but in her panic she worried it might be a little too cute – especially for work. Jack noticed details like that.

Hurrying out the door before Jack broke Vincent's concentration and caused him to come out of his laboratory, she rushed down the hallway. Forcing a smile, she said in a hush, 'Jack, what are you doing here?'

He paused, looking confused and a little hurt. 'Am I not welcome . . .?'

Kat stayed quiet as she passed Vincent's door, only to assure him quietly, 'No, I didn't mean it like that.'

Jack's corduroy blazer was a switch from the T-shirts and sweaters she was used to seeing him in. He wore a new pair of blue jeans and brown boots. As he was an actor, she didn't give much thought to his attire. He could show up wearing a military uniform or a Roman toga and she'd not think anything about it. 'It's just Dr Richmond doesn't like to be disturbed when he's working. He likes his quiet.'

'Ah, sorry. I forgot you worked for a cranky old guy.'

'Yeah.' she laughed nervously.

Unlike the last time they met, he pulled her into a big affectionate hug and swung her lightly back and forth before letting her go. 'I missed you, Kat.'

'I missed you too, Jack,' she said. It wasn't a lie. She couldn't just turn off years of friendship because they no longer wanted to be with each other intimately. Besides, there was something familiar and warm about Jack's embrace, even if it wasn't fused with sexual desire anymore. No, that flame had died.

'I came by because I wanted to give you some tickets,' he said. 'I got your message, but I've been really busy. The show was put back on under a new director and I want you to be there for the opening. It's a week from tomorrow.'

'Oh, Jack,' Kat said, happy for him. She looked at the tickets and saw the address. 'Broadway? It was moved to Broadway? Oh, Jack, that's great!'

'I thought you could bring Zoe with you,' he said.

'Oh, um...' She thought of Vincent. Of course she couldn't bring him. 'Yeah, yeah, maybe. That would be great. She got a promotion at work and is really busy these days, but I'll definitely ask her.'

'I would've gotten tickets for all your sisters, but they only give me so many to hand out.'

'No, this is wonderful. Thank you for dropping them by.' Kat grabbed his arm and tried to urge him back down the hall. He was talking a little louder than she would have liked.

'I have a confession.' Jack was stronger than she was and stopped her insistent pull easily. 'The tickets are just an excuse, Kat. I really came because I wanted to talk to you. I need to talk to you.'

'Oh, how about we just sneak out for coffee?' she again grabbed his arm and tried to lure him out of the building.

'I'm sorry. I have to do this now, Kat. I can't wait any longer and I want you to know I'm quite serious this time,' said Jack. Kat was on the verge of forcibly hauling him towards the front door when the worst possible thing happened – she heard Vincent's door open just as Jack pulled away from her and started to bend down on one knee.

'Katarina Matthews,' Jack said, in a tone every woman instantly understood. Jack was proposing marriage to her – and in front of Vincent!

'Butterfly, who's your guest?' Vincent said behind her.

Kat was so tense she couldn't react as fast as she should have. Time stopped and each second seemed to draw out into a hellish eternity. She saw every detail of Jack's face as it turned from blinking confusion to horror when Vincent slid his arm along her waist and kissed her temple.

'Sweetheart?' Vincent asked his tone questioning. She wasn't fooled. He knew what he was doing – staking claim to her as his woman.

Kat laughed nervously. Jack slowly rose to his feet. That's when she saw the ring in his hand. The diamond glinted in the hallway light. Jack hadn't been lying – he was quite serious.

'Kat?' Jack asked, his voice unsure. The look of hurt on his face tore at her.

'Ah,' Kat tried to speak but nothing would come out. Her stomach was in knots. The awkward silence only lasted a few seconds, but to Kat it felt a lot longer. She was mortified, unsure what she should do or say, and she was embarrassed for Jack. It was hard enough for a man like him to propose, let alone to have that proposal seen by the woman's boyfriend. For Vincent made certain Jack knew where he stood in Kat's life.

'Old man, huh,' Jack said, scowling at her. She knew he was as embarrassed as she was, maybe more so as he had humiliation on top of it.

'Jack, I'm sorry. I can't do this,' she said, trying to be gentle and not sure he heard her. Jack stormed out of the building in anger. Vincent's hand on her was like a weight. She pulled away from him. 'Damn it, Vincent. Did you have to embarrass him like that?'

'Who is he, Kat?' Vincent demanded, his voice losing all the sweetness it had held moments before. 'Another boyfriend?'

Kat blinked several times, trying to make sense of what was happening. It was the first time Vincent had ever referred to himself as her boyfriend. Part of her wanted to shout for joy, the other part of her wanted to slap him for being insensitive to Jack's feelings.

'Damn it, Vincent!' Kat lifted her hands as if she could strangle him without touching him. With a growl of frustration, she ran after Jack. 'Jack, wait up.'

When Kat got outside it was to find Jack already halfway into a cab. His eyes met her briefly. He was livid. She tried calling to him, but he slammed the door and the car took off before she could reach him.

'Damn it!' she yelled, as she turned to confront Vincent. She stormed back inside, her chest heaving as she tried to catch her breath. Jack had been on bended knee. He was going to propose and Vincent saw it. She didn't want to marry Jack, would've told him no, but she would have done it gently, sweetly, and not with Vincent pawing her like a piece of property!

'Who is he?' Vincent demanded. He hadn't moved from the hall. Kat walked around the empty reception desk to face him. 'You mind telling me exactly what's going on, Katarina? How many of us are you seeing? Because I have a really hard time believing some stranger walked in off the street and decided to marry the first girl he found in this building.'

Even angry, she had to admit his jealousy was really sexy. She'd never seen him so worked up before – not even when she squished his milking spider.

'For your information, that was Jack. The friend I told you about. We broke up the day I met you.' Kat marched up to him and pushed at his chest. 'I've seen him one time since then and had no idea he was going to show up here today.'

'Ka –'

'You have no right treating me like I'm some piece of meat to be fought over by a couple of lions. And you have no right accusing me of anything.'

'Why? Because I'm not your boyfriend?'

'No, because I have too much integrity to cheat on you, you stupid ape!' There was an animal magnetism to the moment, a hot fire that crackled its way over her body. 'And for you to imply I could is deeply insulting. If you want to know anything from me, all you have to do is ask me.'

'Are you saying we're exclusive?' His words were still heated and he was breathing hard, his chest rising and falling in hard pants.

'I'm not going to answer that.'

'But, you just said –'

'I don't like your tone,' she yelled.

Unable to resist, she growled as she grabbed his face in her hands. She pulled him roughly against her, as she fought her way into his mouth with her tongue. Angrily, she ripped his lab coat open, causing the snaps to part in a series of hard pops. His teeth bit into her lips as he kissed her back just as hard. Within seconds, he had her pressed up against the wall. The wood bit into her back, but she didn't care.

'You had no reason to hurt his feelings like that,' she said, breaking away long enough to take a long gulp of air.

'Quit talking about him,' Vincent demanded. His hands flew to his waist and he unbuttoned his pants. They slithered down his legs to the floor. Kissing her neck, he scraped his teeth along her pulse, sucking and nipping her like he was a vampire about to bite. The sting of his kiss felt nice, powerful. Her nipples ached but she didn't want to waste time undressing.

'You're one to talk. You didn't tell your boss about us, or Dr Waters. You called me Ms Matthews like you were ashamed of me.' Kat lifted her skirt and pulled off her underwear, kicking them aside.

'I knew you were mad at me,' he exclaimed. 'I knew it wasn't just your period.'

'Damn right I was mad at you! You acted like you were ashamed to be with me. I bet you still haven't told them. I bet you haven't told anyone about us!'

'That's not true. I told my family last night. Oh, and what about you? If you saw that guy since we've been together, you obviously didn't tell him you were taken.' Vincent's hands gripped into her arms before he roughly caressed his way down her body. 'I bet you haven't told anyone anything, have you?'

'And what would you have me tell people? Huh?'

Vincent grabbed her by the thighs and lifted her up

against the wall, holding her body open. She grabbed his shoulders, clawing into his flesh. Her body was wet and she was highly aroused by this dominant side of him. The tip of his cock slid along her wet folds, so warm and alive.

'That you're mine,' he said passionately, right before he thrust inside her.

Kat gasped, her mouth opened wide. The stunning combination of his words combined with his body's claim was too much. There was something more intimate about this time, about the hard pumping way his hips slammed into her with an angry driving force. He'd never taken her like this, his cock hammering into her, fucking her like he was trying to stake claim to her pussy, to her soul.

'Vincent,' she gasped.

His hands dug into her ass, squeezing the cheeks hard as he supported her weight. He buried his face in her neck, breathing harshly against her. The sound of it was loud in her ear. She gripped his arms, digging her nails hard into his skin. Vincent groaned, she knew he liked a bit of pain with his sex. The slapping of their joining flesh stimulated her clit, hitting again and again in stings of intense pleasure.

'Oh, shit, I'm coming!' Kat tensed, her body tightening on his as he continued to take her hard. When he pulled away from her neck, his face was unguarded, completely thrown in passion for her. The look was raw, erotic, real. She climaxed, clawing at him as the pleasure completely overrode all thoughts in her head. Vincent grunted, slamming into her one last time. Stiffening, he came, buried inside her.

She draped weakly against him. Vincent let go of her legs and she slid back down to the floor. For a long moment, they stood together, breathing hard, unable to speak. Then, slowly, he leaned over and pulled up his pants.

'I'm sorry,' he said, his voice low.

'No condom?' She read the concern in his eyes, automatically knowing he wasn't apologising for the rough sex. They'd both gotten off.

He nodded.

'I've been tested.'

'We already discussed that,' he said. 'I believe you.'

'I'm sure we're fine,' she said, not wanting to think of the possibility of getting pregnant, as she tried to remember if she'd taken her birth control pill that morning. The thing was easy to forget but the shots made her queasy.

He nodded and said no more about it. The mistake was done, there wasn't anything to say anyway.

'Did you mean it?' In the aftermath of release, she couldn't find the anger she had before. 'When you said I'm yours, did you mean it?'

'Do you want to be mine?' He stroked her cheek.

'I...' There was tenderness in him. She couldn't answer. Not now. She couldn't have a moment as special as this rooted in deceit. To say she cared for him, that she might even love him would be wrong. No, there had to be honesty between them first – complete and unfettered honesty. She had to make things right.

'Katarina? Butterfly?'

'I want to meet your parents.' Kat knew what she had to do.

'My parents?' He laughed in surprise.

'Yes. I want to meet your family. You said you told them about me, well I'd like to meet them.'

'All right.' he nodded. 'We'll go this weekend if you like. I'll call my mother right now. She's always trying to get me over for Sunday dinner. But, I'm warning you, they're eccentric.'

Kat nodded. That was putting it mildly. She knew she should tell him the truth right now, that he'd given her the perfect opportunity to confess all, but she couldn't form the words. She was too scared of his leaving her. No, she had to tell Mr and Mrs Richmond no first and then she could confess. Until then, she wouldn't have any deeds to back her sentiments. She'd sound more sincere if she could tell him she'd already told his parents she didn't want their offer – not like this.

When he smiled at her, he seemed happy. His eyes gleamed with an inner light, so sexy and playful. 'What about your parents? Can I meet them as well?'

'Why don't we take it one set of parents at a time? Let's see how this weekend goes first. If we survive your parents, I'll introduce you to mine.'

'OK,' he agreed.

'Though, I'm warning you. They're a little eccentric as well. My father has an odd love for Walt Whitman and my mother is ... Well, she's a flake. There really is no other way of putting it.'

'My father has an odd love for Italian silk and my mother is more than an ordinary flake, she's a debutant flake.'

Kat chuckled. Vincent had described the couple perfectly. 'Besides, mine are moving to a small apartment here in Manhattan this weekend and it would work better for them if we waited a week or two. Otherwise, we'll get enlisted for moving detail.'

'I don't mind helping.'

'No, trust me. Besides, I promised I would go over there tomorrow. I'd invite you, but they want a family thing. With Ella finally out of high school and joining the Navy, they said they wanted to be closer to the rest of us.' She gave a small laugh. 'The irony is we all moved to Manhattan to get some space.'

'That's nothing. I don't know where my parents are half the time. They have three houses and an apartment here in the city. Sometimes, if I need to get a hold of them, I have to call all three houses, my father's work and a hotel in Italy.'

'Oh yeah, poor you.' Kat laughed. Then, thinking of what he did have to deal with, she instantly wished she could take the teasing back.

Leaning over he pressed a soft kiss to her mouth and moaned softly. He looked into her eyes, as if he wanted to say something more. Her breath caught and she waited, her heart pounding in excitement and nervousness. Whatever it was, he didn't say it. Finally, he pulled back. 'I'll call them right now.'

Kat managed a smile and watched him walk away. Then, leaning over, she picked up her discarded panties and pulled them back on before smoothing down her skirt. Her hand strayed on to her stomach, but she couldn't think about their small mistake in not using a condom. It was stupid of both of them, they knew better. Now she'd spend every day until her next period worried about what could be.

'Not right now, though,' she whispered, dropping her hand from her flat stomach. 'I have enough things to worry about.'

Just two more days and she'd finally have a free conscience. Now the decision to give up Faux Pas was made, she felt hope in their future together. There was a little sadness at the thought of lost chances, but she knew she was doing the right thing. She'd just have to work harder for her dream. If anything, Kat wasn't scared of hard work.

Standing in the hall, she didn't move to follow Vincent. She didn't want to hear his conversation with his parents. And, as she waited for him to come back and tell her Sunday would work, she held onto the small hope everything might still work out with Faux Pas after all.

Vincent looked at the office door, knowing Kat was just down the hall. He was sorry for losing his temper about Jack, but he couldn't help it. When he saw that man down on one knee and heard the tone in his voice, he'd just exploded. The thought of Kat being with any other man tore his insides.

But now hope replaced the anger. She wanted to meet his parents. It had to be a good sign, right? Only women who were serious with a man wanted to meet his family.

'Richmond residence,' Walter, his parents' butler, answered.

'Hi, Walt, it's the younger Vincent. Is my father available?' Vincent sat on the edge of his desk.

'I'm sorry, sir, but Mr Richmond is at the office,' Walter said, his tone flat. It reminded him of being a child, growing up around the servants.

'Of course he is,' Vincent said, knowing his father to be a workaholic. He also knew he had to have inherited the trait from someone. 'What about my mother?'

'One moment please, sir,' Walter said.

Vincent heard a clink and knew the butler had put the phone down on a pewter tray his parents kept for just such a purpose. He could envision the old butler, in his black suit, walking with slow dignity across the house to where his mother was, which was probably out having cocktails on the terrace.

'Thank you, Walter.' He heard his mother's voice before she answered, 'Hello.'

'Mother,' Vincent said.

'Vinnie, honey, I was just about to call you,' she said.

'I hate it when you call me Vinnie,' he said.

'I hate it when you call me mother,' she answered. There was a tinkling in the background mixed with the sound of wind blowing against the phone's mouthpiece. He'd guessed right. She was drinking outside. 'You know you only do it to annoy me.'

He didn't feel like discussing his childhood with her. It always ended up in irritation on both sides.

'I thought I'd stop by for Sunday dinner if you don't have any plans. There's a woman I'd like you to meet.'

He waited as silence filled the line. 'Mom? Is that all right? Or do you have plans?'

'Did you just tell me you are bringing a woman home to meet us?' Mimi exclaimed.

'Yes, Mother,' he said, only to correct himself, 'Mom. Yes, Mom.'

'Who is she? Is she special?'

'Yes, I think she's special.' He glanced at the door, remembering the feel of Kat in his arms. He never thought of himself as a wholly passionate being, but when he was with her, he felt alive and his libido kicked up several hundred notches. He felt like an eighteen year old, always thinking about sex with Kat, wanting her, masturbating to her, needing her.

'Well then, by all means, come to dinner on Sunday,' Mimi said. 'Are there any special requests, or should I just have the cook make whatever she feels like?'

'I trust your judgment,' he said diplomatically.

She snorted. 'If that were true, you'd be married to Lily La Rue and I'd have a grandchild by now. You know, she's still single. Want me to call and invite her?'

'I'm bringing a date, mom, you did get that right?'

'Fine, fine, but Lily –'

'I have to go, but I'll see you Sunday.'

'Oh, bye-bye darling,' Mimi said. 'We'll see you Sunday.'

Vincent hung up the phone with a sigh. He hoped his parents didn't put Kat off. But, she didn't seem the type to judge a man by his mother.

Chapter Twelve

'I hate photographers. Reporters are bad enough, but I really hate photographers and their stupid migraine-inducing flashes,' Megan announced, joining her sisters on the small balcony patio of their parents' new home located on Ninety-Sixth Street and Columbus. There wasn't much of a view, just some old brick buildings. They couldn't even see the street, but at least it was outside.

'Hey, now! Easy.' Kat wrinkled her nose at her older sister.

'Not you, Kat, news photographers,' Megan corrected.

Kat was glad her sisters were around. They'd always done a good job of taking her mind off things and she really needed to stop thinking of the awkward 'first meeting' with Vincent's parents. She tried to imagine what it would be like to have him with her, meeting her family. Thinking of it only made her more nervous. What if her family liked him, but then Mimi blew her cover and ruined her chances with him? Then she'd spend the rest of her life hearing about 'That nice boy, Vincent, Kat used to date'.

The location of her parents' new home was a little too close to Kat's for her comfort, but what could she do besides change the locks on her door and pretend to never be home when her mother stopped in for unannounced visits? Kat loved her mother, but she liked having distance from her as well. They were just two different kinds of people.

However, the house was pretty on the inside – much

nicer than Kat's run-down place, but not nearly as extravagant as Vincent's home on the Upper East. The classic pre-war building was of art deco influence. It had an elevator in it, which was nice since her father was 53 and had a hard time climbing too many steps. There was a sunken living room, separate dining area and a newly renovated kitchen and bathroom. The girls were sure their mother would do her best to un-renovate them into her wacky personal style. It was almost too bad to think that all the wonderful mouldings would end up covered in tacky little knick-knacks and embarrassing family photos.

'I would've been here earlier,' Megan continued, drawing Kat from her nervous thoughts, 'but they hounded me the second I walked out of the precinct.'

'At least you look cute,' Zoe said, nodding at Megan's outfit. For once their sister wasn't dressed like a detective on the case. Her low-rise blue jeans and tucked-in white T-shirt were a huge change from the drab black.

'Well, all except for that stain on your boob.' Kat laughed, her eye for detail instantly picking it up. 'I bet the tabloids blow that up really big, super cop.'

Megan frowned, brushing at a brown trail of dried liquid. 'I know, I spilled my coffee in the car – again. And don't call me super cop or I'll have you arrested. It is bad enough I have to read it in the papers. All I want to do is go to work and do my job.'

The sisters laughed, all except Megan who tried to maintain her frown of disapproval.

'You know, it's funny,' Kat said. She pointed at Megan in her blue jeans and Zoe, who wore a pair of dark pink track pants and grey T-shirt instead of her usual chef ensemble, 'Here you two are out of uniform for once and –' Kat swung her finger over to Ella in tight camouflage shorts and a grey T-shirt that read NAVY, '– she's in uniform.'

'This isn't my uniform,' Ella said.

'Close enough,' Sasha teased. Both Kat and Sasha had on dark cropped pants that reached down to the calf and tank tops. They hadn't planned to match, it just happened, though Sasha wore navy and pink and Kat had on black and light blue.

'It would be if you were an exotic dancer,' Kat said. The teasing was doing wonders to take her mind off Vincent. So long as the conversation didn't turn to her love life, she'd be fine. 'Where did you find camo hot pants anyway, sis? Are those regulation? What exactly are your plans in the military?'

'Shut up,' Ella grumbled, pouting her lower lip as she tried to hide her smile.

'Ah, look everyone,' said Sasha, 'little Ella's all grown up now. Soon she'll be drinking beer and struggling in the job market like the rest of us.'

'I already drink beer,' Ella said, making a face. 'And you're one to talk. Struggling in the job market? What major are you on now? Your fiftieth?'

'Shut up,' Sasha said, wrinkling her nose.

'Ooo, Megan, did you hear that? Your baby sister is a-breakin' the law! Drinking beer before her twenty-first birthday.' Kat ran behind Ella and put her chin on her shoulder as she peeked at Megan. 'Quick, you'd better arrest her.'

'If you're taking her, you'll have to take me too,' Zoe said, stepping between Ella and Megan like a mock sacrificial lamb. 'I jaywalked this morning.'

'I, ah, littered,' Sasha said, stepping in front of Zoe.

'And I'm an evil photographer,' Kat laughed not moving from behind Ella, 'who smokes "the pot".'

'You guys suck,' Megan said, rolling her eyes.

'Come on, Megs, time to fess up. You ever break the law?' Sasha asked.

'Nope, never,' Megan said. 'To do so would make me a hypocrite.'

'Are you kidding?' Zoe asked. 'She's never even broken

a rule. If curfew was ten o'clock she was in by nine forty-five.'

'Better than Kat,' Megan said. 'If curfew was ten o'clock, she came in at three in the morning ... a week later.'

'Yeah? Well I think you got into policing for the accessories,' Kat teased.

'Yeah, Megan, especially the handcuffs,' said Ella.

'Yeah, Megs, do a lot of cops like using unnecessary force in the bedroom?' Zoe smiled sweetly.

'I don't date cops,' Megan said.

'Too hard to decide who's in charge?' Sasha asked. The sisters laughed. 'Can't decide who should be doing the frisking?'

'I am not discussing my love life with you guys,' Megan said.

'That's because you have to experience a love life to discuss one.' Sasha stretched her arms over her head. 'If you happen to find one though, can you see if he has a brother? I need a love life, too.'

'None of us have one, well, except for Katarina.' Zoe winked. 'She and science boy like to play doctor.'

'Sleepin' with the boss.' Sasha clicked her tongue. 'Very naughty of you, Kat.'

'You slept with a professor,' Ella said. 'What grade was it he gave you, again?'

'Ah! You promised not to tell,' Sasha gasped, laughing as she hit at the youngest sister. 'And I earned that A.'

'I'm sure you did,' Ella said wryly.

'Um, you told all of us about it,' Kat said. She loved being with her sisters. There was something freeing about being around people who knew all your dirty secrets and loved you anyway. When she set things straight with Vincent and gave their relationship a clean start could he be such a person to her? The banter had taken her mind off him, but he was never too far from her thoughts. She again thought of what she had to do the next day when she met his parents. Kat forced a smile, not wanting to draw attention to herself. If her sisters even sensed she was nervous, they'd pounce until they'd pried all the details out of her. She wasn't ready for details.

'Yeah, Sash, you did.' Megan grinned. 'It was Christmas and Ella spilled mom's homemade apple juice on your white pants.'

'Oh, you had to bring up the white pants.' Ella cringed.

'Do you remember when we were kids and Megan here kept that notebook detailing all the things we did when we were little so she could submit her reports to mom and dad?' Kat asked the group at large, making a pointed effort to keep the conversation off herself. She knew they remembered it. How could they not? That damned thing had gotten them all into trouble more times than not. Sure, they deserved it, and Megan always told the truth about what happened – even if it got her into trouble as well.

'They put me in charge,' Megan defended. 'And don't think I don't know you all stole it from me.'

'What can we say? Just another notch on our crime spree belts,' Zoe said, shooting her fingers like pretend guns. 'First your tattletale notebook, next The World Bank.'

Even Megan laughed that time.

'Ah, look at this!' Beatrice Matthews stood on the other side of the opened patio door. 'All my girls at home, just like when you were little. See, Douglas! I told you moving closer to them was a good idea! Oh, now we can do this every weekend!'

Beatrice smiled brightly at her girls, her blue eyes sparkling. Their mother wore a yellow jumpsuit, the colour brilliant enough to rival the sun. Pink flowers were embroidered down one of the sides with a matching pattern along the hems. Her short blonde hair had streaks of what should've been a strawberry blonde, but instead had turned an almost coppery orange. It didn't help that the woman insisted on making her own hair products – which included her all-natural dyes. Unfortunately, the concoctions didn't really work out. Even though she was almost fifty, she looked great and none of it was unnaturally enhanced.

Kat wanted to groan and was sure her sisters were right there with her. Instead of committing to an every weekend family dinner, she lied, 'Something smells good.'

'Oh, I've started Mediterranean cooking classes,' Beatrice said. She looked at Kat and her smile began to fade.

Knowing her mother sensed something, Kat prompted, 'Really? Mediterranean?'

'Oh,' Beatrice said, her attention successfully diverted. 'I'm making Moroccan couscous. You girls just wait right here. I won't be a moment.'

When their mother was gone, they all groaned.

'I heard that.' Douglas Matthews grinned at his daughters from the opened door, appearing where Beatrice had been moments before. If their mother was a bit of a neurotic flake, their father was just the opposite. He had dark-brown hair and eyes. A retired English professor, he favoured his old tweed suits. 'And I'm warning you now. I saw about fifty peppers go into the kitchen that are unaccounted for.'

'Want me to order the pizza this time?' Megan asked, laughing.

'I'll go see if I can help her out,' Zoe said, going through the door. She kissed her father on the cheek as she passed.

'See if you can up the microwave time when she's not looking and burn it for us,' he told Zoe.

'Oh, god! She's put it in the microwave?' They could hear Zoe running towards their parents' new kitchen.

'So, how are my girls?' Douglas asked, joining them on the patio.

'Megan's famous,' Sasha offered.

Douglas nodded. 'Better than infamous.'

'Sasha's switched majors again,' Ella said.

'Glad to see she's keeping her options open,' he replied.

'Ella's going into exotic dancing to entertain the troops on those big ol' Navy ships,' Kat offered.

'Ah!' Ella gasped, smacking Kat on the arm. 'You're awful.'

'I got nothing for that one.' Douglas laughed.

'Well, Kat's got a big secret,' Megan said, giving Kat a pointed look.

'Oh?' Douglas said, looking at Kat expectantly. Kat was sure she was going to be sick. Not her father. She didn't want them to tell her father about him. Not until she set things right. Not until there was a chance he'd meet Vincent as her boyfriend.

'Oh, yeah, it's a good one,' Ella said.

'Really good one,' Sasha said.

'Do tell, Katarina,' Douglas said.

'I got a job,' Kat said weakly. It was foolish of her, and she knew it, but she really hoped her sisters would leave it at that. 'And a commission to put together a catalogue of insect specimens.'

'That's great,' her father said. 'This the same job Ella was saying something about? The one with bugs in the building?'

Kat nodded, feeling nauseous. When no one said anything, her stomach started to ease up.

'Kat has a boyfriend and it's not Jack,' Ella blurted.

Kat wanted to slug her.

'What happened to Jack?' he asked.

Kat took a deep breath. There was no way her parents knew the nature of her relationship with Jack. She closed her eyes briefly. Apparently, she didn't understand the nature of her relationship with Jack. She'd completely underestimated his feelings on the matter. 'We decided to make a clean break of it.'

'Best way,' her father said, nodding.

'Her new man's a scientist.' Ella draped an arm over Kat's shoulder.

'Oh?' His eyes lit up at that.

Kat was hard pressed not to laugh at the look, even as she wished the balcony would break away and take her with it. Trust her father to instantly like another intellectual.

'An entomologist,' Megan said. 'He's the one who helped me out on that case.'

'The insect killer thing?' he asked. Megan nodded. 'Is this serious?'

Kat bit her lip and shrugged. This was her father. She couldn't lie to him, but she didn't like herself too much or what she'd agreed to do in 'trick-dating' Vincent.

'I think Kat likes him.' Sasha teased.

'I like him.' Ella hugged Kat to her, shaking her lightly. It was all Kat could do to laugh. 'He's cool. He milks spiders.'

'Well, if Ella says she likes the guy, that must be something.' Their father nodded. 'You should bring him over for dinner.' He glanced at the patio door, in the direction of the kitchen. 'Or, better yet, we should all go out for dinner.'

'Maybe,' Kat said. 'We'll see.'

'We'll see about what?' Zoe asked at the door.

'Dad wants to meet Dr Vin,' Ella answered, 'and Kat's avoiding saying yes.'

'Oh, I like him. He's very nice.' Zoe winked at Ella. 'I think you should bring him by, Kat.'

'Zoe's biased,' Kat said.

'Is that the one you were telling us about? Kat's friend who called your boss and facilitated the promotion you would've eventually got anyway?' Douglas asked. Kat hid her smile. Their father always believed the best in them. It never occurred to him Zoe wouldn't have been promoted on her own. Zoe and Kat knew the world wasn't always fair. Whereas Zoe should've been promoted several times by now, it was Vincent's phone call that paved the way.

'Yep, that's him all right.' Zoe nodded.

'Hmm.' He nodded in approval.

'Oh! No, no, no, no, no!' came Beatrice's scream from inside, punctuated by the sudden blaring sound of the smoke alarm. Kat had never been so glad to smell burnt food in her life.

Her sisters started laughing and even Kat managed to force a small chuckle. Ella gave Zoe a high five.

The blaring stopped and Beatrice showed up at the patio door, looking very dignified. Smiling, she said, 'Take out, anyone? I decided against the couscous.'

'I'll call for pizza,' Megan said, pulling her cellular phone out of her front pocket.

'Cheese,' Ella said.

Pepperoni,' Zoe and Beatrice said in unison.

'I know, I know,' Megan said, waving for silence as she walked to the far side of the balcony. Leaning against the rail, she began ordering into the phone.

'I like anchovies,' Douglas said.

'Sorry, Daddy, they're all out,' Megan yelled, before talking into the phone once more.

'She always says that,' he grumbled good-naturedly. 'How is it I'm the only one in this family who likes anchovies?'

'So, Kat,' Beatrice said. 'Zoe tells me you have a new boyfriend.'

Kat made a face at Zoe. Ugh, not again. 'Thanks a lot, Zoe.'

'What?' Zoe laughed, not caring that her mother could hear her. 'She was getting at me for not having one, I had to throw something at her.'

'So you sacrificed me?' Kat shook her head. 'For shame.'

'Pish,' Beatrice said, though she hardly took offence to her daughters' banter. 'Let me guess. It's that Richmond boy, Mimi's son, isn't it, Kat? I knew you two would hit it off!'

'You knew?' Kat gasped.

'Well.' Beatrice waved her hand.

'You met him?' Kat asked.

'No, not directly.' Beatrice said.

'What's this? Knew what?' Douglas asked. 'Met who?'

'I told you about Mimi Richmond, dear. Kat and I met her when we were in Colorado.' Beatrice smiled at her husband, but Douglas looked to be at a complete loss. 'You know, the one who looks half her age?' Douglas shrugged. Beatrice rolled her eyes and gave him a tolerant smile. 'Anyway, I was all alone one day in the hotel's restaurant drinking some tea and in walks Mimi. She sat down and we had a nice little chat about our families. Turns out, she has a son that needs a push and I have five daughters, none of whom brings home a fiancé or even gives us hope they're going to marry anytime soon.'

'I just graduated, Mom,' Ella protested. 'You want me married already?'

'Yeah, Mom, that's not right. And I'm still in college,' Sasha said. 'You really want some guy coming along derailing all my hard work?'

'No, of course I don't mean you two.' Beatrice turned to Megan, Zoe and Kat. Sasha and Ella grinned, like two little girls who'd just gotten out of trouble. 'But you three –'

'Bea? Your story?' Douglas interrupted, saving his three oldest from the marriage lecture. Unlike his wife, he was in no hurry to see his daughters settle down.

'Oh, yes, yes. The story.' Beatrice leaned against the patio door's frame. 'Anyway, the woman was distraught, poor thing. I thought a blind date might be fun and even suggested we set up her son with Megan, but then, as I finished my tea, there in the bottom of the cup was –'

'Not the tea leaves,' Kat groaned, unable to take any more. The stress was too much. If the balcony didn't break off naturally, she just might have to start jumping up and down until it did. 'Mother! Tell me you didn't use the leaves in front of Mrs Richmond.'

'What?' Beatrice asked, as if she couldn't understand why on earth her daughter would be horrified about such a thing as divination. 'She was very curious about tasseography, even asked me to do a reading for her.'

Kat groaned again, this time louder. Her sisters snickered. Her father's face was blank, as it always was when his wife went on about such things. He never corrected her, but he never agreed with her either.

'The tea leaves have never proven wrong yet,' Beatrice said, 'even when you were young girls. How do you think I managed to keep five daughters safe? Why, Sasha, you would've been hit by several cars growing up, had I not paid attention to the signs and kept you out of harm's way. And, Megan, the leaves saved you from a pretty bad broken leg once.'

'It's a wonder any of us are sane,' Kat said to the sky, shaking her head. 'Our mother is certifiable.'

'Having gifts is not certifiable. My mother had them, as did my grandmother.' Beatrice put her hands on her hips, looking upset. 'You all inherited them, if you'd ever take the time to learn the art.'

The girls said nothing.

'Anyway,' Beatrice continued. 'They did good by you, didn't they, Miss Katarina?'

'So what did the leaves say, Mom?' Ella asked. 'Finish your story. I want to hear what happened.'

Kat glanced over her shoulder, and wrinkled her nose at Ella who just shot her an amused glance in return.

'As I was saying,' Beatrice said, continuing her story where she'd left off. 'There Mimi Richmond and I were, talking about our children, though she only has one to my five and couldn't believe I've kept my figure without plastic surgery, when I mentioned Kat being on vacation with me.' Beatrice paused, giving a self-satisfied giggle.

Their mother had a penchant for babbling, but with a lifetime of practice, Kat followed her easily. 'I took my last sip and there, right in front of me, was the unmistakable image of a cat along the side of the teacup as if walking along the bottom. By its tail was a bell for good news and a daisy, which means love. Knowing our Kat would never agree to going on a blind date with anyone I chose for her, I hinted to Mimi you were an actress once, and a very good one at that –'

'Mom, I was an old Chinese man. I was horrible,' Kat said.

'– and that perhaps she should consider hiring an actress to help bring her son out of his shell. I also mentioned you were a magnificent photographer,' her mother continued as if Kat hadn't interrupted. 'She said she had a friend at some hoity-toity art gallery to tempt Kat with. The idea took off and, somewhere between cucumber sandwiches and the bill, a plan was made.'

'Ew, cucumber sandwiches are gross,' Sasha said. They ignored her.

Kat stared at her mother. Here she thought things couldn't get worse, only to find out her mother was behind her meeting Vincent. 'You? You came up with this plan? You plotted against your own daughter?'

Beatrice grinned, clearly pleased with herself. 'It was very sneaky of me, I know.'

'But, I thought you said they wanted me to take their family portrait. You didn't let on.' Kat rubbed her temples.

'We did discuss you doing that, briefly, as a way you could meet their son,' Beatrice said. 'But I knew if I asked you to meet him and ask him out on a date you'd say no.'

'You would've said no,' Ella agreed.

'Yeah, Kat, you can be pretty stubborn.' Sasha nodded

'Of course I would've said no,' Kat exclaimed, throwing out her hands 'You divined my love life in a tea cup.'

'Would you have preferred I used a crystal ball?' Beatrice giggled.

'I would've preferred you not meddle in my love life.' Kat wasn't amused. It was weird, knowing her mother had facilitated her meeting Vincent. And, what was worse, she talked about divination to a woman like Mimi Richmond.

'Oh, Kat, you're just upset because mom had a hand in it,' Zoe whispered at her side so the others couldn't hear.

'What would you have said, if I'd asked you to take a friend's son out on a few dates?' Beatrice asked. 'Hmm?'

'No,' Kat muttered.

'But you wouldn't have said no to Faux Pas,' Zoe said thoughtfully. 'Well done, Mom.'

'Thank you, dear,' Beatrice said.

'You're not helping, Zoe,' Kat said.

'Sorry.' Zoe didn't look too apologetic though.

'Why didn't you tell me? You could've said something about this,' Kat said.

'You never asked,' Beatrice answered, smiling sweetly.

'No,' Kat whined. 'Please tell me you're making this up.'

'Wait, I'm not following,' Douglas said. 'Why's Kat upset? I thought she liked this scientist.'

'Because mom used the tea,' Sasha clarified.

'That's not it,' Kat protested, torn between screaming and running away. Like her situation with Vincent wasn't stressful enough.

'Then what is it?' Douglas asked, looking her straight in the eye.

Kat felt like a little kid, as all eyes turned to her expectantly – all but Megan, whose voice drifted over to them from the other side of the balcony, 'I've been on hold. I'd like to finish ordering.'

With a little pout on her face, Kat said, 'Because mom used the tea leaves and I really like this guy.'

Sasha, Zoe and Ella started laughing. Beatrice smiled, threading her arm through her husband's.

Megan joined them, a confused frown on her face. 'What? What did I miss?'

'Kat's in love,' Ella said.

'I didn't say that!' Kat protested.

'You didn't have to, dear,' Beatrice answered. 'Your family knows.'

'My family is crazy,' Kat said.

Megan turned to their mother expectantly. Beatrice smiled and started her story over.

Kat shook her head and walked past them to go inside. She couldn't listen to it again. Sidestepping the boxes lining the hall that still needed to be unpacked, she went into the bathroom and locked the door.

She leaned against the wall, staring at her reflection in the mirror. Groaning, she said in disbelief, 'I can't believe mom used the tea leaves.'

Chapter Thirteen

Mr and Mrs Richmond's penthouse apartment on West Eighty-Seventh Street was intimidating. The building was full service, with a 24-hour doorman, pool, laundry service and fitness centre. She'd expected the grandeur, told herself it didn't matter how much money they had, that people were people, but somehow being under the high ceilings and surrounded by the oversized gold and red lobby furniture made her feel small.

Vincent appeared completely at ease, walking confidently as if he owned the whole building. The doorman greeted him by name, 'Good evening, Dr Richmond', as did the elevator attendant. He merely nodded in return.

There was a rigid quality to Vincent's posture, regal and refined, just like some 1940s movie star. She'd seen the tendency in him before at work, but somehow observing him in his element was an eye opener – and that was only after a small limo ride and walking into the apartment building's front lobby. It was in the way he moved and spoke, a fine breeding the rest of her male acquaintances didn't seem to have. He'd slicked his hair back, and she really wished he'd leave it loose to frame his eyes. Regardless of how he wore his hair, he was still handsome. He'd come a long way from the mess of a scientist she first met.

Kat glanced down, nervously smoothing the skirt of her evening dress. She was glad Megan had said something about dinner with the Richmonds most likely being a formal affair, otherwise she would have been in slacks and a nice blouse. As it was, she had the foresight to borrow the brown satin halter gown from Zoe. Her sister kept a few formal gowns due to the sometimes elitist nature of her job. Whenever there was a dinner party with some of the more well-known chefs, Zoe needed to look her best while hobnobbing.

When Vincent showed up at her apartment in a very debonair black pinstripe three button wool suit with flat-front trousers, she had been waiting in her bathrobe. He chuckled as she hurriedly put on the dress laid out on her bed instead of the pants and blouse, all the while telling her how charming and beautiful he thought she was. She'd pulled her hair up into a simple twist, letting wisps fall around her face in a way which would match either style.

'You look sexy,' Vincent whispered, brushing a light kiss along the nape of her neck, as they rode the elevator up to the Richmonds' penthouse. Her gown dipped low in the back, exposing her skin all the way from her neck to her waist, just high enough to cover the butterfly tattoo. She couldn't wear a bra with the dress, but it came with some built-in support that kept her nipples from showing each time Vincent's hand gently touched her flesh. He ran the backs of his fingers down the length of her spine, before his hand turned and his fingers naughtily dipped below the hem, caressing in small circles along the band of her lace panties.

Kat shivered, trying to still the desire that built within her. The elevator attendant smiled at her as they stepped out into the narrow hall. Aside from a table with a vase of flowers, there was nothing extraordinary about it. Two doors, one leading to each side of the building marked the fact that there were only two homes on top of the building. Vincent walked towards the farthest door and knocked.

'Have I told you, you're beautiful?' Vincent asked. Kat gave a nervous laugh as she stared at the door, waiting.

'There is no need to be nervous about meeting my parents, butterfly. They're just ordinary people.'

Kat suppressed a snort. The Richmonds ordinary? Not very likely.

The same butler, who'd brought her the note from Mimi, answered the door to let them in. He was in uniform, wearing an identical black suit as he had on the first time she saw him. He didn't look twice in her direction, as if they'd never met. Kat breathed a small sigh of relief. The butler bid them to wait as he announced their arrival. She thought it odd the Richmonds would demand their son's arrival be announced – especially since she and her sisters just walked into their parents' house whenever they wanted.

The luxurious home was obviously acquired by wealth. It was the most incredible Kat had ever seen in real life. A chandelier graced the large entryway and living room. Deep, jewel-tone colours were everywhere. The intense sapphires, lush garnets and dazzling emeralds mixed with the dark mahogany woodwork. Where there wasn't wood flooring, there were exotic rugs with intricate patterns.

As they waited in the foyer, she felt like a princess on Vincent's arm, but deep in her heart she knew she wasn't princess material. It would be fun for one night, but she couldn't see herself living the lavish lifestyle. It just wasn't her.

'Is something wrong?' Vincent asked, whispering in her ear. His warm breath fanned over her neck, causing her to shiver.

'No, nothing,' she lied.

'You look great.'

Kat laughed. 'You mentioned that already.'

'What can I say? It's true.' He leaned over and nipped at her neck.

The butler came back only to say, 'Mrs Richmond requests you join them in the drawing room.'

As the man led the way, staying several paces ahead of them, Kat suppressed a laugh. To Vincent, she said quietly, 'Drawing room? Did we just step into the seventeenth century?'

'Walter's old-fashioned and my mother insists he calls the parlour that,' Vincent said. 'I think she believes it to sound more affluent. In the Victorian era, drawing rooms were the most prestigious in the house, basically used to entertain guests and show off wealth.'

'Thanks for the history lesson, professor,' Kat teased, smiling to lighten her comment.

'Sorry.' Vincent laughed.

Walter opened a set of double doors and stepped back. At the same moment, a grandfather clock chimed eight o'clock. It was a soft yet stately sound. Instantly, Kat recognised Mimi. She hadn't changed much since Colorado. Her short red hair was slicked into spikes. She wore a black chiffon dress with smocked sleeves. They billowed around her forearms as she lifted them to the side in greeting. Near her, seated on a leather chair smoking a pipe, was Mr Richmond. His moustache had only seemed to grow larger, like some wild animal attacking his upper lip. The Italian silk suit and slicked hair were just as tacky as before.

The parlour looked more like a gentleman's study, with a leather settee and matching chairs. Bookcases lined one of the walls, filled with books bound to look old-fashioned though they were obviously brand new. Kat wondered if they'd ever been read. Two doors leading to a balcony were open, letting in a cool breeze. They were high up and the sound of traffic was only a faint echo.

In the corner, they had an interesting, almost square-shaped piano. It was near the patio doors and surrounded by plants. The instrument wasn't shaped like a typical grand piano, at least none Kat had seen, but it wasn't an upright either. She couldn't help but wonder if anyone even played it.

'Dear, we're so glad you could join us,' Mimi said, crossing over to her son.

'Mother,' Vincent said, 'I'd like you to meet Katarina Matthews.'

'Katarina, is it?' Mimi said, looking at her.

'Kat, please.' Kat wondered at the sick feeling she got in the pit of her stomach. It wasn't as if his parents were confessing to him about her. They were pretending as if they didn't know her. Would telling Vincent the truth later cause problems between him and his parents? She wondered why the thought hadn't occurred to her before that moment. She'd been so worried about what Vincent would say to her, that she hadn't thought about the effect it would have on his relationship with his parents. How would he feel, knowing they schemed against him? Even if that scheming was well intended?

'Kat, this is my mother –'

'Mimi,' Mimi interrupted. 'And this is my husband, Vincent. But, when we get the two of them together, we usually just call the youngest Vinnie.'

'Only you do that,' Mr Richmond said to his wife. Then, to his son, he nodded once, 'Vincent.'

Mr Richmond was much more stoic than when she'd met him in Colorado. He looked down his nose at her, but didn't say anything to greet her.

'Father.' Vincent repeated the curt gesture he'd been given.

'Oh, you'll never guess who's here,' Mimi said. 'Come, dear, I believe she's out on the terrace.'

Kat stiffened at the look Mimi gave her. Mr Richmond finally nodded politely at her, but made no gesture to make her feel welcome. Unconsciously, she grabbed Vincent's arm, holding onto him as he led her outdoors.

The stone terrace wrapped around the side of the

building, surrounded by thick stone walls along the edge. Beyond the stone wall railing was a stunning view of the city, complete with the Hudson River. An elegant patio furniture set was near the door. The scrolling ironwork and thick floral pads were the most feminine looking thing she'd seen in the house so far. A discarded champagne flute with a smudge of red lipstick was on the glass top. Glancing at Mimi, Kat noticed the lipstick matched. As they'd walked out, the woman had picked up another drink and was halfway through it.

Kat frowned, wondering who Mimi was talking about when she said Vincent would never guess who was there. Just as she was about to get Vincent's attention to ask, a woman with long blonde hair walked around the corner as if she were on a runway. Her long legs crossed in front of each other with each step of her high heeled, smooth black leather boots. Decorative belt straps wrapped around them, held together by gold buckles. She was tall, lean and everything other women hated. Kat automatically straightened her shoulders and sucked in her gut. She wasn't normally weight-conscious, but who wouldn't be in front of the walking stick? The breeze blew and the woman's intentionally messy hair lifted around her face.

Ah, come on now, Kat thought. What is that all about? The woman isn't drop-dead gorgeous enough on her own, the wind has to help her out?

But it wasn't just her stunning face, or the way the lavender silk georgette of her gown clung to her slender frame, that made jealousy bubble inside Kat. It was the way her perfect blue eyes landed and stayed fixed on Vincent, the way her full lips pursed, like the beginning of a kiss. When she walked, her shoulders were thrown back, her elbows pointed behind her. The gown was a halter just like Kat's, only model girl's neckline was deeper in the front, showcasing the centre of her chest and her small, perky breasts. The skirt fell to her knees in a jagged split hem. Even her skin glowed like she'd been doused in a vat of glittery bronzer.

I hate you, Kat thought as she stared at the woman. Like she wasn't nervous enough, now she had supermodel competition eyeing up her boyfriend like he was on the menu.

'Vincent!' the woman exclaimed when she was close. 'It's been so long.'

Oh, perfect, she has a cute pouty French accent, Kat thought sarcastically. The gods are indeed cruel. Even her voice is sexy.

'Hello, Lily,' Vincent answered.

The woman placed her hands on his shoulders. She matched him in height. Leaning forwards, she brushed her full lips against one corner of his mouth and then the other. Kat stared at the touch, watching Vincent's lips to see if he returned the intimate greeting. He did. It was the tiniest of lip movements, but he returned the gesture.

Kat bit the inside of her lip and she stiffened in jealous irritation. Lily pulled away, but didn't remove her hands from Vincent's body. Instead, she trailed them down the front of his chest.

'Vincent, I almost didn't recognise you,' Lily said. She reached to stroke his cheek. 'You look so handsome.'

'Hi,' Kat said, a little too loudly. She couldn't take it anymore. If she had to watch little Miss Lily paw Vincent any longer, she'd be tempted to push the woman over the side of the building. 'I'm Kat.'

The woman was slow to acknowledge her and even slower to pull away from Vincent. She smiled, though it didn't reach her eyes.

'Lily La Rue,' she said, as if Kat should know the name.

'Kat Matthews,' Kat said, in the same tone.

'Yes, you said.' Lily nodded.

'I ran into Lily yesterday after we spoke. I just had to invite her,' Mimi said.

'How's the family?' Vincent asked, leaning his weight in Kat's direction. She wasn't the only one who noticed. Lily's eyes narrowed in on the space between Kat and Vincent's bodies. Staking her claim, Kat slid her hand onto Vincent's arm.

'They are in France,' Lily said.

'Dinner is served,' Walter announced from the patio door.

'Lovely!' Mimi exclaimed. She handed her empty flute to the butler as she walked inside.

Vincent put his hand over Kat's, holding her to his arm as he led the way inside. Lily instantly took up his other arm and began chatting in French. *'Ça va?'*

'Bien,' Vincent answered her in kind, as if it were the most natural thing in the world.

Hey! Kat thought. *Not fair.*

Lilly arched a brow and gave a pointed glance at Kat.

Vincent said something, but all she could make out was, *'coup de foudre.'*

'Quoi!' Lily threw back her head and laughed, hitting Vincent's arm. She started speaking in a rush of words, so fast that they all ran together in a train of nonsense to Kat's ears.

'Vincent, darling, you know I hate it when you two get all cosy like that,' Mimi said. 'It reminds me of when you were in college.'

Mr Richmond said nothing.

Lily laughed harder, as if at a private joke. 'My apologies, Mimi.'

Kat felt sufficiently out of place as they crossed through the home to the formal dining room. The intricately carved Chippendale mahogany chairs and pedestal dining table were polished to a high gleam and set with fine china and silver. There were even place cards. Mr and Mrs Richmond were on the ends and Lily was seated next to Vincent. Kat was by herself on the other side, left staring at her boyfriend and the French model.

As soon as they were seated, the server came in with salads and placed them on the plates. Kat put a cloth napkin across her lap and stared at her place setting. On the left side of the plate were three forks and on the right there were two knives and a spoon. Then, on top they'd set three glasses, another knife, spoon, fork and a smaller plate.

What in the world was she supposed to do with all this stuff? She looked up at Vincent. This night wasn't going anyway close to what she'd pictured in her head. Instead of a dress, she should've gotten dining lessons from Zoe. Watching Vincent, she picked up the fork he used.

'Lily,' Mr Richmond said, 'I think you will like the wine we chose for dinner. It's the Grand Cru Pinot Noir your mother sent us from France.'

'Lovely,' said Lily. Kat tried not to wrinkle her nose and mimic the woman's perfect speech.

As course after course was served, from sesame shrimp and asparagus to odd-tasting plum pudding, Mimi dominated most of the conversation. She drank too much, talked too loud and after the fifth compliment of how cute Lily looked next to her son it became obvious Mimi was again playing matchmaker for Vincent – only this time it wasn't Kat she wanted him to date.

The only thing that made the meal tolerable was that Vincent made no move to sit closer to Lily, or to touch her. In fact, he put off every one of his mother's comments with a wry one of his own. A couple of times, he even winked at Kat when no one was watching.

By the time dessert was served, Kat felt irritated, unfulfilled by the food and never so sure in her life that she wanted Vincent. Just seeing him next to Lily, imagining what it would feel like if he was dating the disgustingly perfect woman at his side, she burned with jealousy.

Taking a small bite of berries in sabayon sauce, sorbet

and fresh whipped cream, she felt movement by her foot. Glancing up, she saw Vincent's eyes on hers. He nudged her again, under the table, gently caressing his shoe along her heel. It appeared a little adolescent to be playing footsies under his parents' table, but she was thankful for the contact.

'Ah, delicious,' Mimi announced, proving to Kat that money couldn't buy good taste. She laid her napkin on the table and smiled. The rest of the dining party followed suit. Mimi led the way back towards the drawing room, before stopping. 'Vincent, be a dear and go select another bottle of wine for us. Lily, you go with him. Find that Château, ah, you know the one with the white grapes.'

'Château Margaux,' Lily said.

'Yes, that's it,' Mimi agreed. 'Go with Vincent. Help him get it.'

Lily nodded, threaded her arm through Vincent's and led him away.

'They look good together, don't you think?' Mimi asked. Before Kat could answer, she said, 'It's so good to see you again Kat. Let's go sit down, shall we?'

Kat sat on one of the leather chairs, feeling very much like the day they'd hired her to date their son. Only now, she was before them, thoroughly prepared to quit.

'Kat, I can't thank you enough for all you've done for Vincent. He's come so far in such a short time.' Mimi smiled at her husband, who nodded his head.

'Thank you,' Kat said.

'Yes, I'd say you've more than held up your end of the bargain,' Mr Richmond said.

'I almost didn't believe my eyes when I saw him last week,' Mimi continued. 'I hardly recognised him. You cleaned him up, got him out of the office and into the actual world. I even think he might be ready to rejoin fine society and take his place in this family.'

'We're prepared to let you out of our agreement early,'

Mr Richmond said. 'We'd like you to go ahead and break it off with him tonight.'

'Tell him you're seeing someone else.' Mimi drew her finger over her bottom lip thoughtfully. 'That you're getting back together with an old boyfriend.'

Jack? There was something in the way the woman said it that made Kat stiffen. No, she can't know about Jack.

'But, it's only been a few months,' Kat said in surprise.

'Yes, but who knew a little attention would draw him out so well.' Mimi tilted her head to the side. 'Again, we can't thank you enough for your fine work.'

'I...' Kat didn't know what to say. 'I work for him though. He'll know I'm lying. We have a project for the museum...'

'I think with your new art show at Faux Pas, Vincent will understand you can't work for him anymore.' Mr Richmond looked her straight in the eye.

'But...' Kat couldn't believe this. She was going to call off this nonsense and here they were doing it for her. 'I promised the museum –'

'We'll take care of the museum.' Mr Richmond reached into his pocket and pulled out a cigar. 'From what I understand, the photographs they needed you to do are done. There's no reason why you need to work with our son to finish the page layouts.'

Not see Vincent? Were they serious?

'Yes, I've already contacted the college that supplies Vincent with interns. A new male intern will be replacing you as his assistant.' Mr Richmond lit the cigar, puffing it several times as a billow of smoke rose over his head.

'But, I like the job. He doesn't need an intern. I can do both. He could lose his funding if they find out he scared the last one off.' Kat's heart raced and she felt faint. How in the world did they know so much about what had been happening? What else did they know?

'His father saw to all that, dear. It's amazing what the promise of a new business department building will do to ease the way for such things,' Mimi said. 'I don't think Dr Huxley will mind the replacement. But, they do mind a woman without a working knowledge of entomology staying on to represent the department beyond her duties as a photographer.'

This was not the same woman from Colorado. Mimi was a shrew.

'But, Vincent says I help him.' Kat started to stand, but Mimi's stern look caused her to sit back down. 'Why interfere with what is working?'

'Well, yes, dear, I'm sure you do help him.' Mimi looked down her nose at Kat, snorting slightly.

'No,' Kat said. 'No, I won't do it. No.'

'Be reasonable,' Mimi demanded, her tone hard.

'I won't break it off with him. I lo—'

'We interfere because he's getting too attached to you,' Mr Richmond said. 'Let's be frank. Women like you are good mistresses for men like my son, but Vincent is going to marry Lily La Rue. It's been the plan since he was little.'

'Does Vincent know this?' Kat asked, unable to stop herself and unsure as to why she should even try.

'How could he not?' Mimi laughed. 'It's been well understood since he was a kid. They went to the same schools, on the same vacations.'

'And he ...' Kat couldn't believe it, but they seemed so sure. Vincent had never mentioned Lily to her, and he did seem very at ease with her.

'Yes. He will marry Lily,' Mr Richmond assured her.

'You see, my dear,' Mimi said. Kat was sure if the woman called her 'dear' one more time she'd reach over and smack her. 'It's a matter of family money. Marriages are alliances and if you find love, so much the better, but more importantly, they are a merger. If Vincent was to be with someone of your economically challenged state that would be a bad business decision. The rich keep their fortunes by doing what is good for the family money. Should he decide to have an affair with you after the wedding is in place, so be it. But you can't honestly believe he'd marry the help's daughter, do you?'

'The help?' Kat asked.

'Your mother works for me now. She does my psychic readings with the tea leaves.'

Kat didn't know what was more unbelievable – that Mimi hired her mother to read her future in tea leaves, or that she was refusing her on Vincent's behalf because her mother 'worked' for her.

Mimi snorted softly. 'We only chose you because you're obviously promiscuous. Take the way you dress,' she waved at Kat's gown, 'not now obviously. That's a Nicole Miller, isn't it?'

What?! The woman was insulting her and wanted to talk about whose designer label was on her gown?

'What is wrong with the way I normally dress?' Kat demanded in anger.

'Your style does tend to scream, "I'm a cheap date ready to get laid", doesn't it?' Mimi looked at her, as if she had no reason to be embarrassed by her words. 'Don't worry, soon you'll be back to your gem-studded mini-skirts and orange hair.'

Kat couldn't speak. What did she say to such anti-quated, cruel comments? Mimi was talking social rank-ing and class order. This was the new millennium and she was defending arranged marriages.

'Break it off with him,' Mr Richmond ordered. 'There is no need for this to be a nasty ordeal.'

'What do you mean?' Kat whispered, unable to look at them. She stared at her hands, wringing them in her lap.

'Another advantage to being rich is we are in a position to offer you what you most desire,' he said.

'Faux Pas.' Kat nodded her head in understanding. He was right. They were in a position to make great things happen. But, it would seem they were also in the position to make bad things happen as well.

'Yes,' Mimi said. 'Your dream, is it not?'

Kat again nodded.

'Good girl. I knew we weren't mistaken when we hired you for our son.' Mimi smiled, looking suddenly as if all the nasty business was behind them and all was well with her deranged world.

'Then it's settled,' Mr Richmond decreed. 'When Vincent comes back out here you'll –'

'She'll what?' Vincent said from the doorway. Kat gasped, turning in her seat. His eyes burned with betrayal.

'Vincent,' she said, trying to find the right words. How much had he heard? She glanced at Mr and Mrs Richmond. They smiled widely at their son, as if they hadn't been caught doing anything wrong.

'You'll what, Kat?' he demanded, stepping into the drawing room. Lily was behind him, her head cocked to the side as she watched carefully.

'Vincent,' she said again, but nothing else would come. She looked at the beautiful Lily, the woman his parents said he was meant to marry. What else could she really say? She knew Vincent well enough to know he wouldn't marry a woman he didn't love. Where Lily fitted into the picture with him, she didn't know. Wherever it was, they were definitely friends.

Kat slowly stood.

'Please leave.' There was a finality to his angry tone and when he looked at her, he glared into her eyes before turning his back on her.

'Vincent,' Lily said.

'This doesn't concern you, Lily.' Vincent didn't move.

Kat stared at him. A tear streamed down her face. His shoulders were straight and proud, even as his head hung slightly. Closing her eyes, she took a mental picture of him. She'd spent her whole life looking for the perfect photograph, the kind that moved a person, the kind that time would stand still for. If she had her camera, this would've been it. That's when she realised something. Work wasn't everything. This was her life and she was thinking about photographs. 'Vincent, please.'

'Go!' he yelled, spinning around to face her. Pointing at his parents, he continued, 'I expected something like this from them. But you?'

She jolted in shock as he yelled. He never raised his voice, not like that.

'May I be of service,' the butler asked from the doorway.

'Walter, please see Ms Matthews out,' Mr Richmond ordered.

'Don't bother, Walter,' Kat said between clenched teeth. 'I can find my own way. It's what us poor girls are good at.' Then to Mimi, she said, 'And by the way, I've never in my life put on a gem-studded miniskirt!'

She stormed towards the door, only slowing as she glanced back to look into Vincent's hard eyes. He looked like his father in that moment, cold and heartless and arrogant. Pushing past Lily, she couldn't get out fast enough.

Chapter Fourteen

'That didn't go as well as could be hoped,' Mr Richmond said, puffing on his cigar. He hadn't moved since Vincent walked into the room.

'Ah, did you get the wine?' Mimi asked, looking them both over. In his anger, he had thrust the bottle at Lily, who now held it cradled in her arm. Crossing the room, she set it down on the table near Mimi. 'Wonderful, dear, thank you.'

Vincent glared at his parents. 'It's never going to end, is it?'

'What's that, dear?' Mimi stood, smiling at him. He saw through her smiles.

'Your meddling in my life!' Vincent yelled.

'Dear, watch your voice,' Mimi warned. 'Civilised men don't yell.'

'Don't you get it? I don't want all this, I don't want to be you and I'm never going to marry Lily.' Vincent glanced at his long-time friend. Growing up they'd known everything about each other, things they'd never told anyone else. In adulthood, they'd grown apart, but the bonds of friendship were there. Whenever they saw each other, it was as if time hadn't passed. They were both from rich families with overbearing, controlling parents. 'Never.'

'Son, don't. She's standing right here –' Mimi began, only to be interrupted by her husband.

'You won't marry her? Why ever not?' his father demanded. 'She's perfect.'

'Thank you,' Lily said, her tone light. Mr Richmond nodded in her direction.

'I can't tell you –' Vincent began.

'I don't see what you have to complain about,' his father interrupted. 'All we want is for you to have a fulfilling life.'

'Married to the person you choose,' Vincent grumbled.

'Yes, and with children to carry on your family name,' his father agreed.

'I am not some stud,' Vincent gestured towards Lily, 'and she's not a brood mare waiting to be impregnated with Richmond seed.'

'Vincent!' Mimi scolded.

'What, Mother? Not delicate enough for you? You're the ones who started this nonsense.' Vincent shook his head. 'I can't believe you hired a woman to date me.'

'Fine,' Mimi shot back. 'If you want to be common, I'll speak plainly. We sought to get you laid and she's the type of girl to do that sort of thing on a first date. We thought if some nobody lured you out of your shell, let you have her a few times, then you'd come around to understanding you don't need to play with your silly bugs all day.'

'Do you not see how sick it is for you, my parents, to be buying me prostitutes? Do you honestly not see what's wrong with that?' Vincent looked helplessly about him.

'Get over yourself, Vincent,' Mimi said. 'You're thirty-three. We're all adults here and you, my son, aren't getting any younger. I'd like to have grandchildren before I'm too old to be seen in public with them.'

'Don't worry, Mother, I'm sure your plastic surgeon will still be in business well into your nineties,' Vincent quipped. Mimi looked like he'd slapped her.

Vincent didn't care if he hurt his mother's feelings, though he doubted he could. He was so angry and wanted to strike out, but it was more than just anger. Frustration welled up inside him, pouring out of his broken heart. When he'd heard Kat's voice, talking about dating him as if it were a business transaction, he'd been crushed. The sound of his pulse had beaten loudly in his ears and he didn't hear the whole conversation, but he'd heard enough. Kat was being compensated to date him. He knew his parents well enough to guess their motive in hiring her. They wanted him dating, wanted him to stop working. And, obviously, she had her motive in agreeing – Faux Pas, a high society art gallery owned by his parents' friend, Mr Faustino. Vincent knew enough about art to know what kind of opportunity it would be for a woman like Kat.

'Vincent, when I die, you will inherit everything.' His father tapped his cigar on a nearby ashtray. 'Not only our money and our homes, but also my businesses, my social standing and position. There are many responsibilities a woman like her just won't understand. Her kind is –'

'You make her sound like an alien species,' Vincent said. He looked at the door, but fought the urge to chase after Kat. Whatever he had to say to her, it would be best if he was clearheaded first.

'Metaphorically, yes.' His father waved his cigar as he spoke, using it to punctuate his points. 'She is different to us. A woman like her will spend your money until you're broke because she's never had it before and won't know how to keep it. You need a woman like Lily.'

'For the last time, I will never marry Lily,' he said.

'Why ever not? She's –' his father began.

'Because I'm a lesbian,' Lily announced. 'Have been since, well, forever. Vincent's been kind in keeping my secret for me, but I feel you must know. There is no reason to hope I would ever marry Vincent, not even as a token husband. I just don't need him. I have my own inheritance and will be taken care of my whole life. Besides, I don't want children. Luckily, I don't have to have them. My brother Charlie is the breeder in the family, not I. Oh, and I like Kat.'

Mimi's mouth dropped open and she fell back in her chair. Vincent had never seen her at a loss of words.

'You're not a lesbian,' his father said, dumbfounded.

'You're too pretty,' Mimi insisted.

Vincent shared a look with his friend. She didn't even try to protest at that stupidity. There were times when he was thoroughly ashamed of his parents.

'Vincent, promise me you'll visit me before I leave for Hawaii,' Lily said, then to his parents, she added, 'Vincent, Mimi, thank you for a lovely dinner.'

'Wait, Lily, I'll give you a ride home.' Vincent frowned at his parents. 'As for you two, stay out of my life or I swear I'll get a vasectomy just to spite you and end this crazy family line of ours. Then, after you die, I'll leave all your money to an animal hospital. The family legacy will be our name right under a huge sign that reminds people to neuter their pets.'

Mimi paled, weakly saying, 'Oh, oh, oh . . .'

'Vincent,' his father demanded.

Vincent turned his back on them. Lily walked at his side. They were silent all the way down the elevator. The attendant didn't say a word to them. Then, as they waited for the limo to pull around, Vincent said, 'Lesbian?'

Lily laughed. 'It shut them up didn't it? No offence, but I don't want to marry you either. It would be like marrying my brother Charlie and that's just wrong.'

Vincent would've chuckled if not for the deep ache inside his chest. 'It did do that. I owe you one. You do realise my mother is calling yours right this moment.'

Lily shrugged. 'I don't care. I'll just tell them I'm bisexual. They'll think it's very Hollywood of me.'

Vincent opened the limo door and helped Lily inside. She sat across from him.

It was a small, six passenger sedan, with plush black interior and silver handles. The long seats were against the sides, set across a narrow mirrored bar with an etched crystal decanter and matching square glasses. The bar was fully stocked and he knew he'd be charged for whatever they drank.

Vincent had planned on taking a long limo ride with Kat after dinner, maybe peeling off that sexy brown satin dress of hers and making love to her on the very seat he was on now. The ache inside him only deepened, until he felt as if his heart was being ripped from his chest. Knots formed in his stomach and he had to close his eyes to keep from tearing up.

All day he'd been having fantasies about Kat in many sordid positions, about riding with the sunroof open so the breeze would keep them cool as she kneeled between his thighs sucking his cock deep into her throat. He liked the way she took him into her mouth, rolling his balls in her palm as she scratched his chest. Just thinking about it made his dick harden in arousal.

'Just drive,' Lily told the driver. Vincent opened his eyes, acutely disappointed it was Lily with him and not Kat. His desire would be going unanswered tonight. The car started and Lily rolled up the privacy window. When they could no longer be overheard, she said, 'You were pretty hard on her.'

'You heard them as well as I did. My parents hired her to date me. I should've guessed they'd eventually resort to something like that.' Vincent leaned his head back. On their trip to get the wine, he'd told Lily all about Kat – how they met and he'd mistaken her for Margaret in his exhaustion, of how she killed his spider, disorganised his notes and how he seemed to get more work done just knowing she was in the building with him. 'You know, I never did ask her what she was doing in my office that day I hired her. She was just there with her camera and I never thought to question my good fortune.'

'Why would you have?' Lily sighed. She leaned forwards and lifted a few bottles, reading the labels as she riffled through them. Finding a brandy, she opened the bottle and poured some of the dark liquor into a glass. 'There aren't any brandy snifters in here.'

Vincent didn't care if he was drinking brandy out of a square glass and not the proper glass. He wasn't like his parents. He didn't need to put on airs. 'Thanks.'

'I teased her with my affection for you and I am sorry if I hurt her feelings, but I saw what I needed to.' Lily poured herself a drink and sat back in her seat. 'She cares for you, Vincent.'

'Me or what dating me will bring her?' Vincent shook his head. That evening on his way to pick up Kat, he'd been full of hope. Now he was in a well of despair.

'Did you tell her you love her?'

'No.'

'Then I don't see what the big deal is. Faux Pas is a great chance for an artist,' Lily said. 'I admire her for going after what she wants.'

'Can we please remember I am the damaged party in this arrangement?'

'Sorry.' Lily gave him a sheepish smile before turning to glance out the window. The cityscape rolled by slowly. It was later in the evening, but the streets were still filled with people. Blue and red light caressed her pretty face. She turned back to him. 'You're staring, Vincent.'

He shook his head, coming out of his thoughts. 'Sorry. I was just thinking how you deserve happiness.'

'We're talking about you, not me.'

'She used me.'

'Why do you care so much? Didn't you use her as well? She slept with you, gave you her body.' Lily arched a brow. 'You'll give her an art show. What's the big deal?'

'It's not the same,' he protested.

'Why isn't it? Men and women use each other all the time. By her dating you, you get help with work, your catalogue done and sex. And she gets Faux Pas. It really isn't a bad trade. I'd take the sex, but then, I don't have any dreams my father's money can't buy for me.'

'I thought it was your looks that opened doors, not the money,' Vincent teased half-heartedly.

'Fine. Those too.' She shot him a sour look.

'Don't get mad at me. I don't think you're beautiful at all.'

'That's sweet of you to say,' she laughed lightly. 'So, will you go to her? Forgive her?'

'No, I can't.' Vincent took a deep breath, lifting his hand to rest over his heart.

'Why? Give her a chance to explain her side,' Lily insisted. She put up her glass and moved to sit next to him, taking his glass and putting it up as well. She draped her arm across his shoulders, before laying her head on his shoulder. 'If you are merely dating, and enjoying each other's company, why not continue to see her? She might be famous some day and you can say you dated her. Plus, think of how irritated your parents would be.'

Vincent took a deep breath and dropped his hand to his lap. 'Because, for me, it wasn't just about sex. I have no problem with her using me, so long as she would've been honest about it. I want Kat to have a chance at her dreams. But she put on a show tonight, pretending never to have met my parents. She lied to me. I don't even know if she truly likes me or if she was just with me to fulfil some bargain. How can I care for someone who lies to me? I feel like I've dated a stranger. It's quite possible she doesn't even want me.'

'You should ask her,' Lily said. 'During sex, have you looked into her eyes? Women always reveal their feeling in their eyes.'

'That's nonsense,' he dismissed.

'I'm French, what do you expect?' Lily laughed.

'You're only half French,' he corrected.

'But I am still one hundred per cent right. Just ask her if she wants to keep seeing you. If she says no, then you know. If she says yes, then make her tell you why. Let her know that you don't care about being used so long as she's honest about it. I saw the chemistry between you during dinner. She will say yes.'

Slowly, he dug his hand into his pants pocket and pulled out a little black box. Handing it to Lily, he looked out the window. Lily sat up and he heard her breath catch. 'It's a butterfly.'

'Yes. She likes them and I call her my butterfly.' He gave a short laugh. 'Stupid, eh?'

'She is it for you, isn't she?' Lily was in awe.

'Yes. I thought she was. Can you see my point now?' Vincent forced his eyes down to the engagement ring Lily held. The gold was twined into a stylised butterfly, with a large oval diamond in the middle. When he'd seen the jeweller, he'd just known Kat would want something different from every other woman. He had discussed it with the man for some time before coming up with the concept for a butterfly. 'I was going to ask her tonight, if it felt right, you know, not too rushed. I bought every florist in New York out of purple and white roses. My home looks like a garden bloomed overnight.'

'No wonder you're so hurt.' Lily closed the box and handed it to him. Her accent was thicker. 'A new girlfriend does such a thing and you can forgive her, but your heart was involved and that's a different story. And here I thought you were kidding when you told me it was *coup de foudre*, love at first sight.'

Vincent had told her as much. They'd spoken in French in front of his parents, knowing they wouldn't be understood. It was an old habit. Only too late did he realise Kat might have thought it rude and stopped.

'That's not all. A man, her old boyfriend to be exact, stopped by work and I caught him proposing to her. She looked horrified to be caught and even got mad at me for being rude to him. She ran after him to stop him.'

'How did she explain?'

'She said that it was over between them, but now I

wonder if she was lying to me because of this deal. That maybe her panic wasn't because she didn't want Jack and was sorry for him, but because she did and she couldn't say yes to him in front of me or risk losing everything my parents promised her.'

'I don't envy you,' Lily said, again resting her head on his shoulder.

'It's just that I finally found something worth having and then . . .' What else could he say? Kat had broken his heart. 'I'm a pathetic fool, Lily. I can't imagine a future without her.'

'Then you fight for it,' Lily whispered, putting her hand over his as she hugged herself to his side. 'If you truly love her like that, you grab on and don't let go. None of the rest matters.'

'I don't know.' He stared out the window. 'This is all so fast. I think I need just a little bit of time.

'Can I have some cash for the taxi?' Kat stood in Zoe's entryway, shaking as she tried not to cry. It was obvious by the horrified look on Zoe's face that she looked atrocious. Her sister was dressed for bed, in a pair of red polka dot pyjama shorts, a white tank top and nothing else.

'Yeah,' Zoe said, nodding frantically. She hurried into her small apartment and grabbed her wallet off a table near the front door. Handing it to Kat, she waited while Kat ran down the flight of stairs and paid the taxi driver.

'Oh, Kat,' Zoe said, holding the door open for her as she came back up. 'Sweetie, I'm so sorry. It didn't go well, did it?'

Kat merely shook her head in denial, unable to answer.

Zoe's apartment was small, but it was near her job and that's what mattered to her sister. Rugs covered the old floors, hiding the warped boards. Kat had helped her decorate and knew most of the posters and scarves hanging on the walls covered holes in the old plaster.

There was a small living room, an even smaller kitchen, one bedroom and a bathroom smaller than Kat's closet.

Kat put Zoe's wallet on an old table in the small entryway. When she looked up, her pale face stared back at her from the tarnished antique mirror. Black eyeliner had dried in trails down her cheeks from when she'd been crying. Her hair was a mess, held halfway up in the twist. She pulled at it, letting it fall over her shoulders. It was still messy, but she didn't care. Kat rubbed at her cheek, but the black only smeared.

Zoe came up behind her, slipping a hand onto her shoulder. Kat rubbed harder at her face. Gently, her sister touched her cheek, stilling Kat's hand. Turning, she looked at Zoe, shook her head and threw her arms around her sister, crying.

'Oh, Kat,' Zoe whispered, holding her. They stood in the hall, not talking about what had happened, not needing to. 'I'm so sorry.'

Chapter Fifteen

'That's it!' Zoe marched into Kat's apartment, followed by Sasha, Megan, Ella and Flora. 'You've been hiding out, listening to . . . what is this music anyway?'

' "Why Can't I?" by Liz Phair,' Ella said.

'She's had it on repeat again today,' Flora added. 'I'll turn it off.'

Kat hid her head in the couch, burrowing into the pillow as she refused to get up. The music stopped.

'I'll start the shower,' Megan said.

'I'll make food,' Flora added. 'Zoe, would you mind putting the groceries in the kitchen for me?'

'Yeah, I'll help you,' Zoe said.

'Great,' Sasha's voice was closer than any of them, but Kat still refused to look up as she heard them bustling around her apartment. 'That leaves Ella and me to get your lazy ass off this couch.'

'Ah, there, some light,' Ella announced from the direction of the windows.

Kat groaned, not wanting to look.

'Let in some fresh air,' Zoe called. 'The air is so stale in here and it's a beautiful day.'

'All right, sis, come on. You smell like ass,' said Sasha. Kat felt a pull on her arm and groaned louder. 'Get. Up. Now.'

Sasha pulled her off the side of the couch, dragging her onto the floor along with her pillow. Kat finally looked up to find Ella and Sasha staring down at her.

'This really isn't the way to handle your problems,' Ella said, shaking her head.

'What would you know?' Kat grumbled, curling up on the floor. 'You've never felt like this.'

'And you're only going to continue to feel like this if you don't get off your smelly ass and do something about it,' Sasha said.

'I hate you,' Kat groaned. 'Leave my lazy smelly ass alone. I hate all of you. Leave me be.'

'Well, that's just something we'll have to live with,' Megan walked over to her feet. 'Now, do I restrain you to get you in that shower, or do you go willingly?'

'Don't play cop with me,' Kat mumbled, hugging her pillow tighter.

'The hard way, my favourite,' Megan announced. She grabbed Kat's foot and started dragging her and her pillow across the floor.

Kat couldn't help herself, she chuckled and kicked her foot. 'Fine, I'm going. Get off me.'

'Damn, and I was so looking forward to handcuffing you to the shower,' Megan teased.

Kat stood, carrying her pillow with her as she trudged towards the bathroom. 'You know, it's only been three days. A girl is allowed a week minimum to wallow in self-pity.'

'Kat, it's Friday,' Ella corrected. 'It's been five days.'

Friday? What happened to the two days she lost? Kat paused, scratching her head. Her hair felt gross and she drew her hand away.

'Ella, come help me carry this pile of laundry down to the basement. Zoe doesn't need me meddling in the kitchen,' Flora said. 'And from the looks of it, Kat won't have a clean thing to wear when she gets out of the shower.'

Kat shut the bathroom door and stepped into the shower. The hot water beat down on her, stinging her skin. For a long time she stood, soaking in the warmth, unable to do more than just breathe with her eyes closed. Finally, she grabbed her shampoo and began washing her hair, feeling better the cleaner she got. Somehow, she even found the energy to shave.

Stepping out, she glanced around. Her robe was missing and a folded towel was on the floor. She dried off and wrapped up in the towel. The faint smell of food was in the air and her stomach growled in response. Zoe was cooking. That always aroused her appetite. Going to her bedroom, she looked around for something to wear. 'Where are all my clothes?'

'Ella and Flora took them,' Megan yelled.

'They weren't all dirty,' Kat said.

'They were all on the floor,' Megan answered.

Frowning, Kat went to her dresser and opened a drawer. The only thing she found was an ugly frock dress she used on laundry day, if even then. Its shapeless form fit her like a garbage bag. She put on an old tank top with it. The thing had holes, but the dress covered them

'Whoo hoo,' Sasha teased. 'The fashion queen arrives.'

'Shut up,' Kat mumbled. 'Someone stole all my other clothes. It was either this or a towel. And if you think this looks bad, you should see the grannie panties I've got on.'

'I'll get a brush,' Sasha offered.

Kat sat down by her drafting table. Pictures of bugs stared up at her and she had to turn her back on them. Anytime she saw a bug, she'd think of Vincent. She'd never be free of him.

'Here we go.' Sasha set to work brushing her hair.

Kat reached up, stopping her hand. 'Thank you.'

'That's what sisters are for, Kat. Now, just let us take care of you.' Sasha again started brushing her hair. 'Everything's going to be all right now. We're here and we're going to work it all out. You'll see, we're going to come up with the perfect plan.'

'I don't think there is one,' Kat said.

'What about your things? You still need to go to the office and pick up your stuff. It's a perfect excuse.'

'It would be, but Mimi had them delivered for me.' Kat reached behind her, and grabbed a piece of parchment. 'It came with this.'

Sasha picked up the note and read, 'Miss Matthews, for your convenience your personal belongings will be following shortly by courier. Thank you for a job well done. Mr Howard Faustino is expecting you Friday at one o'clock.'

'Lovely, eh?' Kat said.

'That's today, Kat,' Sasha said. 'You can still make it. We'll help you put together a portfolio, if you want.'

'What's going on?' Zoe asked from the door. She wore an apron that was lightly covered in flour.

'Kat's got an appointment today to show some work to the owner of Faux Pas.' Sasha lifted the note towards Zoe.

'What?' Zoe took it and read. When she'd finished, she asked, 'Are you going?'

'No.' Kat shook her head.

'But, there is still time to –' Sasha began.

'No,' she said louder. 'I don't want it anymore. Not this way. Faux Pas is tainted for me now.'

'But, if you don't show up, Mr Faustino may never see you again,' Sasha insisted. 'What about your dream? This is what you've always wanted.'

'Sasha,' Zoe said quietly, shaking her head. 'Don't push.'

'But . . .?' Sasha shrugged. 'OK. Fine.'

'Don't worry about it, Sash,' Kat said. 'You're right. I did want my own art show more than anything, but now I want something else. I want Vincent. I love him.'

'Then we'll find a way to get him.' Sasha placed her hands on her shoulders and leaned over to kiss her cheek.

'Who's backing the show, Jack?' Kat asked, forcing her way into her ex-boyfriend's home. The air smelled of incense and candles, a little too chokingly so.

Jack stood in his blue jeans and nothing else. Frowning as she passed him, he said, 'Do come in.'

'Don't get grumpy with me,' Kat snapped. The front door opened into his living room, but she didn't make a move to go much further into his home.

Jack shut his door and crossed over to his black leather couch. Sitting, he stretched his arms along the back. 'What do you want me to say?'

'I want you to tell me the truth. Something about the look on your face when you proposed really bothers me,' Kat said.

'It should. You turned me down.'

'Oh, just stop it.' She crossed her arms over her chest and lifted a brow.

'You look good, Kat,' he said. 'Is that a new dress?'

Automatically she glanced down to the ugly, shapeless grey frock she wore over the old white tank top. 'Shut up.'

'Touchy,' he said under his breath.

'Stop pretending to be hurt over my rejection,' Kat said. 'Now tell me who your backer is.'

'I don't see how it matters.'

'It's the Richmonds, isn't it? They backed your show, didn't they?' she insisted. He didn't have to speak. She read the answer on his face. 'What did they demand in return, Jack?'

Looking away, he didn't answer.

'I knew it. They got to you. That's what they do. They offer what you want most and make you do things. They offered to back your show and move it to Broadway if you proposed to me and got me to leave Vincent. That's why you were so mad. You were scared since I said no that you wouldn't get your show after all.'

'I'm sorry, Kat.' Jack's eyes met hers. 'But, it's Broadway.'

'For me it was Faux Pas,' Kat answered, plopping down in his chair. She gave a small laugh.

'You?' Jack sat up in surprise. 'The scientist? Their son? They bribed you to be with him? And then they bribed me to get you away from him? But why?'

'That's just what they do.' Kat closed her eyes, sighing. 'They manipulate.'

'I am sorry, Kat, but I can't give up the Broadway show. I was mad the day I proposed, but only because I thought they'd take it away, but it was too late. It was already in the papers and tickets had been sold. Anyway, it turned out they really didn't care if you said yes, just as long as their son saw me give the proposal. I am sorry, Kat, but I want this too much. This is my chance. It's Broadway.'

She slowly stood. The way Jack said it reminded her of what she must have sounded like when they first offered her a chance at Faux Pas. 'I know. I'm not here to ask you to give up the show. I just came for the truth.'

'I'm glad the truth's out. That day, when you saw me coming out of your sister's restaurant, I was sure you were there to bust Mr Richmond.'

'Mr Richmond was the man Zoe saw you with?' Kat asked.

He nodded. 'Richmond was checking your sister out as well, I think. I'm sorry for doing that to you, Kat. I really would have married you,' Jack stood, 'if that's what you wanted.'

'Thanks, but I think we've both had enough of the convenience of being with each other.' She turned to go. 'Good luck with the show. Knock 'em dead.'

'Wait, what about you? Are you going to tell me about Faux Pas? We're still friends, Kat. I want to go to your show. I still believe in you.'

Kat laughed softly. 'No. There isn't going to be a show. There is no way the Richmonds would set it up for me now. And even if they did, I wouldn't take it.'

'Why? Oh my ... Kat! It's because of the scientist, isn't it? That Victor guy.'

'Vincent,' she corrected.

'You like him, don't you?' Jack asked in awe. 'You like their son. They hired you to do one thing and now you really like him.'

'No, Jack,' Kat looked him straight in the eye, 'I love him.'

'Would you choose him over Faux Pas?'

Kat looked at the clock on his VCR. It was one fifteen. She gave him a sad smile and nodded. 'I already have.'

The city rolled by the taxi, a backdrop to the reflection of her pale face in the window. A streak of orange slashed through her bangs, falling across her face. Her make-up was dark around the eyes, with the faintest hint of orange and red eye shadow. The orange in her hair matched her orange bohemian style dress. It had a high waistline and a tiered peasant skirt that flowed when she walked. Maybe this was a mistake. Maybe she needed to dye her hair back to a blonde-brown and put on a more elegant dress.

No, Kat told herself. He needs to see me for me. No more lies.

She'd been up late with her sisters. They'd camped out on her living room floor, all but Megan who was called into work. The oldest Matthews left around ten o'clock, but not before offering to have Vincent arrested if he didn't forgive her. It was around the same time Flora fell asleep on the couch.

Spending all that time with her family did much to boost her morale, but now as the taxi pulled in front of Vincent's building, she shivered with fear. What if he didn't want to see her? Already she had gone to his office to find him and it had taken her a half hour before she worked up the nerve to go inside. The front door was locked signifying he wasn't there. Now she was in front of his house.

Glancing both ways down the tree-lined sidewalk,

before gazing up the side of the building to the top where she knew Vincent's apartment was, she took a deep breath. This was it. The moment of truth.

'Miss?'

Kat blinked, looking around.

'Miss? Can I help you?' It was the doorman speaking.

'Dr Richmond,' she whispered, her whole body trembling.

'Excuse me, Miss?'

'I'm here to see Dr Richmond,' she said louder, gesturing needlessly up towards the roof.

The man smiled and opened the door for her. She nodded as she passed. The ride up to the penthouse was a blur and too soon she found herself standing in front of Vincent's door, staring at the hard wood.

Kat's heart thundered in her chest and she lifted her hand several times before she got the courage to knock. She tried to remember all the things she wanted to say to him, the words she'd practised in her head until they should've been memorised. Her mind was blank.

The door opened, and she blurted, 'I love you.'

Mimi stood before her, blinking in surprise.

'Ugh, not you,' Kat said, pushing past her before the woman could speak. 'I don't love you. I don't even like you very much.'

'Excuse me,' Mimi said, her tone dripping with disdain.

'You're excused,' Kat said dismissively, before yelling, 'Vincent, I love you. I'm sorry and I love you!'

Her words echoed off the high ceilings, resounding over them. She looked around the large living room, but the room was empty. Mimi was behind her, saying something, but Kat ignored the annoying woman as she headed through the archway towards the kitchen.

'Vincent,' she yelled, entering the pristine white kitchen. 'I love you and I'm sorry. I didn't meet with Howard Faustino. I didn't –'

'What?' Mimi demanded, pulling Kat's arm to stop her

from leaving the kitchen. 'I told Howard you'd be there. I gave my word.'

'You shouldn't have.' Kat jerked her arm away. 'It's time you learned, Mimi, that you don't own people. You're not the queen of New York and you certainly are not a good person. If you meddle in my life, or the lives of my friends again, I will dedicate myself to making you sorry. Do you understand?'

Mimi huffed. 'How dare you?'

'Quite easily,' Kat said through clenched teeth.

'I blame your influence on my son's behaviour,' Mimi said. 'Whoever heard of a mother being told to "butt out" of her son's life?'

Kat opened her mouth, but she realised the woman wasn't worth it.

'You missed your only chance.' There was a desperate tone to the woman's voice and Kat realised Mimi just couldn't help herself. And, if everything went according to plan and Vincent forgave her, Mimi would be a part of her life. They would have to find a happy balance.

'No, Mimi, my only chance is somewhere in this apartment.' Kat smiled at the woman, hoping she'd understand. 'Your son is what will make me happy. He's what I want and this is my chance.'

Mimi opened her mouth and shut it several times before shrugging helplessly.

Turning, she pushed open the door to the dining room. 'Vincent! I . . .'

She stopped. Vincent stood on the other side of the dining room, looking as if he'd just come from his bedroom. He was gorgeous. His dark hair was tousled about his head and dark circles were under his eyes. It was late in the day but he wore navy and white striped pyjama bottoms and a grey T-shirt. Kat couldn't remember seeing him so dressed down. She wouldn't have thought he owned pyjama pants.

Breathing hard, Kat took a step forwards and stopped.

The side of the cherry wood dining table was between them. Her limbs went numb as she waited for him to speak. Blood rushed in her ears, punctuated by her loud pulse. His eyes roamed over her dress and hair. Finally he prompted, 'You?'

'I . . .' Her mouth worked and she tried to remember all she was supposed to say. Just seeing him caused a hot spark of desire in her, made worse because she couldn't run and jump into his arms. A tear slipped down her cheek. 'I love you, Vincent. I love you.'

'I was hoping that was you screaming and not my mother.' He gave a small laugh, as if trying to smile.

'It was me,' she said. Unable to stay back as she looked at him, his features as hopeful as she felt, she went to him. Throwing her arms around his neck, she kissed him.

'Ah!' Mimi gasped behind them.

Vincent broke the kiss and turned to look at his mother. 'I thought I told you to leave.'

'Well.' Mimi pouted. 'How long do I have to stay away this time?'

'Two months,' Vincent said.

'Two?' Mimi gasped.

'You want me to make it three?' Vincent demanded.

'No, two.' Mimi shook her head in defeat and left.

'This time?' Kat asked, smoothing back his hair and tucking it behind his ear.

'Whenever she invades too much into my life, I banish her,' he admitted, cupping her cheek. 'It's hardly perfect, but it works. Two months to the day she'll be over here with some sort of peace offering, acting like nothing happened. How do you think I got this dining table I don't need?'

'I'm so sorry, Vincent. I want you to know I didn't go to Faux Pas.' She ran her hands over his chest, liking the feel of his muscles beneath the T-shirt.

'You should have. What about your dreams?'

'None of that matters. I don't care about the art gallery. I don't want the chance, not like that. I only want you.'

'I love you too, Kat.' Vincent kissed her, lifting her up off the floor. Kat ran her fingers into his hair, holding his mouth tight to hers. Their tongues touched as the kiss deepened into a passionate embrace. Her body settled into his familiar one, feeling the unmistakable press of his hard cock. His hands roamed down over her back to grab her butt and squeeze. She pulled back with a half laugh, half groan. 'We really need to talk, but do you mind if we go to the bedroom first?'

He lifted her into his arms, holding her tight. 'I think we can definitely do that, butterfly.'

Kat smiled, feeling giddy. She loved it when he called her butterfly. Vincent carried her to his bedroom, hitting the door open with his shoulder. Gently, he laid her on the blue and grey comforter. The thick curtains were drawn and it was darker in the room, with only a strip of light showing. It was enough. She could still make out his handsome face as he crawled on top of her.

Kat reached behind her head and untied her dress. Pulling the straps forwards, she drew the halter bodice down, revealing her naked breasts. Vincent groaned, leaning over to kiss her breasts. He flicked his tongue over her nipples before sucking them between his lips. Burying his face in her cleavage, he pushed her breasts up to smother his face and stifled a groan.

She pulled at his T-shirt and he leaned back to take it off. His thighs pinned hers to the bed. Her stomach tightened and she bit her lip. Vincent touched every-where, moving his hands over her flesh. Slowly, he pulled up her skirt. Starting at her toes, he kissed a hot trail up her leg. When he grabbed her panties and worked them off her hips, she couldn't help but wiggle in anticipation.

Vincent positioned himself between her thighs, hold-ing her open. His eyes met hers as he slowly probed her slit with his tongue. Concentrating his efforts, he circled the tip of his tongue over the sensitive bud hidden within her folds.

'Mmm,' Kat moaned, digging her fingers into his hair. She thrashed back and forth on the bed, making incoherent noises of pleasure. He slipped a thick finger inside her pussy, working it in and out of her opening, rubbing her sweet spot. She clamped her thighs down hard on his head, holding him to her as she rocked her hips to his mouth. Then, feeling she was getting close, she pulled lightly on him, 'Come here.'

Vincent came above her, joining his lips to hers. Kat's dress was bunched around her waist, but she didn't move to take it all the way off. She reached for his pyjama pants, eagerly diving her fingers into them to feel the hard, ready length of his cock. She groaned in excitement, stroking his length.

Pulling back, so his mouth hovered above hers, he said, 'Say you'll marry me. This last week without you was hell. I don't want to lose you again. Marry me, Kat.'

Pleasure shot through her, causing her to gasp, 'Yes, oh, yes!'

'Do you mean it?' he asked. 'You're not just –'

'Yes, I mean it.' Kat nodded, stroking his cheek.

Vincent grinned and she couldn't stop staring at him. This is where she wanted to be for the rest of her life. Things like art shows and careers didn't matter. Everything she needed to be happy was right there with her.

Kat angled her hips towards him, bringing the head of his cock to her sex. She dug her heels in to the bed, wiggling her hips to urge him inside. He thrust, filling her completely. The rhythm started slow, building with each push until their bodies writhed together in a crescendo of passion.

She loved him, loved being with him. He touched her and she felt her insides melt and when he looked at her, called her his butterfly, she felt as if she were the only woman left in the world. Vincent circled his hips, knowing just how to stroke her, how to make her feel beautiful and loved and sexy.

Soon, the steady rhythm wasn't enough. She needed more. Lifting her leg, she put it over his strong shoulder, opening up her body to his. Vincent grunted softly with each marvellous pass. He braced his weight on one hand, using the other to reach between them. He found her clit, thumbing it to send delightfully erotic pleasures throughout her body.

Kat gripped his arms, digging in her nails as her body strained towards that perfect climax. Each time they came together, it was wonderful. It was utter perfection.

His movements became stiff and erratic as he bit his lip. She knew he was keeping himself from coming, waiting for her to explode with release. Then, suddenly, she did, her body shaking and trembling, so weak and yet soaring with passionate strength. She gave herself over completely to him, barely able to breathe. Seconds later, he grunted, his mouth opened wide as he kept his cock buried deep in her pussy.

Collapsing against her, Vincent's harsh breath fanned over her neck. Kat stroked along his spine, feeling the light sheen of sweat on his body. The smell of him engulfed her senses. It was the smell of lightly scented shampoo, soap and physical exertion. She loved that smell. She loved everything about him, even his faults.

'I must be squishing you,' he said, rolling to her side.

Vincent gathered her close to him, cradling her against his chest. Their clothes were a mess. Her orange dress was bunched along her waist, exposing her pussy and her breasts. His navy and white pyjama pants were caught around his upper thighs. The comforter was messed up from their passion. Kat didn't care, she nestled, wiggling until she was comfortable next to him.

'I'm so happy,' she said. 'There were so many things I know I wanted to say to you, but I can't think of any of them right now. My bones feel like they melted and my limbs have all gone numb.'

'I meant it when I said I love you, Kat, and that I wanted you to be my wife.' Vincent held her closer. 'I know it's fast, but there are some things I just know to be fact. One of them is that I want you in my life, forever.'

Kat was so happy, she felt like she was going to cry. 'I'm so sorry for everything.'

'No, you don't have to explain. My mother confessed everything,' he said.

'Then she told you how she bribed Jack to propose to me?'

'Well, let me rephrase, she told me everything about how they hired you to date me. Between her ramblings and what I've seen of you with my own eyes, I pretty much figured out the truth of what went on.' He brushed a kiss against the top of her head.

'I never should have agreed to trick you.'

Vincent chuckled, 'I'm glad you did. Otherwise we may never have met and, even if we had, you might not have been able to put up with me as long as you did. I know I'm not always the easiest person to be around, but –'

'Shh, don't apologise.' Kat lightly kissed him. 'You are so noble and your work is important. I understand that. You're dedicated to your research and that is one of the reasons I love and admire you. I used to think taking pictures was so important and, don't get me wrong, I do love it, but what you do...' Kat sighed. 'I could never make the difference you do.'

'Thank you, butterfly.'

'I love it when you call me that,' Kat giggled. It was as if the last week of tension and sadness just rolled away, leaving them in the moment of bliss.

'I like what you've done with your hair,' he said, picking up an orange strand and twining it in his fingers.

'I'm glad, because I get the impulse to change my style

often. I came over here to show you the real me. All of me.'

'Well, I love it. I love you. I think you're sexy no matter what you wear.' Vincent's eyelids lowered and he reached up to cup her breast. Lightly, he grazed his thumb over her nipple, causing it to become erect.

'Really?' She giggled. 'Because lately I have to tell you, I've been having a lab coat fetish. I see you in it and I just can't seem to control myself.'

'They come in different colours you know.' He wagged his eyebrows suggestively.

'Ooh, do they now?' She turned more fully against him. 'Well, then, I'm going to have to resubmit my application for that assistant job and we're going to have to see about these different colours.'

'You want your job back?' he asked.

'Who else is going to pay me seven hundred a week to look cute?' she teased.

'It was six hundred.'

'I'll do it for five.'

'I'd pay seven.'

Kat ran her hands up and down his chest, playing with his nipples as he was with hers. When they were two hard points, she scratched a trail down the middle of his chest. 'Seriously, Vin, I miss being with you all day. I miss working at the office. I even miss the insect collection.'

'To tell the truth, I did want to beg you to come back to work. The guy the college sent over is a nightmare. He leans over my shoulder, breathing down my neck, and he's not nearly as sexy in a dress as you are.'

Kat tossed her head back and laughed.

'And,' he said, grabbing her hand and urging it lower until her fingers wrapped around his semi-erect cock. 'Only you can seem to relieve the tension I feel when I'm working on deadline, which is pretty much all the time.'

Kat played with his balls, rolling them in her palm

before lightly teasing his shaft with the tips of her fingers. 'Oh, do I now?'

His breathing deepened and he closed his eyes, moaning softly in agreement, 'Mmm-hmm.'

Kat arched her brow, giving him a seductive look. She sat up and crawled down the bed, pushing her dress completely off her body so she was naked. Then, standing at the end of the bed, she tugged at his pyjama pants. He let her undress him and she looked at his sexy, muscled body in the dim, intimate light.

His playing with her nipples had stirred her desires for him once more and she was wet with anticipation. But, because of her recent release, she was able to stop from attacking him.

'Wait,' he said, just as she was about to begin her exploration of his body. Vincent jumped out of bed and ran out of the room. Kat gasped, her mouth falling open, speechless. Just as quickly, he came back into the room. Before she could eek out a word, he was kneeling on one knee before her, looking up her naked body into her eyes. 'I didn't ask you properly.'

Vincent held up a ring and, as his mouth opened, she gasped, 'Yes!', grabbed the ring from him and was sliding it on her finger in admiration.

'Will you marry me?' he said belatedly.

'Yes,' she said, over and over as she looked at the delicate butterfly engagement ring. 'This is so perfect. I love it.'

'Hmm.' His tone dropped and his hands slip up along her thighs. 'Well, while I'm down here . . .'

Vincent's head leaned over towards her pussy, his tongue reaching out as if he would gladly pleasure her right where they were. Kat let him get a few strokes against her clit, as his hands reached behind her to grab her ass, spreading her cheeks as he gripped into them.

'Sorry, buddy, it's my turn to play. Back on the bed, Dr

Richmond. I'm about to give you a thorough examination.'

Vincent glanced up, interest shining in his eyes. He hurried back onto the bed, lying where he was before he'd run off to get the ring. Kat grinned, unable to resist as she lightly rubbed her breasts in front of him, dipping her hands down her flat stomach to her sex.

'You make me so hot,' she said, touching herself intimately. Vincent grabbed his cock and began stroking it as he stared at her naked body. Kat nearly groaned at the erotic sight of his hand on his own cock. Starting at his foot, she licked, kissed and scratched her way up one leg and then the other. Biting his hip hard, she quickly soothed the sting with her tongue. Vincent jerked. His cock bobbed close to her cheek as he angled it towards her mouth. But, Kat wasn't ready to suck him just yet. She continued the trail up, exploring his hips, his stomach, his chest and arms.

Vincent reached for her. Kat shook her head. Grabbing her discarded dress, she grinned wickedly at him. She anchored it against the headboard making a thick rope, which she used to tie his wrists above his head. It wasn't the best binding tool, but it held him in place. Only if he were to strain really hard would his arms break free.

'Oh, you never cease to surprise me,' he said passionately.

Kat raked her nails down his chest as she settled her legs between his thighs. Coming to his hips, she drew circles on them, watching his cock twitch as he squirmed for more.

'Ah, please, butterfly,' he begged. Vincent balled his hands onto the dress, holding himself in place more effectively than the makeshift rope.

'I want to do so many things to you,' Kat purred, licking her lips.

'Do them,' he breathed.

'But there are so many.' She gave a fake pout, even as she stuck her finger into her mouth to wet it. 'It's so hard to decide which.'

'Ah, please, Kat.' His hips arched.

'Please what?'

'Please suck my cock. You have such a beautiful mouth.'

How could she deny him? Kat slowly wrapped her lips around his shaft, using her hands to help pleasure him. Suddenly, Vincent broke free, pulling her up so she was astride his body. The heat of him pressed against her sex. Her stomach tightened, anticipating that first deep plunge. He stroked her clit, thrusting deeper at the same time until he filled her completely. His free hand massaged her breasts as he took her with slow, shallow thrusts, the kind that drove her past the point of sweet, blissful insanity.

'I love you,' she said, looking deep into his eyes.

'I love you, too,' he answered, unflinchingly.

He rubbed her swollen clit, massaging it harder the closer she got to release. His body glided within hers and her climax came over her in a tender rush. Vincent kept moving, rocking his hips up into her, until finally his body jerked with release. Groaning softly, she fell onto his chest. His hands roamed over her back, holding her close.

'Perfect,' Kat whispered. 'Now this is perfect.'

Epilogue

Jack's Broadway career lasted a total of four weeks, but it was the best four weeks of his life. Though critics hated the show and deemed it a failure, it gave him the acting credit he needed to get a number of off-Broadway parts. He's currently pursuing a woman as gorgeous as he is. She's French and looks like a supermodel.

Mr and Mrs Richmond are still enjoying the prestige of high society, using the trauma of having a son who married beneath himself as a way to dominate party conversations. Mimi no longer feels the need to discuss how she keeps her looks, though she does keep the plastic surgeon on speed dial. Mr Richmond still spends too much time talking on the phone during vacations.

Beatrice Matthews' career reading Mrs Richmond's future lasted one session. She saw a clear image of a shark on the bottom of the cup, which every good practitioner of tasseography knows means bankruptcy. Mimi wasn't too happy to hear this and fired Beatrice on the spot.

Flora, after years of Mills begging for a commitment, finally took pity on the man and let him move in with her so she could take care of him. She claims it was to give the poor fellow something to do besides sitting in the lobby scaring children. Emboldened because he'd made progress with his dream gal, Mills is determined to spend the rest of his life asking Flora to marry him. Every morning he gets down on one knee and asks. Every morning Flora says no.

Kat and Vincent were married on a Saturday – exactly

three weeks after he proposed. The ban on Mr and Mrs Richmond was lifted for the day so they could attend. Mimi was horrified by the lack of pink silk and Mr Richmond took exactly one phone call during the ceremony, at which time Kat's dad took his phone away. As Vincent kissed his bride, a swarm of butterflies were released around them.

Kat never did get her art show in Faux Pas, but she got something much better – a fulfilling life with Vincent. However, Katarina Richmond's photography is renowned by animal enthusiasts and entomologists alike. As for her sisters . . . their love lives are another story altogether.